SAN CARLOS

Neil Forsyth was born in Glasgow in 1978. He is the author of five previous books including *Other People's Money*, his biography of teenage fraudster Elliot Castro which has been published in six countries and is being adapted by Forsyth as a feature film. His trilogy of Bob Servant humour books are international cult favourites, likened to the absurdist comedy of Peter Cook and Spike Milligan they have been adapted by Forsyth for both Radio Four and for BBC Television in the sitcom *Bob Servant Independent*. His debut novel *Let Them Come Through* was critically acclaimed in both Britain and the United States. Forsyth currently writes for TV for the BBC and in the USA for Universal Studios. He lives in West Sussex.

NEIL FORYSTH

San Carlos

VINTAGE BOOKS
London

Published by Vintage 2014

2 4 6 8 10 9 7 5 3 1

Copyright © Neil Forsyth 2012

Neil Forsyth has asserted his right under the Copyright, Designs
and Patents Act 1988 to be identified as the author of this work

First published in Great Britain in 2012 by
Jonathan Cape

Vintage
Random House, 20 Vauxhall Bridge Road,
London SW1V 2SA

www.vintage-books.co.uk

Addresses for companies within The Random House Group Limited
can be found at: www.randomhouse.co.uk/offices.htm

The Random House Group Limited Reg. No. 954009

A CIP catalogue record for this book
is available from the British Library

ISBN 9780099555896

The Random House Group Limited supports the Forest Stewardship
Council® (FSC®), the leading international forest-certification
organisation. Our books carrying the FSC label are printed on FSC®-
certified paper. FSC is the only forest-certification scheme supported
by the leading environmental organisations, including Greenpeace.
Our paper procurement policy can be found at:
www.randomhouse.co.uk/environment

Typeset in Bembo by Palimpsest Book Production Limited
Falkirk, Stirlingshire

Printed and bound by Clays Ltd, St Ives plc

For my pals

'Spain is a rubbish dump full of Nazis.'

Violetta Friedman, Auschwitz survivor,
January 1995

Friday

You hope, you just fucking hope, that once she's looked at you and not said anything and taken off her jacket and put her handbag on that stool, that she'll say to you while she's doing something else, 'By the way, they can't meet us tonight.'

You'd burn up when she said *they*, like it's only you, her and those two in the world and you'd burn up because that's how it would feel. But she doesn't say they can't meet you tonight. She doesn't say anything. She just comes in and legs it upstairs. So you're meeting them tonight. You look at the clock. Bang on five. Every night.

You're standing in the lounge next to the couch and chairs that she picked out and you paid for at MFI. You walk through to the back bedroom where the bed's against the wall. Not pushed up against the wall but lifted on its edge and leaning right into the wall like that.

When you got the free weights and the rail it was OK to just push the bed against the wall. When you got the Lat Attack the room was a bit crowded. When you got the Shoulder Moulder it didn't fit. You'd put down the Shoulder Moulder, still in its box with the photo of some boy in a leotard pretending to use the Shoulder Moulder, and had a good look at the back bedroom. Then you'd walked over and lifted the bed on its edge. The first time she came in and saw the bed like that you were on the Lat Attack doing three sets of 20–25–20. You were toiling like a bastard through the last sequence and she was holding a frozen dinner for one. You finished and waited.

3

'You'll have to bring that back down when my parents come,' she said.

You didn't say anything, just looked through the window to the patio where you and her once stood and talked about barbecues and sunloungers, about eating outdoors in the evenings and potted plants. None of that had happened. The patio looked the same as the day you arrived. Behind the glass that she called French windows.

'Just put it back down when my parents come, OK?'

'Yeah, of course, no problem.'

Her parents never came. The day you lifted the bed on its side must have been three months after you took the house and that was already too far in. The first few weeks, no later, they could have come and it would have been all right. It wouldn't have looked too bad back then, you and her, and the way you spoke and looked at each other. You'd have faced a few awkward questions right enough but you would have coped like you always do. You would have said you fancied a change and that you'd lived in the north your whole life. *The bright lights of Peterborough* you might even have tried, with a wink at her mum and a check on her dad's drink.

But after those first weeks there was no way her parents or anyone else was going to come. It was too obvious, spectacularly obvious, that you'd both made a mistake. And now, Jesus Christ, it's got worse. It's almost a year since you took the house. The lease is running out and there's not been a word from either of you about it because you both know that conversation is not going to be much fun.

Peterborough was temporary. Get yourself together after the trials. Talk to John Dickinson, take it easy. But it wasn't too relaxing, truth be told, sitting in that flat with its shite furniture and no Lat Attack even though it was top of the list you gave Dickinson. Anything you want, he'd told you and that had been number one.

No Lat Attack and not allowed to join a gym because of the list that John Dickinson had given you when you gave him yours. Football matches, gyms, political demonstrations, city-centre bars at the weekend, airports, seaports, train stations *only by agreement*. And on it went, page after page of places you couldn't go and stuff you couldn't do.

'What's this bollocks, John? What's this about gyms?'

John Dickinson said that he didn't make the rules. He said this was only for the first year after the trials and then the risk would be reassessed. You'd been left with nothing to do but sit in your new flat in Peterborough and think about what had happened. About the lawyers and the shouting and your finger pointing across the courtroom. Time and time again. *And do you see that man here today?* Yes, you'd said. And pointed. And pointed. And pointed.

There's only so much thinking a man can take and you took more than most. A summer of living by John Dickinson's rules had been enough. When the clocks were about to change you ironed a shirt and went into town. Saturday night. City-centre bars at the weekend. You'd found the busiest pub there was. The Moon Under Water. Next to the Dixons where you'd bought a washing machine and kept the receipt for John Dickinson. You'd only just got your lemonade when her mate was at your elbow saying they'd been wondering if you were a weightlifter. You looked over and she was beautiful, that night in the Moon Under Water.

You'd phoned John Dickinson at his office in London. Got through the password bollocks and told him you were staying on in Peterborough. You'd met someone. He cracked up.

'In Peterborough?'

The two of you had laughed like you sometimes did because he really wasn't a bad lad, John Dickinson, and he'd done a lot for you. But you'd done more for him.

So you stayed. You and her. The cinema, restaurants, bars if you couldn't avoid it. Her curling her little hand over your arm. You guiding her along the streets with the slightest touch on her back. You got on well, to be fair. Next thing you knew you were standing on the patio with her at the house. The estate agent was waiting in the sitting room while you talked about barbecues. You'd gone back inside and signed the forms with that strange new signature.

You moved in and almost straight away it was game over. You'd got a bit carried away. Both of you, you'd lost your marbles. You didn't even know each other and suddenly it was just you and her and bad, bad feelings. Anger and silence and regret. And the worst thing of all was that it just kept going. You don't know why she's kept it going. You don't really know why you have. But the lease, that's going to be what does it. There's no way round it and it's not long now. A relief, that's what it'll be. She can't be enjoying this any more than you are and most of the time you'd guess she's enjoying it less.

Here you are. Gripping the handles of the Lat Attack in the back bedroom while she's upstairs getting changed so you can go and meet those two again. You're flying through the reps. Your back's buzzing. *Latissimus dorsi*. From the armpit to the spine. Your back's seizing up. You let go and the rail hits the pulley. The sweat's in your eyes. You wipe them with your palms. Through the stinging you see the bed. You know you won't ever be taking it down.

'Here they are!' shouts Rog and the two of them stand up from the table.

They've sat facing the door so they can welcome you as if it's their house. Like you should thank them for letting you in the door. Like they own the restaurant. If Rog had time to run a restaurant when his job was so important then that would be impressive. If his missus, Claire, had time to run a restaurant when she was so busy being a cunt then that would be a miracle.

'All right?'

You kiss Claire and you shake his hand. You want to crush it and ask if it will affect the golf. You sit down and she sits beside you and apologises that you're late. She says her work is *a nightmare at the moment*. Her work isn't a nightmare at the moment. Her work is a piece of piss. Administration, home at five. But she has to get this in first and they smile and nod and wait for her to finish and then off they go.

'Well, I've had some week myself.' Rog shakes his head. He makes himself yawn and look like he's on the verge of falling asleep right there and then. You want to suggest that if he's that tired he just heads off home to bed. You want to tell him that he can have your car keys and get forty winks on the back seat.

'I'm sure the two of you have seen the state of the market. It's been absolute madness, mayhem. I mean, I did very well in the end but, Christ, it's taken a lot out of me.'

You want to tell him that you don't know too much about the stock market but you imagine that selling life insurance in Peterborough must put him right at the centre of it all. Every time the Yanks on Wall Street or the boys in the City pull a stroke, they must be thinking, What about Rog though? How's this going to affect old Rog?

'How are you finding it in the construction industry, Craig? Tensions mounting over there?'

Craig Turner, that's what John Dickinson gave you. You wanted Don something after Don Hutchins, Bradford City's number 9. When you were a kid you used to see Don Hutchins at the chippy on Union Street on Sunday nights. The others would chase him up the road but you'd cycle on the other side of the pavement, too embarrassed to go over. You remember him in the *Bradford Mail* saying he was a City man through and through. Then he signed for Scarborough. But, come on now, he was

Don Hutchins, City's number 9. John Dickinson said it couldn't be done. He already had the forms and the passport. Craig Turner.

'It's not too bad. I think people are putting a brave face on it, Rog, you know?'

You think that calling him Rog annoys him. You hope it does.

'Oh, absolutely, Craig, that's what I'm hearing.' He nods and frowns to show he's letting you join him, letting you be part of this great study of the local economy. 'We're just all going to have to ride this one out. I never thought I'd say this, Craig, but Thatcher's looking ropy this time.'

'You're spot on there, Rog.'

You only do three days a week at the site because John Dickinson said any more and you'd violate your compensation. It was all right there, to be fair. Irish and local. A few blacks. Good boys though. They've started sacking and you'll be gone soon because there's no redundancy needed for part-timers. Better you than the others. You've got the money from John Dickinson. Wages, that should be, not money. It's earned.

'Oh God, I've got to tell you,' says Claire as if she's just remembered something she's clearly had in the locker since you walked in, 'where Roger and I are going on our hols.'

You don't want to look to your side. You can sense her stiffen in her seat. This is going to kill her, you think. Whatever Claire, her sister, says is going to kill her.

'The Bahamas!' Claire squeaks.

'Costs an arm and bloody leg, Craig, take it from me,' Rog tells you and shakes his head.

He's so tired he wants to show you, but he'll bravely battle on for now. You want to stick a sleeping bag over his head and zip the fucker up.

'A drop in the ocean for a man of your means, Rog. The Bahamas, eh? That sounds great, doesn't it, love?'

Her smile comes dangerously close to making you laugh. She looks like a ghost.

'Lovely,' she says. 'Shall we order some wine?'

'Slow down,' she says.

You breathe and look out the window at houses you could push over. Look at that rubbish, your mum used to shout whenever there was a southern town on the telly. Two-up two-down, she'd say, give me that any day of the week. The northern way, the Bradford way.

'Slow down,' she says again.

She's pissed and raging. Hardly said a word the whole meal but fairly made up for it over the coffee. She told them she was in for a promotion, that she'd lost half a stone, and that the two of you were thinking of moving to a bigger house. Bollocks, every bit of it.

Her head is slung into the seat belt and bounces gently as the car copes with the new roads between the new houses. You wonder how many of these houses they managed to flog before everything went tits up. You wonder why she does it to herself. Her sister and her life-insurance tycoon of a husband – because of that? You don't have sisters or brothers but you know that's not it. She's slipping away from something. Ten years ago she must have ruled this town. Friday and Saturday nights she could have stopped bars when she walked in. Even now when you're out together you watch the local boys of her age. You see the recognition and then the envy. Not at what she is now, to be fair, but more what she was.

One time she showed you an old newspaper. The *Peterborough Advertiser*. She was on the front page in a swimsuit to promote new water slides at the swimming pool. She told you a modelling agency called her mum from London. They asked for her to be put on the London train so they could take some photos and send her back that night. Her mum said no because she thought they might be paedophiles. And that was that. Her chance gone in the blink of an eye.

She told you this story when she was pissed and holding up the paper which had turned yellow with age. Jesus, you'd thought, what a thing to hold on to. That kind of stuff does more harm than good. You thought of the lads you knew in Bradford who had signed for City as schoolboys before winning a free transfer to the dole or the booze or the drugs or the whole gang. Young talent.

Her car door opens before you've fully stopped. She storms towards the house and all you want to do in the world is turn round and drive away. Drive anywhere. Drive to Bradford. Up and down the estates. Braithwaite, Buttershaw, out to Holme Wood. Lean on the horn and bring them out the pubs. *Look who's back*.

She slams the front door and you imagine her progress, through the sitting room to the kitchen then the fridge for the gin. You know what's ruling that swimsuit protégée head of hers.

Bahamas, Bahamas, Bahamas.

You don't know where the Bahamas are. If those two at the restaurant had pulled out a map of the world, and you wouldn't put it past them, then you could have probably found the rough area. Caribbean, you think, near Jamaica then. You've never been on a plane. Not once. You were meant to go to Tenerife with the boys from the garage a couple of times but it never happened. Sam Albright. You'd tell him you were going to go to Tenerife and he'd say, 'And the struggle, kid, is the struggle going to Tenerife for a little holiday?'

And that would be you not going to Tenerife just so Sam Albright had someone to drive him about and open doors.

'Craig!'

She's at the door and using your new name like it's poisoning her mouth. She waves at you and walks back into the house. You get out the car and walk up the path and wonder what's going to be waiting. Surely not that paper. The swimsuit and the water slides and how her mum should have let her go to London.

'I would have been happy in London,' she said to you last time. Hold on a minute, you thought, they only wanted you there for the *afternoon*.

In the sitting room she's drinking gin and orange. She's on the couch and facing the telly. Teletext. Drinking, drinking, drinking and looking at Teletext. Holidays. Places and prices.

'Get your credit card, Craig.'

'Why?'

'Cos we're going on holiday, that's why, now get your bloody credit card.'

'When?'

'Tomorrow. Look at that.'

It says 'Ibiza – £119 pp HB'.

'What's that?'

'Per person, half board,' she tells you. 'Get your credit card.'

'I'm working Monday,' you say.

She turns round. She's holding her drink and you wonder if she's going to chuck it. It's a pint glass.

'Fuck off, Craig.' The way she's looking at you is unbelievable. 'We're going on holiday tomorrow. Get your credit card.'

You take out your wallet and hand it to her. She can't be serious but you don't want to watch just in case she is. You go upstairs and get undressed as quickly as you can. You pull a T-shirt from the one drawer you're allowed and get into the bed. Downstairs she's on the phone. They would be twenty-four-hour, you think. That's your luck right there. You wonder if you can phone in the morning and cancel. You're sure you can. You can just phone and cancel and she might not even remember. You fall asleep and it feels a long time later that you wake up because she's kicking you in the legs.

'Come on,' she's saying and she's trying not to sound like she hates you quite so much. 'Come on.'

You lie there staring at the gap at the end of the curtain. You can see a bit of sky and a strip of the house next door. A little piece of Peterborough and that's more than enough. It was only temporary. Well, it isn't going to last much longer, that's for sure.

'Wanker,' she says and kicks you a final time.

Saturday

A na has already seen them.

'Here they come,' shouts the Australian.

It had just been Ana and the South African in the dinghy when she crossed to the yacht so the rubber had lifted clear of the water and made her lean forward to keep her balance. Now, though, the dinghy moves differently. It's full of men wearing white T-shirts and they sit in neat rows in front of the South African. They're looking at the yacht, at Ana and at the Australian. The dinghy is slower and it makes a new noise. It struggles and complains while it brings the men.

'You'll be all right.'

The Australian's beside Ana. He touches her back and his hand's wet from the ropes. His face is tanned dark around black sunglasses that show curved reflections of Ana and the water behind her. She gives him what he wants, in her nervous look back.

'Thank you,' she answers and walks to the yacht's bow which points to the pier and the dinghy trying to connect the two. Ana steps round the ropes, lifts her shirt and ties it below her breasts. Her stomach is brown from early mornings beside the hotel's pool.

This is the third job that Ana has done for the Australian but she hasn't worked alone before. The first was early in the summer. He had stopped her in Ibiza Town to ask if she was a model, given her his card and offered her ten thousand pesetas to serve drinks at a party. She'd agreed and that night was driven by two happy Swedish girls to a villa near San Antonio. Four hours of handing out champagne and canapés to people who shouted at each other and took drugs laid out on tables.

The second job for the Australian had been on this yacht. An anniversary party for a Dutch couple. Ana and four other girls earned twelve thousand pesetas for the day. The yacht went to Formentera and back and Ana worked downstairs because she was the new one, opening bottles and refilling the ice. Today, she'd earn her twelve thousand pesetas out on the deck with these people.

The men's voices reach the yacht. They talk, laugh and watch as Ana holds the rail with her hair twitching in the weak wind. The bikini and the shirt are already warm against her skin. In September the days have still been hot. It's only in the nights, which arrive quicker and with hints of different weather, that Ana has felt the summer running from her. Once they were moving it would cool but not too much. The last time, in the room below the deck where music seeped through the wood, Ana realised the yacht was too old and slow to escape the heat.

The Australian is at the ladder, holding it steady. The men are quiet and look up from the dinghy that bangs against the yacht. Their faces are white or red, not used to the sun. Ana smiles at them and moves over to the Australian.

'Welcome to the SS *Victory*, lads,' he shouts. 'I'm your skipper today and this is your gorgeous hostess Ana.'

A few of the men cheer and the first reaches for the ladder. They're a mix of ages. Some old with bellies and bald heads that sparkle with cream, some younger, giving Ana the sharpest looks. When the first few climb the ladder and arrive on the deck she sees that their T-shirts are all the same.

Aztro Bank Boys' Club

Ibiza, September 1989

Ana smiles at each arrival and hands them a can of beer from the plastic cooler. Some are quiet, nervous even, as they receive their drink. Some make a joke not for Ana but for the others. When the last one is on the ladder, the South African takes the dinghy to the back of the yacht and the Australian steps up onto the deck's wooden platform.

'Right, lads. Lifebelts over there if anyone can't swim. Toilet downstairs. Free bar all day, just ask Ana.' His glasses tilt as he looks down at her. 'If you touch her you'll have me to deal with.'

Ana tries to laugh. Twelve thousand pesetas but that doesn't mean she should be here. She should be out on the island's roads, continuing her search, but the money makes this a needed day away from the normal routine. Her wages at the hotel leave life here a struggle. Today would cover two weeks of petrol for the car she'd bought six months ago when she was new in Ibiza, when the fields were full of flowers and Ana had started her search.

The men move around the boat. The South African and the Australian are at the controls with their backs to the rest of them. The engine has started below and Ana only realises they're moving when she looks across the harbour and the walls of Ibiza town slide against the sky.

The yacht was moored at the very end of the harbour, away from the mainland ferries and the smarter boats that park beside the restaurants, so it isn't long before they arc round the town's hill into the open sea. Formentera, the sister island, is stretched flat to the south and it is there that the Australian aims. The waves pass round the yacht and join up again at the other side. Ana is happy that they move so steadily but she knows this is because they move so slowly.

★

You're awake and she's not so you get downstairs quick smart. You can see your credit card but you need the name of the company and a phone number. There's no sign of that. The only thing on the table is one of her magazines with Diana and Fergie on the cover and the headline 'Friends or Enemies?'.

You turn on the TV and get the Teletext up. You only know how to find the sport. You try to find the holidays but it's not going well and you're near enough to losing it when you see TRAVEL. You hit the button and it comes up and then, Jesus Christ, there's 178 pages. You can just about remember what her page looked like, and you can remember the price, but it could take an hour to get there.

You look at the ceiling that's between you and her. Another cracking performance from her there, and topped off with the suggestion of a shag. That's what passes for optimism round here these days.

These fucking adverts. Places and prices and cartoon attempts at planes that don't look too much like planes. You think that Teletext must be a tough gig for a cartoonist. The pages take an age to switch. Who reads this slowly? Lowest common denominator, Sam Albright used to say.

You can't remember the last time you shagged her. Whenever it was you'd have thought of Maxine, the only thing you didn't want to leave behind in Bradford. It wasn't hard to leave your mum the way she was. Sitting in the nursing home, calling you your dad's name and trying to make a phone call using her hairbrush.

Maxine though, that wasn't easy. She was shacked up with an estate agent somewhere up Whetley Hill but she'd still tell you, when she was pissed in Panache nightclub, that she wished it had worked out with you. You'd be shouting in her ear, saying you should give it another go, and she'd shout back that she'd call you Monday and she never did once, even after you bought the answering machine. You still thought it could work though. When you and John Dickinson drove out of Bradford after the sentencing you thought about Maxine and how you were leaving her there. You idiot.

Maxine would have heard of course. Everyone in Bradford heard on the first day of the first trial. You were supposed to be protected. The *Bradford Mail* had called you 'Mr X'. But this was Bradford. Security guards and secretaries, court officers and cleaners. When you ducked in the back door, while the coppers waved their guns at the rioters, your name escaped out the front and wrote itself in the sky above the city. Sam Albright's going down, the people whispered, and guess who's doing it?

The adverts flick by but they're just background now. You're seeing yourself from behind, walking tall in the suit that John Dickinson bought you. Past the side door, up the steps, along the corridor. Waiting, waiting and then through the door. The room was more than full. People were standing at the back. Sam Albright and his four pals sat in a row and looked at you like you'd just told them the secret of life. They looked at you like you were God and the Devil tied together and to them that's what you were when you walked over and sat down in that box.

It doesn't do you no good, though, to think like this. Hard not to. Recently, though, in the last few months, there's been days when you haven't thought about it at all. Progress, no doubt about it. And still no fucking advert. You forgot to remember what page you started on but you must have gone through at least thirty. You could call up your credit-card company. You could say that your card had been nicked. But, no, that wouldn't look too clever when they found out the booking was made from your own house. It would be one daft burglar to sit on your couch and book a holiday off your telly, in your name, with your credit card.

She's up. She runs across the room and pulls the bathroom door closed but you can still hear her puke. A common sound right enough, and no bad thing. Usually you'd leave her up there, groaning and coughing like a tramp, and go through to the Shoulder Moulder and the Lat Attack for an hour.

These pages. Maybe the companies are all the same. Maybe they have all these pages to pretend there's a bit of competition in the marketplace. You should call one and see. That's as close as you're going to get to a plan.

'What you doing?'

She must have tiptoed down the stairs. She's not looking too clever. Her eyes look poisoned and you can smell the drink. She looks at the screen and you can see it's only then that she remembers. She laughs. Laughs and runs round the couch to her magazine. She turns it over and there it is. Ibiza. £119. Half board. The flight times. Four hours from now at Stansted Airport.

'We're not going,' you say, 'I've got work on Monday.'

'We're going,' she says and she's not angry or anything. She just says it then runs back up the stairs.

You stare at the magazine that you didn't turn over. What would be worse, a week there or a week here? You're not sure about the plane journey right enough, but you can't say you don't fancy getting abroad. Making your European debut sort of thing. The more you think about it the more sense it makes. You go to your jacket and pull out your wallet. You put your credit card back and find the bit of paper with the foreman's number.

You're not sure if he'll be there with the Saturday shift but he answers on the first ring. You tell him you need next week off and you realise this is a right result for him. A man down without any effort. He says to give him a call when you're back. That's a long way from saying you'll have a job to come back to.

You go to the foot of the stairs and listen and when you hear the shower you go out the front door and walk to your car. It's first thing Saturday morning and there's not a single person to be seen. In Bradford they'd be out sitting at their doors. Round here people live in houses ten yards apart and act like everyone else is invisible. If you say good morning to one of this mob they near enough have a heart attack.

You open the car door, reach under the dashboard and feel along the back until you find the corner of the paper. You pull it free, fold it in your hand and walk back into the house. The shower's still on so you go to the phone and roll out the paper. You call the woman who gives you a number. You look at the sheet of paper, at the different combinations, and you give her a number back. She tells you to hold and then there's nothing and then there's John Dickinson.

'You've just caught me,' he says, 'I've got to take the kids to tennis.'

You tell him you're going on holiday for a week and he says that's a good idea but he doesn't ask where you're going. He tells you to call him direct while you're away, using his home number that you memorised long ago. He's being a bit funny all round. You ask what's going on and he's quiet and then he shouts at his kids to wait in the car. You take the phone from your ear. The shower's still running. John Dickinson comes back on the phone. He says he wanted to come to Peterborough this week and tell you in person.

'Fuck's sake, John, what is it?'

'Albright's put a price on you. I've got it from a couple of sources now, the prison governor and elsewhere.'

'How much?'

'A hundred. A hundred thousand.'

'He'll get some interest at that,' you tell John Dickinson. 'No doubt about it, John, he'll get some interest at that.'

And John Dickinson can't bring himself to deny it.

*

Some of the men seem drunk already. They smirk when they take beers from Ana and offer each other the ugly smiles she has seen many times on men when they drink like this. It doesn't matter if it's the farmers back home in Komoró or the rich boys at university in Budapest. They all look like this eventually. Everyone watching everyone else, looking for weakness and hiding their own.

The men are against the rails and facing inwards in a rough circle. Sitting on the platform in the centre is a fat man with black glasses and hair flecked by blond dye. Ana has already decided this man would be handsome but his weight won't let him. He holds a can of beer pressed into his right hand but keeps a finger free, pointing it like a gun while he talks loud enough to beat the engine and the breeze that strengthens while they move further from Ibiza.

The fat man's stories involve the other men. He picks one out and describes something that embarrasses his victim and makes the rest laugh. Ana watches from the controls, a small cabin open to the rest of the yacht. She stands behind the Australian and South African who smoke and talk about rugby.

One of the men lifts a crushed can to Ana and she smiles and walks back along the deck, the fat man's voice growing as she nears. She steps into gaps between the men and moves with her feet tight to the hot wood, careful not to sway, knowing that would bring their hands, rapid and grateful, to her skin.

After swapping drinks for empty cans she finds only two beers left in the melting ice of the cooler. She walks back to the controls. Through the window, Formentera is a little closer than it was. The glass is cracked, with lines of fracture springing from a hole in the corner.

'We need more beer,' says Ana.

The Australian turns. His sunglasses are pushed up and onto his head. He looks younger.

'No problem,' he tells her and goes for the hatch and the

ladder leading downwards. 'Bring the cooler over and I'll hand them up.'

The cooler is back beside the men. Ana goes quickly, her eyes to the deck. She takes the end of the cooler but with the melted ice it's heavier than she expects and it slips from her fingers. She senses movement and looks up to see one of the men duck under the mast and drop down beside her. He's only wearing a pair of shorts; they look new.

'Let me,' he says and puts a warm hand on her arm.

He's tall with a thin smile and hair carefully guided by some substance within it. Ana sees a slim body never troubled by sport. His arms are straight lines and his chest hardly pushes beyond his stomach. He looks at Ana with a manner and confidence that seem strange. Practised, she decides, and unreal. She moves to the rail, leaving space for the man.

'There.' Ana points at the hatch and the man drags the cooler along the deck while she walks behind. It tires him more than he would have liked. His back bends and his arms shake a little while he pulls. He is breathing loudly when they arrive and the Australian's hands rise through the gap holding a crate of beer.

'One more to come,' shouts the Australian. He thinks he's talking to Ana but it's the other man who takes the beers, lowers them into the cooler then reaches his hand out to Ana. He gives her his name and also what sounds like his job title. Ana shakes his hand.

'It is nice to meet you,' she says. 'I hope that you're having a good time.'

'Oh,' he says, narrowing his eyes in the same, rehearsed manner, 'I am.'

'Ana,' shouts the Australian and holds another case through the hatch. Once more it is the man who takes it and he's pushing it into the cooler, with water coming out over the sides, when the

Australian climbs the stairs. They are awkward as they face each other.

'Right, cheers for the help, mate,' says the Australian.

'No problem,' the other man answers. He introduces himself to the Australian, without his job title this time, then crouches and pushes the cooler back along the deck. The Australian watches him go.

'Everything all right there?' he asks Ana.

'Yes, thank you,' she answers.

They watch the man. His legs pin to the deck while he braces and pushes, there are no muscles tightening through the skin.

'Are they good guys?'

'Yes,' she replies. Who is a good guy? Is the Australian? At the party at the villa he took drugs with the other people and then tried to kiss Ana when she was washing plates in the kitchen. Later she saw him take one of the Swedish girls upstairs by the hand. On the drive back to Ibiza Town the two girls argued in Swedish while Ana tried to sleep on the back seat.

Ana leaves the Australian and catches up with the man, taking one end of the cooler and helping to pull it into position beside the platform. When the other men see the union of their movement they cheer and shout. The fat man with the glasses has to turn to see them. He twists on the platform, one chubby hand on the wood to steady himself.

'Aye aye,' he shouts. 'Look at fucking Romeo here!'

The men laugh. The man with Ana lifts his palms in response.

'Just getting the beers, boys,' he tells them, rolling his eyes at Ana. She's moved to the other side of the cooler. He can't reach her.

'Don't worry about this lot,' he says.

'OK,' answers Ana. 'Thanks.'

She reaches into the cooler for the beers, her hands magnified by the cold water. She pulls them from the plastic and when she stands up again, the beers dripping in her hands, the man who helped her is back with the others. He has his arm round the shoulders of one and says something that makes his friend laugh and look at Ana.

★

'Slow down,' she says, 'I'd like to get to the airport alive if it's OK with you.'

She doesn't even open her eyes. She's only wearing a little top and you look at those tits of hers and think that maybe this could be just what the two of you need. You might not hate each other over there. You might fuck each other over there. To be fair, you're just glad to be in the car. Leaving Peterborough and leaving the news from John Dickinson.

A hundred grand. Sam Albright phoning up who knows who and saying, 'One hundred thousand, gentlemen,' in that voice of his.

It was a right mystery, Sam Albright's voice. When he talked, just you and him, it was hard to hear what he was saying. If you were in a car and the window was down then all you could see was his mouth opening and closing and you'd just nod and hope he didn't want any answers. Not that he ever did. Sam Albright was put on this earth to give the answers.

But when he spoke to a group of people, it didn't matter if it was a few boys in the street or the crowd in Bradford Square, Sam Albright pulled out a different voice altogether. He'd still be the short-arse with a salesman's smile and comb-over hair and the peacoat with a pocket full of fivers for the kids – *Here you go, boys, now are you happy with that specimen owning that shop? Are you happy with your mother giving that specimen her money every day?* – but his voice would change like he'd flicked a switch.

The first few years, people would turn up at the meetings for want of something better to do. They'd come in and start pissing about. Swaggering and pushing each other and sitting with their feet up on chairs. Then Sam Albright would talk. It didn't matter their age or where they'd come from, when those people left they were silent as the night. Sam Albright had got them just like he got you. Your first day's work at the garage. 1981. Sixteen years old, memorising spanners, and there he was, standing amid the oil and the engines, and saying, 'Now, gentlemen, who is this strapping young man? And is he aware of the struggle?'

★

Ana can see that the Australian is getting angry.

'Guys,' he shouts down to the men, 'we've got to get going.'

They're chasing each other in the water, pushing heads under the surface. Some have taken off their trunks. They wave them in the air and their bodies are white against the sea. The fat man still has his glasses on. He's clinging to the ladder while others swim round him and pull on his legs. *Fuck off*, he's shouting at them, over and over, while he laughs.

'Arseholes,' says the Australian for only Ana and the South African to hear.

The noise isn't reaching the people on the beach but they're still watching. Ana can see the waiters cleaning the restaurant. It will take them a long time. The smashed glasses, the broken tables. The waiters had watched the men with a disgust that had unnerved Ana. She had gone and sat on the sand. The men had started singing in the restaurant but she didn't turn to look. She only looked when the shouting started.

Everyone on the beach had stopped what they were doing when the men came out of the restaurant. People ended their games in the water and those who'd been sunbathing lifted their heads and shaded their eyes. The Englishmen stumbled on the sand, walking backwards from the restaurant with the waiters following them out. Some of the men had put their hands up for calm. Others had carried plastic seats from the restaurant and held them like shields.

Ana had seen the chef come through the restaurant, his running body flickering between the pillars before he was out with the rest of them. The knife caught the sun and flashed white when he waved it. A woman near Ana screamed and pulled her child to her. The Australian and the South African ran between the two groups, speaking in English to one and Spanish to the other.

Ana had stood up, rubbing the sand from her legs, and walked quickly to the dinghy. She'd felt so embarrassed, knowing the people on the beach were watching her move from within them to the Englishmen. She'd sat at the top of the dinghy, facing the sea and the yacht that sat empty and waiting for their return from Formentera's long beach.

The dinghy had been too full. Water had started to collect between the men's legs and, when they were close to the yacht, they made the dinghy turn over by leaning to one side. Ana had swum to the yacht. At the ladder she looked back to see the Australian and the South African scooping water from the dinghy with their hands. The men laughed as they swam round them and they are still laughing in the water now. The fat man with the glasses is the only one who has tried to climb the ladder but his friends won't let him.

'Guys,' shouts the Australian, 'we've got to go. We've got to get back.'

*

Sam Albright. A hundred grand. You wonder who would take the job but it's quicker to decide who wouldn't. You check the time on the dashboard clock. You'd mapped it out in the AA book while she packed her bags. The AI to Cambridge then the MII straight to the airport. An hour if the roads stay like this. The tickets. You lean over.

'You got the confirmation. The numbers and stuff?'

She doesn't move.

'You got the confirmation?'

She nods. A tiny nod. She's not even sleeping, she just couldn't be arsed. You look at her tits again. It'll be hot in Ibiza. You don't take the sun, you burn like a torch. You turn the radio on and she reaches a hand over, feels for the knob, and turns it off. The rest of the way to the airport you think about Sam Albright.

Any excitement when you get there and see the planes coming and going is nicked away by her. You park the car and you wake her up and she's just a proper nightmare. You get the bags out the back and you're carrying the lot which isn't exactly unexpected but the whole way through the car park she's saying that she needs to sit down. Like you'll pull a chair out your pocket or the airline will hear she's struggling and get the pilot to just pick her up from there. She says she's not feeling well. It's called a hangover. People spend a night chucking poison down their throats and then come out with this bollocks, as if they've picked up some mystery illness between drinks.

You walk behind her to the airport. If you walk ahead she'll have a go at you for walking too fast. You walk behind her, trying not to listen to her whining. Inside, she stands below the electronic sign with all the stuff about the flights. She produces a ripped strip of magazine cover.

'Here's the confirmation.'

She sounds bored. You get the desk number from the sign and the two of you find it after trying two wrong aisles. Hooked onto the wall behind the desk is a plastic board that says 'Majestik Holidaze'.

The woman behind the desk looks like she wants to cry. The people in front look like they want her to as well.

'This is absolutely outrageous,' says a man in a hat. 'Is there a plane or is there not a plane? I mean, that should not be too demanding a request from an employee of an airline!'

The woman smiles but it's not much of a smile.

'We will definitely be taking all clients of Majestik Holidaze to Ibiza,' she says to the man in the hat, and the other people which now includes you. 'But there will be a delay. For now we would ask you to check in and proceed through to the departure area.'

Some people moan about that and the man in the hat says he's going to wait in his car. You think that either the departure area's got a bad reputation or he's got a particularly nice car. Everyone else queues up. She's at your elbow, telling you to ask for more information. You breathe and look up at the ceiling.

When you get to the front of the queue you concentrate on the woman's questions about the luggage. You don't ask for more information, just thank the woman and take the tickets. From then on, during the whole time you're in another queue to show someone the tickets and walk through a metal detector, she's at your elbow asking why you didn't ask the woman at Majestik Holidaze for more information.

When you get to the departure area, you go straight for some seats near the window. You look for a plane with Majestik Holidaze on it. There isn't one. She asks why you chose those seats. She asks why you didn't ask the woman at Majestik Holidaze for more information. She asks how long the delay is, and why you didn't ask the woman at Majestik Holidaze how long the delay is. You don't answer. You sit looking at the planes until she falls asleep and then you stand up and go for a walk.

★

The sea gets darker with the sky. The yacht aims to the left of Ibiza Town, for the bottom of the island and the beach of Las

Salinas where the men will be dropped off. Las Salinas is a distant white line with flicks of parasols and people. Ana stands at the controls with the Australian and the South African, holding by her side a long tray that she found below the deck. The tray lets her carry more beers and has meant she's only had to go to the men twice since they finally left Formentera. The Australian and the South African aren't doing much more than swearing or looking back without kindness at the Englishmen.

'Ana, you'd better take them some more drinks,' says the Australian apologetically.

'OK.'

The Australian has moved the cooler to the top of the ladder and away from the men. Ana fills her tray, lifts it carefully and makes her way along the deck. The sun is lower and she doesn't have a free hand to protect her eyes. She walks in nervous steps, with her feet feeling for obstructions, while the men appear as shadows before her. Ana hesitates in front of them and they remove beers without acknowledging her. As she moves among them, their conversation comes to her in bursts.

'It'll be the most expensive car you've ever driven and the most powerful car you've ever driven,' one tells another. 'I know,' answers his friend, 'I'm ready.'

'It's self-belief,' a man announces to two other shadows, 'that's all it is.'

'I told him that's all very well,' says a voice, 'but how much do you actually *make*?'

Ana reaches the platform. There are four men slumped upon it, leaning back on their hands with their faces tilted upwards. They talk across each other and when there is a clash of voices they rise in volume until someone gives way. Ana isn't sure but they seem to be talking about different brands of suitcases. She places the tray between them and they take the last of her beers. Only one looks at her, to wink in a way that suggests he doesn't wink often. Ana leaves them and she can't be far from the controls when she sees white feet before her. The thin man, his hair loosened from its earlier order by the sea.

'I admire you immensely,' he says. His bottom lip drops open, he lifts his chin and looks down with eyes tired by alcohol. 'I love your spirit. You have an extraordinary sex appeal.' Ana has no doubt that these are words he has learnt for moments like this.

'Thank you,' she answers. There's no way to get past him. They are standing where the deck offers the smallest space. Behind Ana are only the other men. She takes hold of the rail and pulls the tray in front of her. She smiles at the man whose attention moves steadily down her body.

'I need to get some more drinks,' says Ana.

'I have a proposition,' he starts. A hand appears on his shoulder. He turns in reaction and the Australian is there, pushing himself sideways between them.

'All right, guys?' says the Australian but he is only looking at Ana.

'Can I help you?' replies the thin man.

'I need to get back,' says Ana, annoyed with herself for sounding shaken.

'Yeah, you do. OK, mate, let her get on with it.' The Australian looks at the thin man who smiles and swings to the side.

'Of course, no problem.'

It's hard for Ana to get through. Her bum touches the Australian but she holds the tray between her and thin man. She walks to the controls. There's no reason to look back but she does. The Australian and the thin man are watching her and both turn quickly away.

*

The airport's bigger than Leeds Bradford but it always felt a bit daft that Bradford owned half an airport next to a golf course in the arse end of nowhere. You picked up Sam Albright there whenever he'd been away. France or Germany, and then that one time he'd flown down to London and on to America where he'd had a burger the size of a dinner plate. *International relations* were what he called those trips and he always came back with something.

Once it was radio. Some French outfit were running adverts about Algerians and Sam reckoned he could get Bradford 103 to do something similar here. And he nearly did. He went in there and you stood beside the door and after an hour Sam had the station manager eating out of his hand. Free speech, Sam told him before working his way round to Winston Churchill and shaking on a deal. The station manager passed on the news to his bosses who must have thought he'd banged his head on the way to work and sacked him on the spot. His bosses hadn't met Sam, though, that was the difference.

The airport's bar is packed out like it's still Friday night and not the fag end of Saturday morning. When you look at these people, at what they're all about, it sometimes makes you proud of what you and Sam and the others did. You know you shouldn't think like that, and you don't really, but just look at these people. Boozers, gamblers, selfish bastards that won't lift a finger if it doesn't come back with a pound note. And then look what you did. April Fool's Day 1987. Bradford Square. Eight thousand of the willing.

That was what it was about for you. Watching something grow and being a part of it. Having Sam Albright lead you into rooms and standing next to him while a dozen faces looked back. Then a hundred faces, then eight thousand. When Sam spoke you watched the others. When they fell for him you felt they fell for you. When things got bigger there were other speakers but you didn't care about them. You'd go and wait in the car. You didn't think that Sam had noticed.

You see a screen, find your flight. IBIZA – MJK135 – DELAYED.

It's supposed to take off in twenty minutes. That's not going to happen. You walk past the bar, past the laughing and the red faces and the master race. The police said that there were five thousand in Bradford Square. There were eight. Minimum. April Fool's Day 1987, not even three years ago. Sam Albright on the back of Whyte's Fish lorry standing behind the speakers that you lifted up by yourself.

'*Ladies and gentlemen, we stand here today as history forms around us . . .*'

'*Britain is an island of land and people. This is the land and you are the people . . .*'

'*Your names will be picked out on the tapestry of this great nation . . .*'

'*They will hear us in London. They will hear us in the furthest reaches of this green and pleasant land . . .*'

The future, the struggle, the taking back. You'd stood at Sam's side, the only other person on Whyte's Fish lorry. Everyone in that crowd knew who you were. They were looking at Sam, listening to Sam, but they knew who you were. And wherever those poor bastards are right now, every single one of them knows what you did a week after Bradford Square.

Even Sam hadn't expected eight thousand. Afterwards you'd gone to the Rose in Holme Wood where they'd put on sandwiches and the kids played with the flags. Sam drank but when you drove him home he wasn't angry like he could be, just quiet. He'd sat with you for a minute outside his house. The little house in Dawson Street that he said he'd never move from because he needed to be with the people.

Sam's face was lit by the street lamp. He asked you if it had gone well. Out of eight thousand people you were the only one he'd asked. He'd never asked you something like that before and he'd never do it again.

'Yeah, Sam,' you'd said, 'it went well,' and Sam Albright smiled in gratitude.

Past the airport's bar there's a bookshop. You can't find an Ibiza book in the travel section so you ask the woman behind the till and she says, 'You'll get something in the Spain books, love.'

You'd thought Ibiza was in Spain but, to be fair, you weren't a hundred per cent sure. There's a big book on Spain with a beach on the front and you take a bit of time with the index because they've made it a lot harder than they need to but there's stuff on Ibiza on page 167. You turn to page 167 and there's a map and you think, Spain's an island?

And then you realise that it's Ibiza that's an island. It's a funny shape, kind of slanted, but it looks nice. Not too small, not too big. You wonder where your hotel's going to be. You check the number of pages on Ibiza in the book. Twelve. In a big book like that. It doesn't seem worth it, but you go and buy the book anyway. On the way back over to her you look at the screen and it doesn't say that your flight's delayed any more, instead it says that you'll be going in two hours' time. You sit down, careful not to touch her and wake her up, and you start reading the twelve pages on Ibiza.

★

The sun hasn't set but it's behind the hills and won't be seen until tomorrow from this side of the island. For the beaches the day is ending and Ana watches the lights from the bars grow brighter across the water. She knows these beaches on the island's southern tip have few houses nearby and there are less people on the beach than she'd hoped for. Other people are what she needs now, to keep things normal, but there are only a few dozen left. They are mostly on their feet, packing their things or walking through the dunes to the car park and the road that travels north, past the airport and on to Ibiza Town.

The yacht is anchored perhaps a hundred yards from the shore and the men are getting ready to leave. They're crowding the ladder above the South African who tells them to wait while he pulls the dinghy into position. The men laugh and push and finally one falls, spinning in the air and landing on his back in the dinghy before bouncing up and into the water. The others shriek with delight while the dinghy rears under the South African who swears and manages to right it.

'Take it easy, guys,' he shouts, clutching the bottom of the ladder. 'OK, come on.'

The men climb down into the dinghy with the extra care of drunks. They talk loudly and look at the beach, apart from one who stares back to Ana. The same face, the same intensity. Ana waves at the thin man and turns gratefully to the Australian. The yacht seems a lot bigger now that it's just the two of them left.

'How am I getting back please?'

'To where?'

'To the town. My car is at the harbour.'

She can see he's not thought of this.

'Up to you, Ana. We've got to stay with them for an hour then they've got taxis coming and we'll take the boat round to the harbour. It'll be a couple of hours by the time we're back or you can head off now. There's buses from the car park to the town, you know?'

'OK.'

'Here you go.'

He hands Ana the banknotes and she pushes them into the top pocket of her shirt.

'Thank you,' she says. 'Let me get my things please.'

She skips across the wood and swings a leg for the ladder. The cabin's dark so Ana moves slowly onto the cold wood. She doesn't know where the light switch is so feels her way along the wall. She finds her jeans and is pulling them on when the Australian arrives, dropping quickly to the floor. There's a click and the lights come on, two bare bulbs hanging from a wire.

'All right then?' He smiles, and walks towards the toilet. 'Just going for a piss. Don't you two leave without me, OK?'

'No.' She smiles back. The fright and then the safety lighten her mood. 'Or maybe, if you are too long.'

The Australian laughs. 'Cheeky Russian bastard,' he says, closing the toilet door behind him.

He has called her Russian before and she didn't correct him. Now it is probably too late. She climbs back up the ladder with her bag's strap across her shoulder, walks to the rail and looks for the men and the dinghy. They've reached the beach and jump into the breaking waves, with the dinghy swinging from side to side in response. On the sand they walk unsteadily towards the bar which has no other customers. The South African turns the dinghy and starts back for the yacht.

Ana thinks of the bus to Ibiza Town, collecting her car and then the drive to Es Cana. She could be back at the hotel in an hour. She finds her watch. Eight o'clock. Her shift at the hotel begins at ten. Enough time to eat and wash.

The Australian bangs closed the hatch. He waves at the South African who approaches in an arc to sweep back in to the ladder.

'I'm going to go now, catch the bus,' says Ana.

'No problem,' answers the Australian. 'We'll deal with these idiots.'

He lets her go down the ladder before him. It's awkward in her jeans because they're stiff and dry against her legs. Ana thinks the South African might try something with his hands, on her hips maybe, but he doesn't. She reaches the dinghy and sits backwards against its side. The Australian jumps in, the South African lifts the stick and the dinghy moves under them.

'I might have another one of these next week. Fancy it?' the Australian asks Ana.

'Yes, if it's in the day. I work nights at the hotel.'

'You're still there?' He's surprised.

'I like it there.'

'Away up in Es Cana? You don't want to be stuck away up there. Why don't you let me speak to the clubs? Amnesia or Pacha. They're always looking for girls like you. Hostessing, stuff like that.'

'I'm happy at the hotel. I live there.'

'You sure?'

'Yes,' Ana tells him, 'thank you.'

The Australian doesn't know that the hotel is not just where she lives and works. It has become her base and it's the point from where she's carved up the island. The only place left to search is the area around the hotel itself. The resort of Es Cana and the older villages in the hills behind. Ana left this until last because it's the easiest. It hadn't seemed possible that she could have the fortune to find what she was looking for so close to Es Cana. Now she is worried that there isn't any fortune to be had at all.

Behind them the water turns in a grey streak while the dinghy skims towards the beach. The men are strung along the wooden bar and Ana can already hear them.

★

You weren't counting on this though. You thought she'd moan her way onto the plane and get back to sleep but in fact she's fairly perked up. You've still got a couple of Ibiza pages in your book to go and now she wants to talk. You never really want to talk to her but right now you don't want to talk to her because, truth be told, you're shitting yourself.

The plane's driving along the tarmac and some bird is showing you all how to blow up a life jacket and what doors to leave by if you crash. It all looks a bit optimistic and you're sweating like a bastard. You want to read the last pages on Ibiza to distract you but she wants to talk.

The only thing you can do is pretend you're so wrapped up in the bird talking about the life jacket that you can't hear anything else, but she's carrying on regardless about the duty-free and about how it might be worth buying a bottle of vodka and keeping it in the hotel room. She says it would save on paying minibar prices. She's an expert on the minibar prices of hotels in Ibiza.

You're beside the window, that's the kind of luck you're having. She's next to you and then there's *another* fucker next to the aisle. Some boy actually *wearing* sunglasses on the plane and, the mood you're in, that sets you off. He's either blind or he's a prick and you can't see a blind boy going on holiday on his own unless he's got a golden retriever in the plane's boot.

Staring at the carpet between your feet, you try to pretend that you're in someone's house. Maybe the bird with the life jacket. You try to tell yourself that you're round at some bird's house and she's decided to show you how to blow up a life jacket. Not too likely a scenario, to be fair, but it buys a few seconds.

Is it too late to go for a piss? It's too late. You're going to piss yourself. No you're not. Yes you are. You're in bits but you can't help thinking it would be worth pissing yourself just to see her face. What about that then, you'd ask and point at your trousers, you going to tell Rog and Claire about this? They'd do well to beat that on the way to the Bahamas. Unless Rog has a shit in the cockpit.

You're giggling like a kid. You're near enough hysterical. The engines are roaring. She reads out something from the duty-free magazine. Something about limits per passenger. She asks you if you think she can use your limit as well. The plane's moving for real now. No messing about. It gets even louder. At least it's louder than her.

You wonder how long the runway is because they're about to run out. They're about to run out of runway. You turn to her. You want to tell her that they're about to run out of runway. You want to tell her that this is it. You're both going to die and you're going to die together and what a joke that is. She doesn't even know your name. She's pointing out the different prices of the different bottles of vodka and she doesn't know your name. You want to tell her that it really doesn't matter about the vodka because you're going to. You're going to. You're in the air. You, her, the plane, you're in the air. Everything's going backwards. The runway, grass, fence, fields, England. That was close, you think. That was definitely close.

'Well?' she says and, believe it or not, she's smiling. 'Shall we just go for it?'

'Yeah,' you say before you look at the page. Her bastard finger has moved to the champagne. £14.99.

Jesus Christ. She's smiling though and you don't want her to stop. If she was to just keep smiling then everything would be OK. But because she won't keep smiling, because she won't even keep smiling for a bit, then there's no way that things can ever be OK. That's just the way it is. Plus, agreeing to spend fifteen quid about ten seconds after the plane takes off is a pricey way to start the holiday. And what about the money as well come to think of it?

'What about money, how do we get their money?'

'We get it there, at the airport. Or we can use a card.'

She says it like you're her kid except it's your card she's talking about. Your money, paid every week by John Dickinson. Paid by the good taxpayers of Great Britain and Northern Ireland. For the loyal service of the silly boy with a hundred grand offered out on him. £180.75 per week. Living allowance. Three days a week on the site too but that looks like it's gone. Still, it's not hard to live on £180.75 a week and so there's a few grand sitting on your card.

Sam Albright went to prison. You get £180.75 a week. That's not why you did it but no one would ever understand that. Not any of the eight thousand in Bradford Square, not any of the rioters at the courthouse, not Maxine, not even Sam Albright. Sam doesn't even know because you never told him why. All he knows is that he's in prison and you're somewhere else. And he wants to know where. And he reckons, for a hundred grand, he's going to find out. But you're up here and he's down there. A little liar in his little cell. Thinking of you while you think of him.

★

The men call Ana over and part to let her get to the bar. She wants to wish them a good night and leave but they're shouting and the Australian and the South African are beside her and, without meaning to, she ends up standing between these two at the bar. If she stays for a few minutes, Ana decides, she can leave without attracting too much attention.

The shirts of the waiters have large smudges of sweat. They must have been pleased at first with this late arrival of customers but they're not pleased any more. Some of the men wrestle and push each other from white plastic chairs that bend and finally there is a snap. The men cheer while one of the waiters runs from the bar, shouting and pointing at the chair. The shouting is returned in English. The thin man steps out from the others.

'OK, Manuel, take it easy,' he says, and the other men laugh. One of them, near Ana, repeats the word *Manuel* in appreciation. The waiter is about to reply when the thin man pulls some notes from his pocket. He starts to sort them and then changes his mind, dropping them on the sand in front of the waiter.

'Sod it,' he says, 'take the lot.'

He tries to make it seem an accident that he looks straight to Ana but she knows it's not. She turns to the beach to avoid him. Other people are leaving for the car park, taking a wide route to avoid the bar. There is so much noise coming from the men, it doesn't seem possible. It feels like there are hundreds of them. The South African pleads with them for calm while the Australian, who seems to have given up, tries to attract a waiter's attention.

'I'm going to go,' Ana tells him quietly.

'You sure?' asks the Australian. 'I can't get you a drink?'

'No thank you, I have to go. Thank you for the work.'

'You OK getting to the bus stop?'

Ana hesitates, but only briefly.

'Yes, I'm fine. I know the way.'

The waiter asks for an order.

'Last chance?' smiles the Australian.

'No thank you,' Ana answers. 'Let me know about next week.'

'Will do,' he tells her. 'Take care.'

He's already lost the waiter's attention to one of the men who climbs the side of the bar, hanging on a wooden pillar and making the roof shake. Ana slips away over the cooling sand and into the dunes. That was a lot easier than she'd feared, she thinks with pleasure while picking her way between the bushes.

From the top of the first dune she can see the fence and the car park beyond. She pulls her shoes from her bag in readiness for the car park's gravel. Down she goes into the dip before the next dune. The sand is heavy and Ana watches for the sharp roots of the bushes. She's tired now that the work is over but she knows she can sleep a little on the bus to the town. She hears breathing that isn't hers. She turns round and it's the last person she wants it to be.

*

By the time they bring the food and drinks you've calmed right down. She's as greedy as always and orders herself a vodka and tonic to go with the wine. You give her your wine to make up a hat-trick and order a Coke instead. They hand out the food and bang, straight away, you're sitting on the brown couch watching *The Comedians* with your old man.

Every week one of them told a joke about aeroplane food and you all used to laugh. You on the floor, your old man in his armchair and your mum watching from the kitchen doorway. You all used to laugh even though none of you had been on a plane. Mum laughed because she liked it when people were laughing, it meant she didn't have to think about money. You laughed because you were just a kid. Dad laughed because he was pissed.

Your old man didn't cause trouble when he was pissed. He just laughed or smiled or tried to sing songs that he didn't really know. You were too young to see anything worse and that was lucky because you don't have enough memories of him to let you afford bad ones. When Mum pulled you out of school and told you in the playground you wanted to run to the hospital and tell him not to bother. You had this feeling that he was dying because he thought that was what you wanted. It didn't make any sense, but that's what you thought – that if you just ran all the way to Bradford Royal and told him that he didn't have to die, then he'd sit up in the bed and say, 'Well, thank fuck for that,' and try to order a drink off a nurse.

But he was already dead and smiling at the ceiling of the funeral directors in Eccleshill. Your aunt said he was smiling at his friends in heaven but you weren't young enough to buy that. If they had made it into heaven, you thought, then they can't be any of the ones you'd met. With their cans of bitter and their *Racing Post*s and their angry wives.

You didn't want to go back to school after that. Any kid who didn't have an old man got called a bastard. They said your mum had shagged the postie, or the milkman, or the pools collector. But Mum said she'd get the jail if you didn't go back so back you went and sure enough they called you a bastard and said your mum had shagged everyone under the sun. Even the ones who knew that your old man had died. Even the Wilkie twins who lived in the same street and came to the funeral in their school uniforms without the ties.

You told your uncle and he gave you this video. It was called *Geordie* and it was about this Scottish kid. He was just a skinny little thing but he read about some boy in London who offered a mailing course in how to bulk up. He wrote away and back came instructions to eat steak and exercise and that's what Geordie did. To cut a long story short, Geordie got himself properly, seriously big and went to the Olympics for Britain and threw the hammer.

You knew the story was bollocks. It had come from your uncle for a start and he used to sit in the Spread Eagle bar in Buttershaw calling out quiz questions. Not in an official capacity, with a microphone and so on. Just shouting out quiz questions when no one had asked him to. Your uncle was a lunatic, but he did right by you when he gave you *Geordie*. It might have been bollocks but it was enough to send you down to Gold's Gym and your mum down to the butcher's two minutes before closing for the cheap steak.

You were thirteen years old and built like a wasp. A year later you were the biggest boy in the school and they'd stopped talking about your mum. A year after that you got suspended eight times for fighting. A year after that you didn't get suspended because no one would fight you. You did all right in your exams, you left, you took the job at the garage on Davidson Street and on your first day, your first day at sixteen years of age, Sam Albright turned up. Half the boys at the garage had been to see him give one of his first talks and there he was to make sure they joined up. Like a ghost. The ghost of things to come. Looking past them to you, sitting on a bonnet, and trying to memorise the sizes of the wheel spanners.

1981.

'Now, gentlemen, who is this strapping young fellow? And is he aware of the struggle?'

★

Ana starts moving again but the thin man catches up in seconds and walks beside her in steps a lot longer and slower than her own.

'Why would you leave without saying goodbye?' he asks her. He sounds surprised. 'Why are you messing me about?'

'I'm sorry,' says Ana. Her voice breaks as she speaks, her mouth is dry. 'I am going home now. It was nice to meet you.' She doesn't look at him.

'I'm too old for games,' he tells her.

In the thin man's voice is an urgency that Ana doesn't want to hear. His hand comes to her hip and holds her in a busy grip, the fingers working against her shirt and the skin below. Ana keeps walking but they reach the top of the next dune and she knows that the car park is too far. She can't see anyone, only sand and the shadows of the bushes. She should try to turn, to go back to the bar, but if she turned there would also be a stop and she doesn't want to stop. Instead the two of them pass down the back of the dune and she sees the wall of bushes. It's enough to force a halt and it is where the fat man with the glasses stands, waiting for them and holding his penis before him.

Ana gasps and tries to scream but there is no sound. The fat man looks at her, but she only knows this from the angle of his face, it's too dark to see anything else. She still can't speak. No one else speaks either. The two men look at each other. Ana knows that when she moves something will start. She stands in the sand and tries and tries to talk, to scream, anything. The fat man flicks his penis back within his shorts, rubs his hands on his T-shirt and says, 'What's going on?'

Ana sees the dampness in front of his feet. A black shape of liquid. Urine. This is what he is doing alone and away from the bar. She sees the opportunity.

'I'm going home now,' she says. 'I need to go home now.'

The fat man nods and looks from Ana to the thin man. Ana doesn't want to see his response. He is standing at her side in silence. The fat man walks over to them. On Ana's shoulder he places the hand that has just held his penis.

'Come on, love,' he says and gives just enough pressure to make her move. He steps heavily beside her and when she stumbles up the dune she senses it is only the two of them. At the dune's narrow crest she looks back to see the slender figure watching them go.

'He's a weirdo,' the fat man says to Ana, then turns back. 'Piss off!' he shouts. 'I'll be speaking to you in a minute.'

The thin man doesn't move.

'Weirdo,' says the fat man again.

He struggles in the sand with his plastic sandals, toiling a couple of yards from her with no suggestion of wanting to be closer. They get to the fence and then the car park where the remaining cars look strange so far from each other. At the bus stop is a queue of people.

'Thank you,' says Ana to the fat man but he's already going through the small gate, turning to the side and lifting his arms in front of his body to make it.

'I'll get you to the bus stop, love,' he says, 'don't you worry.'

Ana slips through the gap and pulls on her shoes. She feels the energy of escape and surprises herself by asking, 'Have you had a nice time?'

The fat man frowns. His T-shirt is on inside out, the label hanging at the back.

'It's been all right, I suppose,' he answers. 'These things drag a bit, you know?'

Ana smiles at the honesty.

'I'd have ducked out of this if I could,' he continues. 'I've just had a kid. But, with this lot, you know? It's expected. It's hard.'

'Yes, it is,' replies Ana.

The people at the bus stop are what she was hoping for. Men, women and children with woven baskets full of towels and parasols. Ana leans to the fat man and kisses him quickly on the cheek. He flinches.

'Thank you,' said Ana, 'I hope you enjoy your holiday.'

'Holiday?' he laughs. 'I wouldn't call it that.'

He walks away with his arms swinging by his sides and his feet battling with the sandals.

★

Maybe it's Peterborough. Maybe it's the house. Things were all right before you moved into the house. She'd come to your flat or you'd turn up at hers with a bottle of wine and she'd lay out two glasses as a joke. The two of you would sit and laugh at some shite on the telly and it really wasn't too bad. And she was gorgeous, to be fair. You look at her on the plane and it's like you're looking at a photo of someone you know but you're not sure if it's them. It's not even been two years but that time has damaged her more than it should have done through booze, unhappiness and frozen dinners for one.

That's not the sky out the window any more, it's the sea. There's a ping and a sign tells you to buckle your belt but you never took it off and then the pilot comes on and says you're approaching Ibiza. The plane's dropping and turning and the sun's in your eyes. It's not far off the horizon but it's still blinding so you turn away and hold the sides of the seat which has you in one big pinch.

You're not looking forward to the landing but then her hand arrives on your arm. You turn to her and the sun glows her face and it's unfair of you to say she's not still a good-looking girl. She smiles at you and you smile back and when the plane hits the runway you're thinking, well, hold tight, you never know, do you?

The pilot drives the plane about a bit and then there's another ping and everyone jumps up and starts getting their stuff together. You're delighted to get out of the seat which isn't built for a man like you. You're only a few rows from the door and when the airline bird who did the life-jacket gig opens it there's this smell that comes in. By the time you reach the door and then the stairs you're breathing in so hard your head goes light. You don't know what it is, it's foreign.

There are hills a lot bigger than you expected and then a flat valley with fields flooded with water. The airport has a big sign saying EIVISSA that you know from the guidebook is just Ibiza in Spanish. It's the state of the fields you don't understand because you can't see them getting that much rain. A couple of boys in fluorescent jackets point you towards the airport. It's a bit of a hike. You wonder why the pilot didn't get a bit closer but then you see a boy waving table-tennis bats in front of the plane so it's hardly the pilot's fault. You look over at the fields. A proper flood – they didn't see that coming.

'Salt,' says a man beside you.

He's not a bad lad, he's not taking the piss, just nodding back at the fields where he saw you looking.

'They're making salt,' he says. 'Look.'

You follow the line of the fields and see a white hill, a hill of salt.

'Oh, right.' You smile at him. 'Thanks, mate, I was just wondering about that.'

'First time here?'

'It is, yeah. Yourself?'

'Oh no, I'm an old-timer,' he tells you. 'La Isla Blanca, I just can't leave it alone.'

47

'Right,' you say and you're not exactly disappointed when she starts coughing and the boy waltzes off. The salt's a funny business. It makes sense, you suppose, salt water makes salt. Strange to see it like that though. You can tell her hangover's back.

'All right, love?'

'Yes,' she says quickly, 'thanks.'

'You got the passports?'

She doesn't answer. In the airport the coppers on the passport desk wear uniforms that look home-made. They're only checking every few people but they're sure to check you. The boy looks at your passport, looks at you, looks at your passport and nods. He checks her too and looks at her for a lot longer than is necessary. You really don't have an opinion on that. Maybe once you'd have been proud. Maybe once you'd have been angry. But as things stand, you just don't have an opinion.

'Why don't I wait for the bags and you get the money?' she says and points at a desk behind a window with big stickers of credit-card-company logos.

'Yeah, OK.'

You go to the desk and some boy nips in front of you, just steals in when you're about two yards away. He's a weedy little bastard and you think how he wouldn't have done that if it was just you, him and a bank machine. But with the Spanish boy behind the desk and everyone else around this boy's just a hero.

You try to work out how much money to get. You look at the exchange rates. One hundred and ninety pesetas to the pound. You're there for a week. You try to work it out over and over and you're starting to get properly wound up and then the lad in front is finished and the Spanish boy is smiling at you and saying, 'Yes, sir, how can I help?' and you're thinking how did he know I was English? You panic and you give him the credit card that John

Dickinson gave you and you say, 'Can you take £180.75 off this and give me it in pesetas please, mate?'

You sign the forms and the Spanish boy hands you the money and you go and find that she's already collected the bags. She's even standing behind the trolley as if she'd be the one to push it.

'Give me that love,' you tell her.

You steer the trolley through to the front part of the airport. Everyone seems to be moving together, following a couple of people in yellow T-shirts who are laughing more than they need to and talking to people who you're pretty sure were on your flight.

Outside you smell it again. It's getting late, the sun's gone and it's not that much warmer than Peterborough, but it's the smell, you don't know, it's like there's some voice in your head just banging on – you're not in England, you're not in England – and when England's the last place in the world that you should be that's not a bad voice to be hearing. The people from your flight are lined up to get on a bus. It looks brand new, with tinted windows and a big cartoon on the side of a family walking along a beach.

'It's a nice bus,' she says.

'It's a nice bus,' you agree, 'but it's not our bus.'

Underneath the family in the cartoon it says SOL VACATIONS.

You've already seen the other bus, parked on the other side of the car park as if it's a bit embarrassed to be too close to a good-looking mate. It's small and old and the sign is wrong. You know it says MAJESTIK HOLIDAZE but if you weren't looking for those words then you wouldn't have known because some of the letters are gone.

'Jesus,' she says, but she's not angry. She's not exactly laughing about it, but she's not angry either and the two of you go over to the Majestik Holidaze bus. The driver throws your stuff into the hold and some bent English lad ticks your name off a clipboard and suggests that you find a seat on the bus. That's what he says, find a seat. You get on the bus. You're the only people on it.

★

The bus stops the way buses stop in Ibiza, as if the driver was only told about it at the last second. Ana is used to this now but some of the other people wave their hands in worry, thinking the driver hasn't seen them. The bus brakes and complains before the tyres hold and it falls back with a sigh. Ana follows the others on, pays her money and walks between the rows of seats.

She knows that the women and the men see her in different ways. The women wonder what she's doing, all alone with her bikini showing through her shirt. The men watch and, if they feel they can, turn in her wake to watch the twin curves of her bottom, shaping and straightening through the jeans while she walks to a seat near the back.

The bus grinds along the road with every move by the driver provoking defiance from the engine. They cut through the salt flats that sit as black fields in what is now the night. There's the hill of salt and then the airport with the large EIVISSA sign lit behind the planes.

A British family sitting a few rows ahead of Ana begin to argue.

'Shut up,' says the mother. 'Shut up or you'll get nothing.'

She's shouting at her son in front, who tries to answer but is crying too much to speak.

'Shut up,' says the mum. 'Will you tell him?'

The father sits facing straight ahead. He says something in a softer voice and the son nods and manages a smile. The mother looks away, shaking her head. There is a silence, the parents both ignoring the son who wipes his nose and watches them. Then he smiles again and he laughs and the parents join in. The mother pretends to hit her son across the head, the father's shoulders shake with laughter. Ana smiles at the boy who is embarrassed when he sees her looking.

Her English is as good as it can be and her accent fades by the day. At university the English classes were the escape from the History. For Ana the History meant rage. The weak professors who stood talking of checks and balances and seeing the situation from both sides. And behind every argument, every debate, was Pál Teleki. *Teleki Will Protect.* A troubled man, argued the professors. His hands tied. No one could have stopped what happened. That's what they called it. What happened.

And then they began with statistics. 400,000 said some. 600,000 said others. Ana had sat in a lecture room in the Árpád building, far emptier than it should have been, while two of the professors spent an hour debating these figures. If anyone had walked in during the lecture they would have thought it was Mathematics or Economics being discussed. It was always the figures, always the sums, and then back to Teleki. The protector. No one could have stopped it, that's what they said.

The English classes were the antidote and Ana found them easy from the beginning. She loved the order and the rules which made the Magyar look wild with its Gypsy variants and local forms. English was stern, strict, and she spoke it whenever she could. It is her English that has enabled her to come here, from Budapest to Jerusalem to Spain, but she is here because of the History. She is here because of Pál Teleki.

★

The bus is a shambles. The driver must want home for his dinner because he leaves the airport like Nigel Mansell. He's steaming down the road and you're glad you twigged that they drive on the wrong side or you'd have bailed out the fire door by now. Then the driver starts overtaking cars he's got no business overtaking. He doesn't give a shit. He just stares straight ahead even when some Spanish boy is halfway out his window screaming at him.

The boy with the clipboard's useless. He's a poof all right, which is his own decision you suppose, but he's lost his backbone in the process. There's only about a dozen of you on the bus but when he stood up to speak you'd have thought he was accepting an Oscar. He was shaking and nervous and apologising for everything under the sun. He said that they'd be stopping at three hotels but he didn't know who would be getting off where because the hotels had the list. When he sat down he ducked out of sight, as if people might start chucking their pesetas at him.

'We've hit the jackpot here,' you tell her but she doesn't find it funny and you wish you hadn't said it.

The bus might be strictly amateur but the island's not big enough for you to bother about the transport. The hotel's the worry and you hope the bus isn't much of an indicator. She starts kipping and you're certainly not going to complain about that. And there it is, just like the photo in the book, in the distance to the right of the road. Ibiza Town. The book said it was two thousand years old. Those walls must be massive up close and you can't blame the boys for building them high. Two thousand years on a small island, you're going to get all sorts of ambitious bastards coming to have a pop.

The bus turns onto a smaller road and soon you can't see the walls because you're in among old buildings and newer hotels. There are plenty of pubs with English names and plenty of English walking about the place. It might be dinner time but this lot haven't exactly spruced up. It's spot the football top. Everton, Spurs, fucking Man Utd, and you think that's Sunderland but it could be Stoke City.

You stop outside a hotel that doesn't look too bad and a woman gets on. She's got her hair scraped back so tightly that, for a few seconds, you reckon she's bald and it's impressive she's such a gobby bird when she's bald and then you see that she's not bald and she's just gobby anyway. She reads out a few names, not yours, and then she's off with all these rules and suggestions. You don't know why you're being subjected to this bollocks and why she can't just wait till the people she's called out are off the bus. Finally she lets them get their gear and head into the hotel and the bus driver starts the engine and pulls off about a ninety-five-point turn in the middle of the road.

The sea is right there at the end of the street but once the driver finishes pissing about you're moving away from it. You get to the edge of town and keep going with the walls behind you. You'd have liked to have been staying in the old town but the book had a few other places that looked decent. Besides, you're out in the country now and it's easy to look at. It's a lot greener than you thought it would be. Not that you were expecting a desert and camels, but it's greener than you expected.

The bus passes a woman standing in a field. She's wearing a black dress and a big old hat. There's a few sheep hanging about but she's not doing much apart from standing there. She looks at the bus and you look at her and she looks like a statue. You think about her all the way to the next town. There's a church on a hill and you're back near the sea. It's smaller than Ibiza Town, more peaceful. The bus stops at a good-looking hotel and another woman gets on. This time she's Spanish but her English is OK.

'Welcome to Santa Eulalia,' she says, and then reels off some names but not Craig Turner.

When the bus leaves it's only you and her and some old couple who look terrified. The woman's checking a guidebook and telling him to say something but he's just kind of smiling with a sad look like he knew he was going to be stitched up one way or another.

53

You wink at him and sit forward in your seat. The boy with the clipboard's head is leaning to the side. Surely he's not having a kip?

'Here, mate,' you say, and then louder, 'Here, mate.'

He turns round.

'Yes?'

He was definitely having a kip. You point out the window at the town you're leaving behind.

'We're getting a bit far from the action, are we not?'

'We're nearly there,' he smiles. 'Two minutes, I promise.'

'Two minutes?'

'Yes,' he tells you. 'Es Cana. You'll love it.'

*

The harbour's car park is a lot busier than it was this morning and it takes a moment for Ana to remember that it's Saturday night and these people are here to enjoy themselves. The heels of the women click on the concrete while the men hold their hands and look at Ana. She finds her car. Inside is trapped warmth from the sun. The engine starts well and she backs into the space, turning the wheel and taking the unpredictable car to the exit.

It had been Francesco's last act of kindness to her. He had picked her up in tennis shorts and a crumpled shirt to drive her to Coches Felices on the airport road. Francesco had done his best at Coches Felices. He banged the bonnet, pressed his keys into the tyres, and rocked the car to and fro. The mechanics had watched in amusement while Ana had hidden hers. Perhaps if he had not worn the tennis shorts, she'd thought, the mechanics would have taken him more seriously. Ana paid eighty thousand pesetas and they said they'd deliver it the next morning. The price on the car window was eighty-five thousand.

It was nearly all she had but she needed a car. After Francesco gave her the files it had taken her only three weeks to finish searching in Ibiza Town. With the rest of the island to cover she decided to base herself somewhere quieter, cheaper and offering paid evening work to go with how she spent her days. She'd mentioned the move to Francesco in little gaps of conversation, without giving opportunity for a response, but on the way back from Coches Felices, he finally reacted.

'You are leaving now, the town?'

'Yes,' she said.

'You will still phone me?'

He put his hand to his face and it shook a little. Ana had reached across and squeezed his other hand on the steering wheel. It tensed under hers and he smiled.

'Of course,' Ana told him as they reached the harbour roundabout.

This is what Ana remembers when she passes the roundabout now, five months from that day with Francesco. She never phoned him, though in the first couple of weeks she missed talking to him a little, and she never returned his calls when he tracked her to the hotel.

When they gave her the bar job, with the rewards of tiny wages and a dirty room, they laid out the many ways she could lose it. One was if they suspected she had someone staying with her in the room, as if that room would be an undeserved pleasure. Francesco would never have seen her room but she did not need the risk of them thinking he might. He was a good man but he had given her the files and it was the files that she'd wanted from the beginning.

The only calls she made from Es Cana were to her father. She had to buy special cards and then it would be two hundred pesetas to hear her father shout for a few minutes. It was strange; on the phone he always seemed to know what was happening, it was the rest of the time that his mind became harder to locate. He told her he hoped that Paris was going well, that her job in the museum was enjoyable, and that she would come back soon. Ana told him she'd be back as soon as she could. She'd stand in the phone box by the hotel, watching her money flicker lower and making promises.

'Soon, Papa,' she'd say, before the beeps came.

There were friends that she could have contacted. The Gera sisters in Budapest, Dora in London, even Kianna in New York, modelling for the same magazines that the four of them used to read together, lying in the grass in Komoró. Talking about travel and escape, dying their hair and listening to the Ramones, designing tattoos they never got and trying to speak in English.

Ana had sent letters to her friends before she left Budapest for Ibiza. She'd told them she was going to Paris to work in a museum and joked that her History classes had finally proven useful. If she called any of them from Ibiza and talked of Paris then they'd know she was lying. They knew her better than her father. Not as well as her mother but her mother was gone.

The car's clock gives Ana an hour before her shift starts at the hotel. She doesn't like driving fast in this car, particularly in the dark, but she has little choice and stays at eighty on the Santa Eulalia road, passing slower cars and glad there are few tourist buses at this time of the night. At Santa Eulalia she thinks once again that she should visit the church. She has meant to do so since seeing it on that first drive to Es Cana with the map on her knees.

Now Ana knows the island like a local. She sweeps through Santa Eulalia and joins the short road to Es Cana. The hotel will be busy because it's Saturday night, when some of the British leave and some more arrive, so she is not surprised to drive down the hotel's street and see a bus outside.

Ana parks her car in a lucky space at this time of the evening and walks quickly up the steps. In the hotel's lobby old and new guests wait for their turn with the receptionist. Ana walks to the lift. The doors have started to close and in the lift is a big man with a small woman who appears shrunken next to her companion. The man is enormous, so big it's hard to look away. To Ana his body seems inflated in the way it grows from him wherever it can, in slabs of muscle on his arms and the heavy blocks of his chest. The man stares at Ana. His eyes are dark points in such a body and his head is shaved tightly. The doors close. Ana moves to the stairs. She only has to go to the first floor.

★

This Es Cana looks all right. There's no church on the hill or anything that looks too old but there's plenty going on. You don't really like the way all the bars have English names right enough or that you can't see anyone who looks remotely Spanish but you're happy enough when you wake her up.

'Come on, love,' you tell her, 'that's us here.'

You, her and the other two get off the bus and the driver pulls out your bags which look stupid in that big space all by themselves. The boy with the clipboard takes you inside the hotel, past a sign reading HOTEL DE JULIO.

Named after a Spanish boy called Julio, you think, no doubt about it. Maybe after the owner like Jackson's Hotel, up next to Bradford Park Station. The reception area's packed but you're just pleased to be off the bus, and if you're pleased, then she's ecstatic. She even holds your hand as you wait in the queue and when you look at her she says, 'Nice, isn't it?'

'Oh yeah,' you answer, 'lovely. Really nice.'

The woman behind reception asks for a credit card or a cash deposit for extras so you hand her John Dickinson's card to swipe. On the wall is a sign saying *The telephone code for the United Kingdom is 00 44. Thank you*, and a poster gives information for ferries to the mainland. You get your keys, the boy with the clipboard gives you a couple of brochures and then you carry your bags to the lift. Some porter boy tries to take them but you're not going to get into that racket.

'You're all right, mate,' you say with a smile.

While she deals with the buttons you see a woman walking towards the lift. The doors are closing. You wonder if you should try and stop them but now the woman's closer and you don't think sensible thoughts like that any more.

She's wearing jeans and a white shirt with a bikini top under it and she's tanned and her hair is kind of brown and blonde at the same time and she's tall and she's coming to the lift and fuck's sake. She's right there walking towards you. Every step she takes lets someone you don't know do something inside you. Her eyes are green or blue, hard to say, but she's looking at you and you're struggling to breathe and then the doors close and you want them to open. You want to rip them apart just to see her again.

★

The hotel gives two different uniforms to the staff, one for the day and one for the night. The daytime uniform is white. A pair of shorts and a T-shirt with *Hotel Julio* printed on the front and *Team Member* on the back. The night-time uniform is black. Trousers for the men, skirts for the women and a black shirt for both with *Hotel Julio* written over the left breast pocket. Ana checks herself, standing in the cheaply made black outfit in front of the bathroom mirror. Later the material will itch when it warms up. She ties her hair back and returns to the cramped bedroom.

She's arranged her work on the bed so when she returns from the bar she cannot go to sleep without facing it. The red folders are lined up and the remaining list of addresses faces her, ready to be checked off once the day's schedule is planned.

For now, though, there is the bar. Ana flicks off the light and leaves the room. The staff accommodation is on the first floor, at the back of the hotel and facing away from the sea. Ana has seen the guest rooms which have space and balconies and modern fittings. From her room she gets the noise from the lobby. Her bed is small and soft and her bathroom reminds her of Hungary. There is no television but she knows that's a good thing. When she feels weak, it would steal her time.

Ana takes the stairs down the single floor and walks through the lobby. She waves at the receptionists and enters the bar where the Irishman waits. Usually he makes jokes or asks Ana to join him at a nightclub later, one of the places that stay open through the night, and Ana politely refuses. Tonight he is too tired to care. He tells her he was at one of these nightclubs until late this morning. His eyes twitch and he looks hunted when he hands her the keys and gratefully leaves her in charge.

Sometimes Ana wants to find the bar deserted, so she can relax and order her thoughts. Sometimes she wants it full to loosen her mind and make her work without thinking until the till is locked at two o'clock. Tonight there are few customers and she's happy with that. She's tired from her day on the boat and the Irishman's been lazy. There are trays of spilt beer to be emptied, fridges to be refilled, spirit bottles to be pulled from their grips and shined with a dry cloth.

*

The bed was your main concern. When you're eighteen stone on a good day you need a decent bed and this one's top notch with a wooden base and a mattress that's eight inches minimum. You put down the bags, place a fist on the mattress and lean. Not much give, perfect.

The room's a fair size, bigger than the bedroom in Peterborough.

59

There's a wardrobe to the side of the door and the bed sticks out from the right-hand wall. To the left are a wicker chair and a table with a TV and then through to the bathroom. She's already at the far side of the room, fiddling with a set of glass doors until they open and she slides one across the other. She steps out to a balcony and spins round with a smile.

'Oh, Craig, come and see it.'

You walk across the white tiles that remind you of swimming-pool changing rooms. You're on the fourth floor so you know there's a chance of a view but it's a lot better than you expected. The hotel looks over the other buildings to a proper bay. It must be half a mile wide, with little hills at each end and the town in between. You can't really make out the water in the darkness but just knowing that it's there gets you going and it'll look even better in the morning.

'It'll look even better in the morning, love,' you tell her.

'Look, Craig.'

She's leaning over the balcony, standing on tiptoes. You look down at the block of water. Around the pool people sit at tables crammed with drinks. Voices are made louder by booze.

'Lovely, isn't it, Craig?'

'Yeah,' you answer, 'lovely.'

It's getting on a bit now. You're not sure what the best plan is or what you should suggest. By rights, the two of you should be going for dinner but she looks knackered.

'What do you think?' you ask. 'Shall we just call it a night, get a good start at it tomorrow?'

'Yeah,' she replies. 'Maybe just a drink here and watch some telly.'

'All right, love,' you say and walk back into the room. You unzip the bags. You tell her you'll unpack for both of you and she thanks you and goes to the TV. She presses a button. It takes a few seconds to warm up and the picture grows from a spot in the centre of the screen. It's a Spanish boy with a moustache sitting wearing a suit behind a desk. He reads from a bit of paper, his voice not much more than a whisper. You know that they can, of course they can, but you can't help thinking that even the Spanish would struggle to follow this boy.

'Must be the news that,' you say. 'Try the other ones.'

You think that there might be some football on the other ones. Real Madrid, Barcelona. Lineker's at Barcelona these days. The Jock striker Archibald and Sparky Hughes were there as well, but you think they've both been binned. That's right, you remember, Sparky Hughes is in Germany now. Heysel, that's what it is. The European ban. If Division One players want European football then they've got to go and play abroad. That's a disgrace, any way you look at it.

She's going through the channel buttons but there's just inter-ference. She gets to the bottom one and says, 'Last chance.'

There's definitely something there. The picture's screwed but there's something there.

'Nearly,' you say. 'Just turn the other thing.'

Her clothes feel like feathers in your hand. She stretches back over to the telly. She turns the dial, the picture waves about a bit and then sharpens. There he is behind his desk, the same lad with the same moustache. She looks at you and purses her lips to stop the laughter but it starts anyway. You join in without trying, your shoulders shake and you drop her clothes onto the bed. You're laughing along to a Spanish boy on the telly, like a couple of spastics really, but it's hard to stop.

★

Ana asks the last people if they'd like another drink but they're old and the woman answers before the man. He looks as if he was going to give a different answer but he smiles at Ana and says, 'There you go.'

She walks back to the bar, locks the till and switches off the fridges. She's started to make her notes for the Irishman when a British man comes into the bar. Ana tells him the bar's closed. He asks for a bottle opener and then something else, but Ana's tired and sends him to the hotel's reception. He seems unsure for a moment then leaves. She thinks she has maybe seen him before.

*

You're still in your clothes and the telly's still on. She's dead to the world, lying in her pyjamas with her face turned away. It doesn't feel like you've been asleep long. There's a game show on the TV. It's based around a bird with big tits who comes through a curtain, holds up a toaster or kettle and then goes back behind the curtain.

You get up and go out to the balcony. There's no one by the pool and the streets are quiet apart from taxis looking for work. You find your watch and go to the bathroom where it's a great disappointment to see the sign telling you not to drink the water. It's two in the morning and you need a drink. You make a decision, take the Spanish money from the table and sneak out of the room.

When you press the button for the lift it's as if the button's wired to a part of your brain because, from nowhere, all you can think about is the woman from earlier. You tell yourself that you don't want to see her, that to see her would be nothing short of a disaster. It doesn't make sense this thing you do. It was the same with Maxine. You'd walk into Panache nightclub, straight in there with the bouncers slapping your back, and you'd be hoping Maxine wasn't about when trying to see Maxine was the only reason you were there. Not for the shite music and the boys shouting in your ear *You all right, mate? You all right, mate? You all right, mate?* and wanting to shake your hand so their mates could see them do it.

The hotel's reception is empty and so is the street but you spot a shop with lights on. You're a bit worried about the Spanish situation but the place is just like a Spar. You pick up the water and, while you're here, grab a bottle of wine for her which isn't the priciest but not the cheapest either, then some crisps and a big bottle of Coke.

When you pay the boy at the counter he smiles and says something in Spanish and you say, 'Yeah, cheers,' and walk towards the hotel and that's when you see the bar. It's next to the hotel's entrance and looks out onto the street. Some tourists sit at tables near the window but you're looking past them to a woman behind the bar. And it *might* be. She's sideways on and it's dark out here and it's hard to see but, well, it might be.

You walk up the hotel's steps into the lobby. There's a glass door through to the bar and she's behind the bar writing in a notepad. There's not much more to say other than the fact that it's her. You, obviously, have stopped moving. You can't just stand here. You start for the lift but your legs appear to be having a rebellion.

This, again, is what happened with Maxine. She'd come into Panache nightclub and walk through the crowd like she was doing everyone a favour by coming in and this is the kind of thing that would happen to you. But this feels much worse. You're staring at the button for the lift as if it's going to grow a mouth and tell you what to do.

Surely to Jesus Christ you're not going to turn round and walk into the bar holding your shopping? Surely to fuck. You lunatic. Are you? You turn round and you walk into the bar holding your shopping.

You know there are other people in there only because you saw them from the street. That feels a long time ago. It's you and it's her and you walk to her like you're walking through deep, deep sand. She looks at you. The bar's shrinking and there's not enough air. Your brain is on strike. Your shopping weighs a ton and a half. She's smiling. She's speaking but at first your ears are too busy to hear her and she has to say it at least once more.

'I'm sorry,' she says, 'the bar's closed.'

Her words travel miles within you before you know them. She's wearing a black shirt that offers a V of brown skin. The tan turns gold where it stretches over her cheekbones. Her eyes look green then brown then green. Her hair is long curls of brown and blonde. You think about lunchtimes at the garage in Davidson Street when the boys stuck on *Scarface* and you all sat and waited for Michelle Pfeiffer in the scene beside the pool or when they stuck on *Top Gun* for that bird that Tom Cruise shagged. She doesn't look exactly like either of them but she's in that department and it's not a big department. Seeing her serving drinks behind a bar is laughable, it doesn't make sense.

'Sorry,' she says again.

'Do you have a bottle opener?' you ask her.

The moment when you think to ask this question, which is just before you do, is one of the best moments of your life. It's you, her and your shopping and you manage to find a connection. She picks something up and stretches her hand over the bar. You take the bottle opener. When you take it and feel the presence of her grip it sends electricity up your arm.

'You can keep it,' she says. 'You've just arrived?'

'Yes,' you answer.

She doesn't say anything. She doesn't say anything because she doesn't have anything to say.

'Where is the best beach?'

It's fair to say that you didn't know, you really had no idea, you were going to say that. Certainly, when you do, you're genuinely surprised. You feel that you should add something but there's not a huge amount to add to a moment like that. Maybe you could ask her to ignore it. Maybe you could pretend she misheard you.

Maybe you could apologise to her and say that you're mentally ill.

'You will get a map from the receptionist,' she says and her smile says The Fucking End.

You walk out the bar and towards the lift. Someone's moved it a hundred miles away. It takes you a week to get there and another week for the doors to open. You get in the lift and the doors close. It takes you up four floors in the time it could take you up Kilimanjaro. The doors open again and you walk down the corridor while you try not to think.

Thankfully, she's still asleep. You get undressed and into bed. You open the water and take a drink. You rest it on your chest and jam the pillows behind so you can sit up.

Where's the best beach?

You drink the water. She works in the hotel and you're going to see her every day for a week. A whole week and that was your opening number. That was how you kicked things off. Standing holding a shopping bag and talking about bottle openers and beaches in the middle of the night. You laugh and nearly choke on the water trying to keep quiet.

Where's the best beach?

You're gasping and you stick a fist in your mouth and bite down. Your eyes water with the silent laughter. What a picture. What a *prick*.

*

On the way back to her room Ana does a deal with herself. She can go to sleep without forming her schedule for tomorrow but she must leave straight away in the morning with no hour by the pool. She can work out her plan for the day once she's begun. It's not the best way to work but the day has been so long with the yacht and then the bar that, when Ana gets to her room and sees her bed, she knows there is no choice but sleep.

She lifts the folders to the ground then undresses quickly, washes and slips under the bed sheets. The last thing she sees, her head turned to the side, are the folders sitting ready for the morning. The last thought she has, and it's only for a second or two, is the sand dunes and the thin man, but her mind sends this away without effort. There is too much else to worry about, too much to do.

Sunday

She's talking about a swim but you're not getting sucked into that. Better stay right here in the shade, under the big umbrella, stretched out on the lounger that's not exactly delighted to have you on board. When you came to lie down after breakfast there was a creaking and for a moment you'd thought the thing was about to give up. You and her had looked at each other, laughing once you realised it would hold. She'd gone straight down to her bikini, covered herself in lotion and dragged her lounger out of the shade. You'd stayed safe from the sun and watched the people arrive.

The old folk came first. Waving over at the two of you and talking about the weather as they passed by to the proper chairs at the end of the pool. They'd produced packs of cards and books and sat there happy enough in short-sleeved shirts and sandals. Soon the families descended with squealing kids and their parents handing out the first rows of the day. You saw the dads and you tried to put yourself in their place but it just didn't work. Not for any of them, even the ones where the kids were quiet enough and the wives were still decent to look at. Best of luck to you, lads, you thought, but not for me.

She'd slept with her face turned to you and thin lines of sweat running through the frown. You'd never met anyone else who frowned when they slept. Now she's woken up. She's on her elbows and blinking at the brightness. She's talking about a swim.

'No thanks, love,' you say, 'I'm all right here.'

With the time that's passed the sunlight has come up and

onto the lounger and reached one of your feet. You stretch an arm to the umbrella and move the shade back. You've left your watch upstairs but it must be getting close to lunchtime.

*

At a corner table of the Argentine restaurant, Ana takes a seat well covered by the parasol. It's early for lunch and the Argentine owner, who named the place after himself, sets up while his wife calls instructions from the kitchen. He waves a hand, or nods, or shouts back, but he never turns. He turned, though, when Ana arrived and he held out hands full of cutlery in welcome.

The potted plants separating the restaurant's terrace from the village's paved square hide wasps that emerge when food is served. Ana likes to come early for this table, at the other side of the terrace and looking back towards the square and the church beyond. That's on days when guilt over a barren morning doesn't keep her working into the afternoon, with hunger a discomfort to go with the frustration.

There had been no difficulty in the decision to come for lunch today. Not only had the morning been productive but Ana was exhausted after the quick start. Within ten minutes of waking she'd been in her car, guiding it out of Es Cana while her body struggled with the suddenness of the day's beginning. Ana had driven from Es Cana through the countryside to the valley headed by the village of San Carlos. At the crossroads on the edge of the village she had taken the road to San Vicente, five miles up the coast towards the island's north-eastern tip. In a car park in San Vicente, Ana had formed her plan.

From San Vicente she progressed gradually back down a section of the road to San Carlos, working through the addresses she had transferred into the day's list of fourteen. Seven houses had been scored from the list by the time she stopped and came to the restaurant in San Carlos. Some had been easy and some harder. She had waited, and visited the neighbours of empty houses, and looped back on herself, but one way or another seven were gone. Half finished, therefore, Ana sits on the terrace of the Argentine restaurant while the owner's wife shouts and he mutters and finishes his tasks.

Ana has made San Carlos her base for the region because the crossroads gives options for major roads. To the east is back to Es Cana and on to Santa Eulalia. To the south the road takes you all the way to Ibiza Town, the west means the hills and dark red fields of the island's centre, and to the north is San Vicente.

The roads would mean nothing without the addresses. When she received Francesco's files and found ways to reduce them, Ana had begun with a little over a thousand addresses for the entire island. By the time she started on this last region it offered a final list of 194. All could be reached off one of the four roads that meet outside San Carlos and that was how she worked them, up and down those four roads and out into the land around them. Ana has only the San Vicente road still to cover. This morning there were forty-five addresses left. Now there are thirty-eight. Thirty-eight from over a thousand. Some would see that as an achievement but Ana can't. Her belief is being cut with each address ruled out. She fights worry, fear, and in recent nights when she has woken with these numbers ruling her mind, there has been panic.

Ana checks the list against the map. Of the seven addresses left for the day, six are near the road and one is up what looks like a private drive in the hills directly behind San Carlos. Ana can see those hills from where she sits. They are steep, banked with pine and looming heavily behind the church. Occasionally, among the trees, a house shows in glimpses of whitewash. When she started her search Ana saw such houses as hiding from her. They would be cowering and anxious, behind the trees and the curled drives, and scared for her threatening arrival. Now, the positions seem to have reversed.

She looks for distraction in the few people who pass across the square, going to the church or the village's other restaurant which is overseen by a waiter who exchanges formal, unfriendly waves with the Argentine. San Carlos is Ana's favourite place on the island. Sometimes, in the early morning, she will turn off before the crossroads and come into the village for just a few minutes. She sits in the square, next to the fountain that she has never seen working, while the day's brightness builds behind the hills. Even in September the sunshine arrives hopefully in San Carlos and this is what Ana needs, with the summer passing by and every day reporting shorter than the one before.

*

You're watching her swim when the young ones drift onto the scene. Teenagers, who arrive rubbing their eyes, holding their backs, groaning like they're returned from the trenches. The morning after the booze and fuck knows what else. At that age hangovers have to be shown and celebrated, particularly when there are birds about and these kids are split down the middle. A group of lads tell stories in voices that travel deliberately down to the girls who sit far enough away to look like they're not listening. The girls stand and stretch and make sure they're being seen from the right angles, and to be fair you're happy with every angle, while the boys pretend they're not looking.

Lads like that. English lads, at that stage and with those minds, well, you know them better than they know themselves. You could pick out the leader from the voices alone. You could pick out their capability at forty miles an hour while they stood at an estate corner, which is exactly what you used to do. You and Sam. You'd have a look and sometimes he'd say, 'Yeah,' and you'd brake and pull a U-turn. They'd see the car and maybe they'd even feel a little brave but then you'd get out and they wouldn't feel brave at all and then Sam would walk over to them and Sam would say,

Afternoon, gentlemen, may I join you for a moment? May I tell you something about this great country of ours?

Like everything else it got easier over the years. By the last months, before Bradford Square and the trials, the car would be waved over. Local celebrity, that's what Sam was by then. He'd be in among them, patting his favourites and reminding everyone about their Youth Subscriptions.

Half price if you're under eighteen, lads. Subscribe to the struggle, gentlemen, just a few quid a week.

You know that all they want, the boys back in Bradford and those ones over there by the pool, is to be told who they are. Once you've done that you can give them the rest. Give them a cause and an enemy. Reasons and instructions. Sam would talk to them on an estate corner and a week later a newsagent, or a mosque, or a bar full of benders got its windows put in. And Youth Subscriptions would be paid.

She climbs out of the pool, stands at the steps and pulls her hair back. You watch her come towards you and then dart your eyes to one half of the youngsters. The bold boys are having a good check on her but, it's funny, when you look over they go all Patrick Moore and start staring at the sky.

'We should get lunch,' she says and waves at a waiter. He's wearing shorts and a white T-shirt with the name of the hotel on it. It's not exactly the first time you've thought of the woman at the bar but you could have done without it. The man hands you menus coated with plastic. He asks what you want to drink and you say 'Two waters' to stop her from ordering booze but she doesn't seem to mind. She's drying her hair with a towel and not really listening.

*

The gap between the key turning and the engine responding is no more than a second but Ana is fearful every time. On maybe

73

a dozen occasions the engine has decided not to start and she has been left waiting and trying until finally, finally, it comes to life with reluctance. Of course, she should take it to a garage but that would mean spending money and, besides, it starts more often than not.

Today the engine sounds confident after its lunchtime rest. Ana drives back out of San Carlos onto the San Vicente road that runs up the corner of the valley, giving a view back down to the village and the fields beyond.

A product of the countryside, Ana notices the many jobs that the local farmers ask of their fields. In March she saw the olive trees blossom and their fruits harvested with wooden poles waved from ladders. After the olives had been gathered potatoes were planted in lines that curved round the trees. They would be lifted soon, Ana guessed, and in the meantime goats pick over the ridged soil and chew on the leaves that would otherwise be ground for compost. These fields have much to admire for Ana, while they continue anciently onwards and ignore the villages that have grown into towns because of the tourists.

The road peaks then drops into the long approach to the coast and San Vicente. Ana glides towards the sea before slowing and pulling the car off the road and onto the short drive of a cottage. Straight away the dogs bark.

Ana still doesn't understand Ibiza's dogs. She could be a mile up a private road when plump, healthy specimens chase her car with heads bobbing at the window only for the road to end at an abandoned house. Similarly rootless dogs prowl the island. There are single operators who slink between parked cars in the towns and whole packs that march their threat down beaches while children squeal and parents look on in unease. Ana has known wilder dogs in Komoró, where the men use vizsla hounds against the foxes, but she is frightened more by a bite from one of these strays.

The two dogs that harry her now, Ana sees with relief, look

kept. She has never seen a local dog with a collar but these have cut hair and their barking sounds born from habit rather than anger. She ignores them and they glumly watch her walk to the cottage. The door's opened by a young Spanish mother with infant children fidgeting behind. The name that Ana has for this house looks French and the woman remembers talk of a Frenchman owning it before her parents who had in turn passed it to her. French is not what Ana needs. German, Swiss, Austrian perhaps. But not French. Ana thanks the woman, who is only mildly interested in her unusual visitor, and passes the cowed dogs on her way back to the car.

Such are the exchanges that shape her days. There have been hundreds, if not thousands, of these small excuses for conversations and Ana drives onwards to the next one. Six to go for the day and it is always best to concentrate on the day alone. She looks down, briefly, at the map and the house behind San Carlos that would eventually signal the day's end. The road to it looks strange, sketched almost with hesitation onto the map.

★

You pretend not to see her moving about until she sits on the edge of your lounger. She runs her hands up inside your T-shirt then down onto your legs.

'You going to sit under there all day?'

You look at the empty plates and glasses from your lunch. You could eat the same again, easy.

'For a bit,' you say.

She points over to the pool. There's a lilo floating in the deep end. Down in the shallows, a dad pulls his baby through the water and says things like *That's it* and *Kick your legs*. The kid's barely got hair. It's hard to tell with babies but it doesn't look like it's at the coaching stage.

'Go on that lilo, Craig, get a bit of sun.'

It's not a bad idea. The pool's just quietened down again after the old folk and the youngsters both had a crack at the same time which, to be fair, was a disaster. The kids had chucked a football back and forth while the old ones swum up and down with breaststroke so slow it hardly kept their heads above water. Eventually, as it was always going to, the ball had bounced smack off some old boy's beak and the whole thing descended into laughing and shouting and you shook your head and closed your eyes and thought, *All the way to Ibiza to hear this shite*. But now the old folk have left, the youngsters sleep with arms hanging off loungers like they're dead, and a bit of sun wouldn't hurt.

'Yeah, all right,' you say.

You stand up and take off your T-shirt. You cough while you walk to the pool and a couple of the young lads stir and look over. You know what they're thinking. They're thinking, *Fuck ME*.

It's easy for you to forget about your size despite the gym and the eating and the muscle rotation and the supplements and, if we're going to be honest here, the steroids until the trials when John Dickinson said it would make you an unreliable witness. What with all that, you're a lot bigger than most others on this earth and that makes people look at you. And invariably, no matter who it is, the reaction is the staring and the *fuck ME*. That's what these lads are offering and she'll be watching and enjoying it because she's always loved the way other men react. The two of you walk into a bar and any boy shouting loses his voice before the door closes behind you. She likes that and all the rest.

You dive in and it's colder than you expected. You go towards the bottom, letting some of your air out and feeling your body tighten in surprise. Down there, under the water, you think of the swimming pool in Bradford where your old man dragged you on a Saturday morning. He'd take you to the baths and pay you in and then he'd go round the corner to the Royal Arch and forget to come back. You'd walk to the Royal Arch with your trunks rolled in your towel and he'd shout, 'Ah, the sailor, back from the sea,' and mess about with your wet hair for the barman's benefit.

You swing your legs to the tiles and push back up, breaking the surface and waiting for your eyes to beat the sun and find the lilo. You tug it towards you but it's a tricky bastard. You try to pull yourself on but it slips away and you go under. When you come back up she's laughing and you're rubbing the chlorine out your eyes.

'That was impressive,' she shouts.

You laugh with her and grab it again. Other people are watching but that's hardly an issue. You tread water and line up the lilo. You pull it beneath you and kick like a mule and launch yourself onto it. It just about works. You squirm your way up until your head reaches the end. With your weight on board the lilo's only an inch clear of the water but that's enough.

'Congratulations,' she calls over.

'Cheers,' you say and close your eyes. Your back is already drying in the sun's heat.

*

If the person who opens the door isn't Spanish then Ana starts with English. She has just enough French and German for what is required but English is where Ana and the foreigners usually meet. These situations are rare, however. In the majority of cases the door is opened by a Spaniard.

It was in Barcelona that Ana learnt Spanish, in those winter months between Jerusalem and Ibiza. She'd spent Christmas alone and handed over too much of her money for Spanish lessons and dictionaries. She had lessons during the day and spent nights with her dictionary in the hostel where beds cost two hundred pesetas and she tied string from her bags to her arm before sleeping. The dictionary and the lessons taught Castilian with some Catalan variation only for Ana to arrive in Ibiza and find the locals had twisted the language once more.

For example, at this second house, Ana tells a man she seeks a German friend who may have lived here some years before. He replies that he has rented the house from a local landlord for ten years and, while reaching for the door, he says *derea*, my pleasure. If he was in Barcelona and staying loyal to the Catalan, Ana knows the man would have said *de res*. If he was in Madrid, working from the Castilian, the dictionary Spanish, Ana would have expected *con mucho gusto*. The Castilian response, thank you for your help, would have been *gràcies per la seva ajuda* and the Catalan variation *gracias por su ayuda*, but Ana knows that with this Ibicinco, who reacts with surprise to her knowledge, the answer is *gracias para ayu*.

Perhaps because of her use of the island's dialect, picked up in instalments since her arrival, the man pauses to tell her of a German who lives nearer San Carlos. Ana thanks him without enthusiasm. There are many Germans who live permanently on the island, and Italian, French and British. There is a European school in Santa Gertrudis where she has watched the blonde-haired children play.

Ana drives onto the San Carlos road and then off to a farm-house. She walks right round the noiseless building and is back at her car when a whistle reaches her from two fields away. Ana takes off her shoes and trudges through the soil to the farmer. He tells her that he bought the farm five years before. Ana smiles while she walks back over the dry soil that yields and leaves her prints behind. *Bona sorti*, the man shouted in wishing her luck, a twist on the Catalan of *bona sort*.

Sometimes Ana thinks about all this knowledge she has gained and does not view it with pride. She views it with nervousness, a regret that it has all been a waste and what that would mean.

★

At first the lads by the pool are just talking about football. The lilo drifts and the water runs through your fingers trailing over the edge. You're not far off falling asleep when they start chanting. *United, United, United.* Fucking Man Utd. Has to be, they're not Geordies. *United, United, United.* To you it sounds like another chant.

You don't want to think about Sam Albright, not here, but you know why you are. It was easy to push the hundred grand away when you had the airport, plane and hotel to deal with. But lying here with your body hot and the water cold under you it's hard not to think about the hundred grand and who it could bring out the woodwork. And from there your thoughts can only really go one way and that's backwards.

United, United, United.

Albright, Albright, Albright.

It was started by the office bearers who swarmed round Whyte's Fish lorry like rats. Sam worked his way through them and they jabbed fingers in the air and began.

Albright, Albright, Albright.

It was a virus that spread to those around them. Sam put his polished shoe on the lorry's registration plate. You pulled him onto the platform and the people saw him and that's when it took off. The cheer didn't even die before it was swallowed by the chant.

Albright, Albright, Albright.

In waves it ran across Bradford Square.

Albright, Albright, Albright.

Sam walked to the microphone and lifted his hands skywards. The gold of the rings. He wanted silence and it came. You looked at Bradford Square and you saw something strange. It wasn't just the punters that were waiting and watching. The police were as well. They weren't facing the crowd, they were facing Sam.

★

At the third house a teenage boy relates the line of owners back to a departed Italian grandfather. At the fourth a worried couple show Ana their certificate of purchase from 1984. At the fifth house the smell of cooking comes through the open door but no one answers her knock. She drives a mile to the sixth house where a man hacks back juniper trees at the end of a brown lawn. He introduces himself as the owner of an Es Cana hotel that Ana knows is small and old but the man talks of grandly. He lights the stub of a cigar and asks Ana to join him for a glass of Hierbas but she is already moving towards the car, thanking and apologising.

She returns to the fifth house. There is this one and one more to go. Still nobody comes, still the door is open and betrays the cooking from inside. Ana never enters a house in this situation. It wouldn't be right and there are the dusty shotguns she has seen hooked above kitchen doors or resting in porches. It's not a large island but many houses rarely have visitors and this can make people nervous. She walks to the car, winds down both windows to let in the faint breeze and pushes her seat back. Sleep is tempting. Instead Ana looks at the map and the last house to come.

This final address has more than enough power to hold off sleep. It belongs to a category that exists separate to the others. It hides among other addresses that appear to play a similar role but that's a decision Ana made to maintain motivation. Those thousand addresses that Francesco had given her had contained around seventy like this. It would have been easy to go straight to these addresses but the risk was, in the event of failure, Ana would return to the neglected bulk of the addresses with her confidence stripped.

The reason that these seventy addresses offered the greatest chance of success, and were therefore the most attractive to Ana, were that they were all properties bought by a foreigner in 1945 and when Francesco's records ended in 1981 they were yet to be sold.

Unlike the others, where she was looking for clues to the previous owner, these houses bore current owners who could offer a lot more. The days when one of these addresses worked itself naturally into her plan provoked extreme reactions in Ana. She left them until the end of the day, allowing the heightened hope to act as motivation, but the disappointment would then arrive different and much stronger than the standard.

A woman hurries up the drive with a basket of bread and vegetables. Final ingredients for the meal cooking inside, Ana guesses. The woman's rushed progress ends in a sudden, surprised halt. She politely explains to Ana that she's lived in the house for four years and has never heard of any foreigners coming before her. Her accent is local and she excuses herself with a gesture to the basket. It is enough and Ana thanks the woman with a gratitude exaggerated by anticipation of the day's final task.

★

The police only gave permission for the rally a week before and that helped get the city on edge. The *Bradford Mail* called it a 'Shock Rise in Extremist Feeling'. The next day the letters page told them it was a long way from a shock rise. It had been coming. It was about jobs, and houses and self-respect. You'd bought the paper and gone to pick up Sam. You'd asked him who'd done that, who'd organised the letters, and he looked at you and told you that no one had.

In that moment you both realised that it had happened. After six years. Six years of you driving Sam to the function rooms of pubs, to community centres booked for birthday parties that didn't exist, to warehouses, garages, to the front rooms of council houses, to motorway service stations where Sam went and spoke to people in the backs of cars, to picket lines and demonstrations that had nothing to do with Sam but he made them have something to do with him. After six years the thing had a life of its own. All you could do, all Sam could do, was direct it.

It had started with twenty men. Five of them had been from the garage where Sam found you. You'd been given a card and on the card it said *Membership Number – 21*.

When you stood on Whyte's Fish lorry six years later you looked down at the National Committee, the Local Organisers, Press Officer, Travel Secretary, Youth Liaison Workers, Logistics Co-ordinator. There had been times when you'd thought Sam had made up these positions on the spot when some new rising star stood with his hand on the flag. It seemed that anyone who came to enough meetings, who clapped in the right places and showed a bit about them, got some sort of title. Once they'd paid. And the one position that never went anywhere was the one for the money. *S. Albright – Party Leader, Treasurer. Membership Number – 1*

It was the office bearers that started the chant, those morons with their laminated membership cards, and when Sam asked for quiet they all called for it as well, as if their feeble voices were needed.

The speakers on the back of Whyte's Fish lorry vibrated when Sam started to talk at Bradford Square. He spoke to the old men with their medals and to the shoppers with their plastic bags. He spoke to the families with kids on dads' shoulders and to the angry unemployed. To the loyalists and the curious, the good voters and the hooligans who didn't like standing next to each other but there you fucking go. And he spoke to the youngsters. Like these ones beside the pool. Doing what they should be doing, going on holiday, pissing about and trying it on with birds. Not standing in Bradford Square listening to a liar.

'Did it go well?'

That's what Sam had asked. After Bradford Square and the pub and the congratulations and everyone saying that this was it, that it had become unstoppable. Outside the house in Dawson Street where he'd always said he lived.

★

There have been times when Ana has felt close. There have been Germans and old men and women who have hardly been able to speak for nerves. Faces have lurked at windows rather than answer doors. Some have shouted through mosquito blinds for Ana to leave or delivered the same message from behind their dogs. Ana always stays, with a smile and an apology and then the questions. Over time Ana has come to see these reactions as meaningless. They can mean many things and guilt is just a possibility among all the others.

There was only one time when Ana thought, really thought, that she'd found him. He was a German man who lived in a villa outside Portinatx, the furthest north of the island's towns, and he lied from the beginning. The first lie was that he had bought the small house, hidden from the road by an ignored garden, in 1978. The second was that it was a holiday home and he was only on Ibiza for a few weeks. He called himself Schwarzer.

From Francesco's files Ana knew the house had not been sold in 1978 and had, in fact, not been sold since 1953. She also knew the house was registered not as a holiday home but as a permanent residence. It was all she could do to concentrate on the road south to Es Cana that night, driving back to the hotel while her mind buzzed with possibility.

She looked at the one photo she had for a long time. The man who called himself Schwarzer seemed too small and, especially, too young, but she had learnt not to use that judgement forcefully in Ibiza. Those on the island who avoided the worst of the sun and followed the local diet of fish, oils and endless salads maintained bright features into old age.

The following morning Ana returned to the German man's house. She parked a little up the road, walked to the end of the drive and forced the mailbox to find a pair of letters. One was from the electricity board to an A. D. Schwarzer and the other was handwritten, posted in Frankfurt, and addressed to a P. Bolzher. It was more evidence that the man's story was different to what he'd offered, but Ana was unsure how to react.

For a week she continued her search of the Portinatx area but at least once a day would stop outside the German man's house, parked far enough away to disguise her intentions while she waited and watched. Ana never saw anyone enter or leave the house and she never saw the man again apart from on the front page of *Ibiza Diario*. She was lying by the hotel's pool in the early morning, reading the *Diario* out of boredom with the sun behind clouds. She sat bolt upright when she saw him and her body was swept with coldness. He was being led in black and white into the Portinatx police station with his hands bound and the Guardia Civil at either side.

Paul Bolzher was a 61-year-old financial adviser from Frankfurt who had embezzled five million Reichmarks from private clients and banks. He had taken the money and slipped into Ibiza a few years ago to hide in the home of his cousin Adrian Schwarzer. The house, the *Diario* concluded, had been empty for many years since the death of Adrian Schwarzer's parents. Bolzher wasn't the man who Ana needed but it was the closest she had come.

Still, she searches. Making her plans and heading out into the alleys of towns and villages and along the country roads. Up dead ends, wrong turns and tracks that twist through the pine trees with crickets droning in the grass. All to reach another address in a car that sometimes stops without asking and is being directed from a map that is now folded down to one last section.

At the San Carlos crossroads Ana takes the Es Cana road and the map guides her to a turning soon after. The road to the day's final house is a surprise. San Carlos is a wealthy area and even private drives like this one have usually been rolled and gritted with stone from the quarry at Port Des Torrent. This road seems almost vandalised such is the state of disrepair. Branches have been left to hang and scratch at the roof of the car which bucks its way upwards through potholes that would stop a more cautious driver. Ana and her car toil together over the unforgiving surface until the road ends in a clearing. The engine sounds grateful when she turns it off but Ana's attention is elsewhere.

This is new, she thinks. This is different.

*

You're awake and you've just got time to shout before you're under the water. You gasp and thrash your arms about and they bounce off the plastic of the lilo which you use to pull yourself back up. You tuck the lilo under your chin and hug it while the panic ends. Your toes skim the tiles and you realise you can stand. Jesus Christ.

'You OK, Craig?'

She's sitting up on her lounger, her hand shading her eyes. There's no one else around apart from a family eating their dinner and an old boy kipping in the corner. It's later.

'Yeah, how long was I asleep?'

'An hour, maybe a bit more,' she says.

Now that you've got the time you feel the sting. You raise a hand and gently push your fingers over the crest of your shoulders. Someone has started a bonfire on your back.

'I'd better get out the sun,' you tell her and wade towards the steps.

You make the shade and sit facing her. She smiles and curls towards you on her lounger, one leg on top of the other.

'Now you've got me sleepy,' she says.

You lay a towel over the lounger and lean slowly into it. This should be manageable as long as you don't move too much. You pick up her magazine and a bottle of water and your back quivers behind you. You read the magazine. A woman is sleeping with her daughter's boyfriend and is wondering if that's a good idea. Another woman's boss has been calling her names based around the size of her tits and she wonders if that's acceptable. Another woman has a photo of a family gathering and wonders if, past the couch and through the conservatory window, she can see the face of her dead husband.

This is the stuff she puts into her head. You read the stories while she sleeps but it's not much of a sleep she's getting and eventually she gives up. She looks around and walks over to the family. She asks them the time and then looks back in surprise to you.

'It's nearly six, Craig,' she says. 'We should get going.'

A whole day gone and you've even enjoyed it. You're excited too but that's not because of the day, it's because of the night to come and what it might bring. The hotel bar and the woman behind it. You stand up and your back doesn't enjoy you pulling your T-shirt over your shoulders. The two of you get your stuff together, walk into the hotel and through to the lift. You consider coming up with an excuse to check the bar now but decide against it. Wait till later, you think, when you've got some decent clobber on.

Up in the room you suggest she goes for the first shower. You take off your T-shirt and make for the balcony. You're looking forward to the view and maybe a bit of a breeze when her voice stops you. It's strange, the minute she starts speaking you know exactly what's happened. You can't quite believe that you never considered this a possibility, even when you felt your back burn and give up secrets.

'Craig,' she says and she's properly shaken up, which is fair enough. 'What the fuck is that?'

★

Two cameras on metal poles peer over the unpainted, concrete wall at either side of a yellow gate. The gate itself must be seven feet high, the wall another foot on top of that and the cameras look down on Ana like birds in the trees. The wall runs off into the pines and sunlight catches on the barbed wire strung along its ridge. Painting this gate yellow, considers Ana, seems a light touch considering the concrete and the wire.

She has never seen such security in Ibiza and it means trucks of bricks and cement have somehow scrabbled up the testing road, the defects of which now appear determined and deliberate, an opening hurdle placed in front of visitors. The road shows no sign of money but the destination shows it clearly.

An intercom system is bolted beside the gate. When Ana presses the button there's no noise or even an indication that the system is in use. From up close Ana can see that paint peels from the gate while the wall bulges and is in need of support. The cameras wear a film of African sand carried by the winter rain and Ana doesn't feel monitored when she looks at them. It is a foolish thought, she counters, that she would instinctively know such a thing.

It's nearing evening and Ana feels her options narrow. She's scared. It's hard not to be when faced by such a surprise at the end of such a road with the sun departing for the day. She is also more intrigued, more alerted, than she has been since Portinatx and the man who would be Paul Bolzher.

For now, Ana decides reluctantly, she will return to the hotel. It's difficult to turn the car but the road is easier to travel down. She presses and releases the brake while negotiating the road's failings and tries unsuccessfully to consider the new addresses to be visited tomorrow. She knows it's to here, to the yellow gate, that she'll drive in the morning.

★

One week after Bradford Square you and John Dickinson had your second conversation and, at the end, you said you wanted your tattoos off. The first conversation was four months earlier. You were standing filling your car at the Shell garage on Albany Road when John Dickinson walked up to you, showed you his badge and asked *just how much* you knew about Sam Albright.

You'd dropped the hose on the ground and it had pissed petrol over the car's wheel. You'd walked round the back of the car and told him to say another word, just one more word. He'd put his hands up and told you to take it easy and then laid his card on the roof of your car. He'd walked away and, while doing so, he'd said, 'Just take the card, that's all I'm asking, and give me a call when you find out. And don't,' he'd added with a finger raised in warning, 'call Bradford Police. If you call anyone when you find out, call me. But don't call Bradford Police.'

You'd picked up the card. *Special Branch*.

He didn't tell you what he knew because he was a clever boy that John Dickinson. If he'd told you from the off then you'd have gone running to Sam Albright who would have denied it and twisted it as easy as breathing. So, just like John Dickinson wanted, you found out by yourself and when you did you'd called him one week after Bradford Square.

He'd told you to meet him the next morning at the Little Chef at Junction 40 on the M1. The next morning you'd sat in the Little Chef and at the end of the conversation, once everything was agreed, you'd told him you had tattoos on your back and you wanted them off. A few weeks later he took you to a private hospital near Hendon where a Jock doctor whistled and said, 'Well, that's some decoration you have there.'

The first day you just got through it, gripping the metal sides of the bed as the doctor did his *Star Wars* stuff with the laser. The second day you tried to lighten the mood a bit.

'So whereabouts you from then up there?' you asked him while you got hunkered down.

'Dundee,' he told you. He started rubbing the cold lotion onto your back and then in went the needle to kick things off. You stared at a poster telling the doctor how to put stuff in the bin. You wondered what kind of doctor struggled to put stuff in the bin.

'Football fan?'

'I am,' he answered as he moved around the room in preparation.

'Rangers or Celtic?'

'Neither. Dundee United.'

'I thought all you lot were Rangers or Celtic?'

He'd stopped moving.

'No,' he said, 'we're not. Listen, we're doing the pigment today. Yesterday we did your stratum corneum, which is the surface. The pigment is below that, so I'm going to have to dig in a bit. It's going to hurt.'

'Fine.'

Miserable Jock, you thought, no surprise. There was a click and a strange, whining noise that wasn't around the day before and then it started. The oil and the injection did what they could but that wasn't much. You stared at the poster but you weren't thinking about putting things into the bin. You'd never known pain like it and you were thinking – *YOU JOCK CUNT YOU JOCK CUNT YOU JOCK CUNT YOU JOCK CUNT YOU JOCK CUNT YOU JOCK CUNT*

And now here you are, standing in the hotel room in Ibiza and she's behind you and asking again.

'What *is* it, Craig?'

You walk past her to the bathroom, turn backwards to the mirror, and look over your shoulder. They're fighting their way out of you and showing white against the deep red of the burnt skin. She comes in and you smile at her.

'It's a tattoo, love, I had it removed.'

She stares at the mirror and you do too. Everything's back to front, but that doesn't make any difference to the situation. You know what it is and she doesn't. You can recognise the blurred shapes and symbols. The badges, the flags, the dates. This was how Sam had tested you. This was what he had done.

To her it's just a mess.

'What was it?'

'A footballer,' you tell her. 'Don Hutchins. He played for City.'

'Why'd you have it taken off though?' She's suspicious but not too much. She's just glad it's not some disease, you can see that easily enough.

'He signed for Scarborough,' you say with your eyes on the mirror. You remember being bare-chested behind Sam on summer days, knowing that the kids were nicking behind you and hearing their admiration.

'Fucking hell, look at that, would ya?' they'd squeak.

'So you had it taken off!' She laughs and puts her hands carefully on your hot shoulders. 'Aw, did you get all upset when he left? Did you cry?'

You look again. The flags and the dates. The names of places and events that Sam told you about. Birthplaces of the movement, he called them. Victories.

★

The receptionist stops Ana.

'That man phoned for you again,' she says, a little cold in her delivery. They are busy at reception and these calls must become irritating.

'OK,' says Ana.

'Francesco,' says the receptionist.

'Yes,' says Ana. 'Thank you.'

She walks away from the receptionist's disapproval. At least the gaps between the calls were growing. This was the first one for weeks. When Ana moved up here, to Es Cana and the hotel, he had phoned almost every day.

Of course, she felt badly about what she'd done. Francesco was an honest man. That had been evident from the opening moments of their relationship, at the bar opposite the *ayuntamiento* in Ibiza Town. It was two days after she arrived on Ibiza by the mainland ferry. The *ayuntamiento* was a large building just outside the town's walls and marked by a row of flags showing the line of command running Spain, Catalonia, the Balearics and then Ibiza itself with that strange flag of the old town shown four times.

At first her plan was this – Ana would approach the *ayuntamiento*, produce her certificates and neatly forged letters of introduction, and announce she was here from Budapest University researching immigration to the Balearics. She envisaged the Spanish officials welcoming this eager Hungarian student and happily throwing open their records.

The plan lasted one awkward conversation in the *ayuntamiento*'s cool entrance hall. The clerk said all record requests had to go to Madrid, a separate request was required for each record and that permission must be given from the individual concerned. Ana wandered dejectedly from the building and into a bar opposite. She took a table and watched the people come and go between the *ayuntamiento*'s uniformed doormen, trying to distract herself from the scale of this setback.

She was surprised how late it had become when she saw workers leaving for the night. They funnelled through the door of the *ayuntamiento*, splitting left and right until one group walked straight ahead towards the bar. They were four young men in short-sleeved white shirts and thick ties. The barman laughed and called out names and started pouring small glasses of beer.

The men sat at the bar. Ana turned in her chair so they could see her and asked loudly for the menu. She ate while the men talked and joked. They drank differently to Hungarians. There was no rush or great need for the beer that sat in front of their folded arms. But they were young and she was there and it wasn't long before one hooked a leg from his stool and approached. He had politely waited, Ana realised, until her plate was cleared. His face was betrayed by nerves.

'My name is Francesco,' he said in heavy English. 'A visitor to our island should never sit alone. Please, would you join us?'

★

It's not easy to find a shirt that's too big for you but you somehow managed it with this one. It's a yellow number from Top Man that you bought without trying it on when you saw the XXL but you're an old friend of XXL and this is a step beyond. Christ knows who'd have bought it if you hadn't. They must have been expecting Geoff Capes through the door. Right now, to be fair, you're glad to have it with you. You roll the sleeves up and it sits off your back, leaving some air around the skin.

She's planted in front of the mirror but she's not far from ready. Her hair's done and there surely can't be much more to go on her face. You're sitting here in your one-man tent of a shirt and trying not to ask her how long. You reach into your bag and take out the bottle of Slazenger she got you for Christmas. You were a bit surprised, you thought they just made tennis rackets, but she told you they'd had a crack at the aftershave market. This one's called Advantage. You put a little on your fingers and rub it into your neck. Obviously, it fucking hurts. You'll not be back in the sun for a while, that can be taken as read.

'Not long,' she says.

'No problem,' you tell her.

She walks through and slips her towel off and you watch her pull on pants and a bra and it's rare to see that they match. She's got her dress laid out already and she pulls it over her head and turns to you. Her skin's got colour to it already, her nose is a little red and she's got a few freckles that you don't think were there before.

'How do I look?'

'Beautiful, love. Great. Now' – you stand up – 'where do you fancy?'

'I don't know, do I?' She laughs.

'I thought we could go for a walk along the front, find a restaurant down there?'

'That sounds nice.'

She looks at her shoes that she's lined up against the wall. You're wearing trainers. Maybe you should wear shoes. Half the clubs in Peterborough won't let you in without shoes and in Bradford it was nearly all of them. Strange stuff that. A lunatic in a pair of shoes is just a lunatic in a pair of shoes. If they said straitjackets, that no one could come in unless they were wearing a straitjacket, well, that would make more sense, especially in Bradford.

She chooses a pair, hooks a finger round the straps and yanks them on.

'OK?' she says, and leads you out the hotel room with her heels tapping on the tiles.

She looks good. You follow her to the lift, watching her arse come and go against the dress while she walks. In the lift you suggest Spanish food and she says that would be nice and then it's a bit awkward until the doors open because you know that you're both wondering what Spanish food is.

You don't want to bump into the woman from the bar, not yet, and you don't even look through the glass door when the two of you pass by. You don't want her to see you with another bird. As if she cares. Jesus Christ, the things that go on in your head.

*

Poor Francesco.

Ana gave the men equal conversation, keeping all four involved while she evaluated the worth of their jobs. One worked for the island's tourism department, another on the school board, and Ana eased both out of her attention. That left Francesco and the fourth man who announced with some pride that he worked in the planning office. Ana was interested until he talked of reviewing hotel developments. Only Francesco was left and yet, as it worked out, only Francesco was needed.

'*Registros*,' he told her, his eyes sliding shyly to the side and his hand reaching for his drink. Ana was silent through excitement but one of the other men misread it.

'Records,' he clarified for her, his tone dismissive. 'Pieces of paper.'

To his colleagues, possibly even to Francesco, the job was apparently an embarrassment. Ana waited until the others were in conversation with the barman before saying quietly to Francesco, 'Do you know the Hotel Verde on Calle Colonial?'

'Yes.'

'That is where I am staying. You should call me there, in the morning.'

That was nearly too much for Francesco. He took a long drink and his eyes widened in alarm. He put down the glass and nodded, with the briefest of looks, to Ana.

'Yes,' he said, his voice wilting. 'I will.'

'Good,' replied Ana.

She stood, touched Francesco lightly on the arm, and passed the others in an arc while she said rapid farewells. The next morning the manager of the Hotel Verde shouted up to Ana and she walked happily down the stairs. Francesco was phoning from the office with other voices coming and going in the background. He invited Ana to meet him for a drink at the Hotel Montesol.

'It was the first hotel on the island,' he said with the English only just making it through his nerves. 'I thought that maybe you would find it interesting.'

In the short time she'd been on Ibiza Ana had noticed the men didn't dress well. The brown suit that Francesco wore to the Hotel Montesol looked passed down by an older relative and did not sit comfortably with his polished black shoes. These, thought Ana from across the table, must be what he sees as his best clothes. In the early-evening sunlight, which afforded a truer view than the first time they met, he wasn't an impressive sight.

He wasn't particularly ugly but he was a man where the only points of interest in his appearance failed to help him. His eyebrows, for example, crept too close together and there was acne here and there that would never leave him now. His appearance wasn't important to Ana, this wasn't going to be a romantic affair, but she worried how unlikely a couple they must look. She couldn't risk others suggesting to him that she might have hidden motives, or the possibility of Francesco himself losing confidence. It was already clear that this was something he held in short supply.

After Ana ordered a glass of wine he made a significant display of requesting the cocktail menu. She watched him eye a list that held only mystery. The waiter frowned at his choice and when Ana saw the drink's majestic approach she bit on the inside of her cheeks to stop the laughter. The glass was a foot tall, tapering outwards from a slender root and holding an explosion of activity. The drink travelled through various colours, held a fistful of chopped fruit, bore twists of glittered tinsel and was topped by a sparkler that fizzed defiantly in Francesco's devastated face.

He battled through the decoration to pull desperately at the alcohol and filled the silence by asking Ana about her academic project, the explanation she'd given for her arrival in Ibiza. She told him she was undertaking a study on immigration to the Balearics and switched to Spanish to try and relax him.

They had a second drink, a beer this time for Francesco, and then he walked her back to the Hotel Verde. She offered him a cheek to kiss and said she hoped to hear from him again.

'Definitely,' he beamed, standing in his brown suit.

There was a lunch in a harbour restaurant where Ana stressed the importance of her studies and took his arm on the walk back along the marina, but it was the third meeting when things changed between them. Ana felt guilt before she did what she did but this was swamped by the motivation behind it. It was four years since the death of her mother and four years can offer a lot of motivation.

The restaurant was Italian and brutally expensive. When Francesco took the menu from the waiter he made a troubled, involuntary groan which he attempted to convert into a cough. While he came to terms with a choice that must have been recommended to him by others, Ana said helpfully that she had eaten a late lunch and would start with only soup for now. Francesco made a weak attempt at encouraging her to order more before asking for pasta.

'A small one,' he said to the unimpressed waiter, 'just to see if I like it.'

He was wearing a white shirt with a collar that seemed larger on one side than the other. Ana was in the best dress that she owned, bought for the leaving ball at Budapest University. It was cut deeply at the front and she leant into the table while she spoke. Francesco stole two, three looks at her breasts, his face vaguely startled in the candlelight.

Ana spoke only of her studies. The real purpose, she said with a glance around that hinted at conspiracy, was to find a German man who had moved to the island in the 1940s. Her family had been trying to trace him for many years without luck. It had been, Ana told Francesco, her mother's last request.

'Before dying?' he asked and was instantly embarrassed at his own directness.

'Yes,' Ana answered.

Over the soup and Francesco's pasta, which came in a large saucer, Ana continued. She'd expected questions and some suspicion but there was nothing. It wasn't that Francesco was stupid, she decided, just that he didn't possess curiosity and it was enough of a victory for him to be sitting with her in a restaurant. This was all he needed and he wasn't going to risk losing it by offering anything other than encouragement.

Francesco began by telling Ana about the island's records that were kept in stone cellars under the *ayuntamiento*. Property ownership and utilities. Historically, he explained, the island's council had controlled the local water supply and also the gas and electricity sent from the Spanish mainland by pipe and cable. It was only six years before, in 1983, that a series of privatisations had removed these tasks from the council. In response the council moved property registration to the Catalan authority in Barcelona, allowing it to close what had been a large *departmento de registros*.

Left down there in the cellars was Francesco and a handful of others pulling old records where required. Ana clarified what he was saying. That from the 1940s until 1983 there were records not just of a property's ownership but also the names of those who paid for the property's utilities.

'Yes. So it is not just landlords, you see, tenants as well,' said Francesco. 'And another thing.'

'Yes?' said Ana. It was hard to conceal her delight.

'If a foreigner came to register ownership or to open an account for gas or power then they went into a different file. *Extranjero*. Foreigner. This man you are looking for, he will be somewhere in that file.'

Francesco was clearly surprised by the opportunity that his job was giving him but when he fully appreciated what that opportunity was he faltered. Ana didn't press him. She finished her soup and moved the conversation to a future beach visit. It was Francesco himself who ended matters. He placed both hands on the table and looked at them as if for guidance.

'I could get you the *extranjero* file,' he said finally. 'It is very large but I could copy it. If . . . you know, this would have to be a big secret.'

He looked tortured by the subterfuge. It would be untrue to say that Ana felt anything but joy.

'Really?' she asked, her eyes childlike. 'You could do this for me?'

*

Down at the sea the sky is pink and blue and the pavement is just wide enough to handle the people who follow the curve of the bay.

'Gorgeous, isn't it, Craig?'

Her face is damp with After Sun and she's holding your hand. It's a decent little scene other than the fact you can only look out to sea for so long before checking you're not about to stroll into some other fucker looking out to sea. They should put lanes on the pavement, you think, arrows.

People nod and smile as they pass by. The older ones, all Brits, say *Good evening* or *Lovely night*. The hotels down here have rooms with balconies pointing straight out over the bay. You wonder what the view must be like from up there and you decide that the view must be outstanding. Having said that, these hotels don't have that woman behind the bar, now do they? But you shouldn't be thinking like that, you should be giving this a chance. She's holding your hand and smiling and she's quick to reply to all the *Good evening*s and *Lovely night*s.

You arrive at a row of restaurants that remind you of the lads at the edge of the dance floor at Panache, elbowing each other out the way, fronting up. With this lot it's a battle of blackboards. There must have been some sort of sit-down and then the decision of one blackboard each and let the punters decide, but some of them had tricks up their sleeves. A couple of these blackboards must have arrived on the back of a lorry.

You stop at one that's bigger than you. The menu is up there five times in five languages with little flags beside them. She points at the menu under the Union Jack and you think all the usual stuff you think when you see that flag.

'This one looks OK,' she says.

> Half Chicken and Chips
> T-bone Steak
> Grilled Sole
> Hamburger (Bun)
> Hamburger (No Bun)
> 'Lasagne'

'Yeah, perfect.'

She laughs.

'Look at these blackboards, Craig, they're ridiculous.'

You laugh and it's natural, you mean it.

'I was just thinking that,' you tell her.

A waiter slaloms through the tables towards you holding menus bound in red leather and looking like the boy from *This Is Your Life*. Aspel. But Aspel would probably have more of his shirt done up.

'A table, señor?'

He only asks you, which is fair enough. It's not like you're going to go in and leave her in the street.

'Yeah, please.'

'This way,' he says.

He takes you to a table, you sit down and he gives her a proper look while he hands her a menu. Non-stop, you think, that's what it is for a lot of boys with the looking and the watching. You, on the other hand, would go for months without bothering and then lose your mind out of nowhere. Maxine, then this one here for a while, and now, well, put it this way – you're looking at the menu and you're wondering what that other woman at the hotel is going to have for her dinner.

You know that you want the T-bone so you put your menu down and let her catch up. Above the restaurant there's different music coming from different balconies and the result is a right old racket. With the music are the voices, young and drunk. Out at sea, where it reaches the sky, there's less and less to choose between the two. It's the night now really, all things considered.

The waiter's on his way back so you jog her along a little.

'You ready, love?'

'Yeah.'

You order first. The T-bone with extra chips and a plate of veg on the side. It probably winds him up a bit, the way that you order by pointing at each item in turn, but it's important to get it right. When you're training proper back home you eat five times a day. You might be on your holidays but the very least you've got to do is maintain. She orders the half chicken. When the waiter takes her menu he rests a hand on her shoulder as if to balance. He's fearless this one. He asks you for your drinks order.

'Coke please,' you say and she asks the waiter what he recommends. He suggests sangria.

'Yes please,' she answers and when he goes she smiles at you.

'All right?' you ask.

'Yeah, this is great, isn't it?'

'Oh yeah, really nice.'

In front of both of you is a bit of paper to stop you messing up the table. It's a map of Ibiza and you both realise this at pretty much the same time.

'Let's find where we are,' she says, and runs her finger over the paper. Her mouth moves a little as she goes through the names. The big towns marked out are San Antonio over on the left of the island, Ibiza Town at the bottom and then Santa Eulalia on the right-hand side. There are lots of places in smaller writing and above Santa Eulalia you see Es Cana.

'That's where we are.' You point and she looks and takes a minute to find the spot on her side.

'Oh,' she says. 'Right.'

Beside Es Cana, maybe an inch in from the coast, it says San Carlos. That sounds nice, you think. You wonder if it's walkable.

'We could go for a walk one day,' you say, 'into the hills.'

But she's not listening to you because the waiter's on his way back. He's carrying a tray with your Coke and then one empty wine glass and a jug of booze that could do four people and you're thinking that this doesn't look too clever.

*

Two nights later, Francesco picked Ana up from the Hotel Verde. She kissed him close enough to the lips, looped her arm within his and ignored the leather holdall that hung heavily from his shoulder. While they walked she tried to calm his obvious nerves by talking of the boats she'd seen that day in the town's harbour.

'They are party yachts,' said Francesco with disapproval. 'They take tourists to Formentera and back.'

Dinner was strained and largely silent. When the coffee came

Ana wanted to offer to pay but decided this would offend Francesco and could be seen as a bribe. From nowhere, perhaps to buy time, he asked her about Hungary. Ana described Komoró and its setting deep in the mountains. She explained that her father had worked as a farmhand and she had left Komoró to attend university in Budapest.

'You are the first person in your family to go to university?'

'On my father's side, yes,' answered Ana. 'There is no family on my mother's side.'

There was a silence while Francesco put that with the greater tragedy of her mother's death. Looking for an exit he asked if he had perhaps misunderstood, did Ana say that her father no longer worked?

'He is sick,' said Ana. 'Since my mother died he has been sick.'

'What type of sickness?' asked Francesco, who looked a little trapped.

'In his head. A depression,' Ana answered and felt the normal flicker of shame. People in Komoró said he was mad. At the hospital they'd told her that in other countries, richer countries, her father would be seen as curable and given medicine but in Hungary they were seen only as mad. Nurses came to the house to feed him soup and put him to bed. When Ana had returned from university it was to watch him sit and read the paper, cover to cover, all day long.

'I have an uncle in San José,' said Francesco, 'he does not leave his house. We think that perhaps he has this also.'

It wasn't where Ana would have chosen to guide the conversation but she hoped his awkwardness was pushing Francesco to his choice. It hadn't been made when they left the restaurant and walked through the streets with the holdall slung wordlessly on Francesco's shoulder. He stopped at a bar and led Ana to a booth in the darkened rear. He ordered drinks and watched the waiter's departure with suspicion before speaking with his hand waving in front of his mouth in some strange defence.

'I have a bag with me tonight,' he said in a voice Ana could only just detect.

'I can see it,' she said helpfully.

'It is the *extranjero* file,' he said.

'Oh,' said Ana. It is surely ridiculous, she thought, to try and generate surprise.

'I have been copying it while the others take their breaks. It is a lot of work, a lot of data.'

'Yes,' said Ana, 'I can see.' The bag's sides were being stretched by the contents.

'If I was found to have done this,' said Francesco, 'I would be ruined.'

Ana thought at first he had got his words wrong. Sacked or fired perhaps, but ruined seemed dramatic. When she looked again and saw his face and thought of how an island must become very small when someone does something very wrong, she realised that he'd meant it. She slipped a hand on top of his.

'You have done a good thing.'

Outside the Hotel Verde Ana let Francesco kiss her on the lips. He kissed her hard and with his mouth closed which was the best she could have hoped for. One of his hands trailed down her back and Ana caught it at the base of her spine before freeing herself with a smile.

That night, she didn't sleep. The files showed every property purchase or utility application made by a foreigner between 1940 and 1983. Where the property had been resold by the foreigner to a local there was a note on the file and Ana removed it. She pulled out all the files giving an address in Ibiza Town, where she would start, then removed everything before 1945. By the time morning loomed she had her first pile, her first selection of addresses to check.

It started. At houses and apartments and farmhouses on the edge of town, Ana knocked and rang bells. There was a Danish couple, tanned and lean in their old age, who invited her into the cottage they'd owned since 1963. The husband showed Ana photos of his paintings being exhibited in Barcelona, while the wife produced books she had written on women's liberation. The meeting gave Ana hope. They were both seventy, she was told proudly, and perfectly healthy. Ana looked at them, these people who were the same age as the man she sought, and she knew that this was possible.

★

She's gone, well gone. Two jugs down. You had tried to talk her out of the second one and it didn't go particularly well.

'How can they afford the Bahamas?'

'I don't know,' you say because out of all the words you know they seem to be the safest.

'He gets £150 for every mortgage he sells, she told me at Christmas. He can't sell that many, can he?'

'Not sure.'

'She's only part-time. Two hundred a week, maximum. She comes to see me in the office sometimes at half twelve. And that's her finished!'

'That's true.'

'Last time she came in she asked if I could come out early for lunch. She said could one of the other receptionists not just cover for me?'

'OK.'

'What?'

You look around the restaurant. The tables next to you are empty. That's lucky because you know she's about to –

'Are you fucking kidding me, Craig?'

She's shouting now. Her words are slower and heavier and she sends them like punches. You can sense heads turning. You look at her and lift your hands in protection.

'Calm down,' you say.

'Calm down?' she screeches. You try just looking at the table. That could help. Don't give her a target.

'It's OK,' you say, even though that's one thing it's not.

'I'm an administrator, Craig, not a receptionist. In case you haven't noticed that's how we pay Asda on Sundays. Your bloody five meals a day. I'm an administrator, one of the best at the company.'

You're delighted with her new tone, a hiss that barely makes it to you let alone anyone else. This food argument is a load of bollocks. Every Sunday she'll drive to Asda and come back with a boot full of shit that you'll go and empty and put away for her in the kitchen. Then on a Monday you'll stop at the butcher's and come back and fill the bottom shelf of the fridge and half the freezer and that'll just about get you through the week.

You don't eat hardly any of her food and if the two of you go out on a Friday night then you pay. So the argument makes no sense but she's tried it a few times. She talks about these Asda trips like she's taking on the North Pole single-handed and you should be ready for her return with a banner and a brass band.

'I know you're an administrator, love. You're doing well.'

Never mind that you pay all the rent, all the bills, all the drinks, all the meals. And, come to think of it, the pesetas for this trip that's turning into Peterborough with sunburn.

'I know I'm doing well, Craig, you don't have to tell me that,' she says in accusation. 'I'll probably get another promotion next year.'

'Great. Shall we ask for the bill?'

'I want another one of these.' She picks up the jug of sangria and holds it like she's won a trophy. You reach across the table and take it from her. It's a risk, but rather that than she drops it.

'Let's go back to the hotel, love, get one there.'

She stops herself saying what she was going to say but only for her own reasons, not out of any consideration for you. She shrugs and you wave at the waiter for the bill who's delighted to get the nod. You give him some pesetas and he darts off to get your change. You keep your eyes on the table while you wait. On her side, the map of Ibiza is covered in food and a circle of red from her glass. Your side is spotless and they shouldn't even bother changing it. The waiter comes back and you work out the tip and leave it sitting there. She says, 'You should leave more than that.'

It's the first time you've got angry. She doesn't even know what coin is what. She doesn't even know how much is there. You stand up and say, 'OK?' and walk out to the pavement. She catches you up. You think she's going to talk about the tip. She doesn't but it's not much better.

'How much is a flight to the Bahamas?' she says. You're two people walking along the pavement beside the sea. Two individuals. You wonder if anything really, genuinely connects you. Peterborough? The house? You can't believe quite how desperate that sounds.

'I don't know. Five hundred? It's a long way.'

'Five hundred quid? It's not that much. Don't be ridiculous, Craig.'

You nod. You agree that £500 is probably a bit high. She keeps talking but you're not listening any more because you're thinking about the woman at the hotel and how, all being well, you're about to see her.

★

There was a problem. Too many of the houses were owned only for holidays. It was early spring, a long way from the holiday season, and Ana was finding the majority of the homes she visited were deserted. She couldn't afford to leave these possibilities behind and her days became filled with return trips. She looked, once more, to Francesco.

He picked her up in his father's car and took her to the casino. Ana had asked him if this was the Casino de Rey, explaining that she had heard of this place, but Francesco told her the Casino de Rey had closed years before.

His tuxedo, Ana decided immediately, was similarly borrowed from his father who must be a smaller man because it is rare for a tuxedo to be worn with the sleeves rolled up. At the casino they were almost the first people in the entire building, let alone the restaurant where tables were still being set and the confused waiter sat them next to the balcony. They watched the cleaners finish their work below. Francesco muttered darkly to himself while Ana wondered who was advising him on where to take her and if the person was a true friend of Francesco.

She told him her problem and asked how she could know if the *extranjero* listed was a permanent resident on the island or was buying the property for holidays. He told her that the file would have this listed, in the *residencia* section. Ana wished she'd asked Francesco this question over the phone instead of committing to what turned into long hours in the casino.

After dinner Francesco insisted they wait for the gaming to begin. Finally a croupier arrived at one of the tables, his tie hanging undone and a cup of coffee in his hand. Ana didn't know how many chips Francesco was expecting for his thousand pesetas but, from his reaction, he certainly expected more than five. Five spins of the roulette wheel later, he silently led her out the casino doors.

A sore stomach was the reason Ana gave for returning straight to the hotel where she ran up the stairs to the Ibiza Town file. There it was. The section in each entry she had missed offered two choices – *residencia* and *tourista*. An hour later, Ana had halved the remainder of the Ibiza Town possibilities. Two weeks later, there were no possibilities left.

To search the rest of the island, Ana realised that she needed a car and had to move from the old town. Francesco's confidence had become overblown. He had taken to arriving at the Hotel Verde without invitation and calling her name from the hallway in a manner that he must have felt was romantic.

The tourist office at the harbour provided escape. There was an advertisement for English-speaking staff at an Es Cana hotel. Ana found Es Cana on her map. It was in the Santa Eulalia region, not too far, and she needed the money. They told her to come up to the hotel for an interview so Ana phoned Francesco and he took her to Coches Felices.

'Happy Cars,' he translated for her with a hopeful smile.

After Coches Felices, on the last day she saw him, Ana granted Francesco an unrushed kiss and he smiled with such delight she felt a genuine pain on his behalf. She got the job, moved to Es Cana and now he calls the hotel and she doesn't call him back. Meanwhile she works in the bar, sorts through the files and spends her days looking.

Six months have passed and the search has grown and then shrunk. One way or another it's nearing an end.

★

This isn't exactly a master plan. If you were to choose a sidekick, for a start, then you wouldn't be picking her, and certainly not in the mood she's in, but it's that or nothing so there you go. You can send her to get a table and go to the bar yourself. You'll get a bit of time up there to prove two things to the woman –

1. You're staying in the hotel.
2. You're not a lunatic.

You consider that it might even work to your advantage, going in there with her, because it'll make you look desirable. You know that this is very much clutching at straws. You wait until the two of you are in the hotel's reception and you say, casual as you like, 'How about a quick drink in the bar, love?'

'Nah,' she says, and keeps walking.

You're in disbelief here. Suddenly she's off the booze. You look through the door to the bar and there's no one there but that doesn't mean anything really.

'Come on, Craig.'

She's already at the lift. The one time she doesn't want a drink, that's your luck. Sometimes you think about your luck and decide there has to be someone else involved. Not God, not any of that bollocks, but someone. Someone has to be watching this and enjoying it. Some sick prick who clocked you early doors and said, 'Leave that one to me, lads. I've got plans for him. I'm going to chase him up a fucking tree.'

You walk to the lift. The doors are already open by the time you get there and she's looking at you strangely. The doors close and you think she might hit you but then she's kissing you. She makes you part your mouth and slips her red tongue inside. It tastes terrible. You wait, hopefully, for the doors to open. When they do she takes your hand and leads you out the lift, along the corridor and into the room. The room's untidy. You should have sorted it before you went out.

She sits on the end of the bed and pulls you to her. Her hands are on your belt and then your jeans are down, crumpled round your knees. She pulls away your pants with one hand and the other is straight onto your cock. You weren't expecting this but your cock is in her mouth now and not having to try too much because you can't say you're not enjoying events. You'd rather be in the bar downstairs, right enough, but this isn't a bad second prize.

Her head dips with a pant here and there. You take your shirt off. You rest one knee to her side and slowly, slowly, you move sideways onto the bed. Her head follows your cock like it's attached. You guide her round until she's right angles to you and her skirt's within reach. You push your hand into the skirt and she opens her legs. She's damp right through her knickers and you slide your fingers in there which makes her frown and moan. Her head rises and falls slower now. You feel yourself getting going so you tug gently at her shoulder and she lets you go. You lift her up and drop her onto her back and she bounces gently on the bed, scrabbling at her knickers while you move heavily on your knees between her legs.

You're on top of her and pushing in and up. Her hands are on your chest and her eyes are closed. You scoop her tits out of her top. They look daft, folded over the material. You're jamming yourself into her, faster as you go. Her eyes stay closed. You wonder who she's thinking of. It's probably not even a bloke, not like that anyway. She's probably thinking about her sister. She's probably thinking about her sister's husband and his mortgage commission rates. She's probably thinking about the Bahamas.

You grab her legs. Pull them to your chest. Hold them up in big V. She's whispering something but you can't hear it. You're firing into her now. Sweating like a bastard. Your legs are rubbing against her dress and it's starting to irritate. You concentrate. You look down at her pussy. You look at her legs. You look at her tits. You look at her face. You look back at her pussy. You come, in a few rolling bursts, each one less than the one before. You think she does as well. You pull out and lie down beside her. A drop of cum falls from your cock and onto your chest. You look down at your cock. It looks right back at you.

*

Of all the people on Ibiza it is the British that Ana understands the least and it is the locals that she understands the best. In Komoró as in Ibiza, the children would run close to naked in the summer and the men worked without shirts and returned home with torsos tanned by outdoor industry. Her father went so dark that the other men made fun of him and talked of the footballer Eusebio. From Komoró Ana also understood the spirit of the Ibicencos and the happiness that can come from living in a reduced universe. Up in the mountains, with bad roads all around and the railway stopping only in Kolcse, Komoró became an island when the winter snows arrived.

She finds it surprisingly easy to tell the mainland Spanish from the Ibicencos, particularly the children. The local kids are brown streaks of energy and have hair that is split, dried and lifted clear of their heads in tangles ruled by the sunshine. The mainlanders have paler skin and their children look pudgy and clumsy when they walk along the beaches.

Among the foreign visitors, the Italians remind Ana of the rich people in Budapest who sit outside the Váci Street restaurants, the men with their sunglasses and the women with long, bare legs that even in winter would slide out of fur above the snow. The Italians walk the alleys of Ibiza Town in linen suits and eat in loud groups at the seafood restaurants. The Germans sit in silent family units on the beaches, the men wearing beach hats and reading while the women, who favour short hair despite looking young for such a decision, look after the obedient children.

The British are different again. The younger ones make sense, they are here to drink alcohol and find people to have sex with, but the older couples mystify Ana as she watches them in the hotel bar, trying to find the reason they have come here. Her life can feel empty and there are many times that she thinks of men and marriage but the British help ease these concerns. If that is marriage, Ana often thinks, it can wait forever.

Ana watches these people while they sit in the hotel bar and drink and look up and away from one another. Each evening they arrive earlier than the one before and have less to talk about once here. By the end of the holiday Ana watches the men stand and point at the glass of the women, who smile sadly and nod with faces reddened by the sun. The women watch the men depart for the bar as if they never want them to return. They are strange, these sad wives who come from Britain for a week that must be little different to the weeks either side.

★

You can't sleep for a lot of reasons but mostly because of her. She's snoring the booze out but her legs are stealing the show with all the twitching and sudden kicks which bury her little heels into your side. You pick up your watch from the bedside table. You used to own a Casio with a light built in but with this one you have to angle it for some moonlight. One in the morning.

While you're getting up and pulling on your clothes you wonder just how much it's her snoring and kicking that's got you up and just how much you were looking for an excuse. Because to be fair there's no great debate about what you're going to do now. Yeah, you decide, this is an inside job.

You close the door gently behind you. In the lift you relax for all of a second before fear arrives with the double whammy. Will she be there and, if she is, how is this going to look? At least you don't have any shopping this time.

The lift opens. You tell yourself, announce to yourself, she won't be there and the bar will be closed. You get to the glass door. She's there and the bar's not closed. You walk in past a couple who are leaving. She's watching you and here you go again with the short breathing and the heat and a thousand ideas coming charging into your head.

★

It's an hour until Ana can close the bar and there are eight people left. Four older tourists play cards. Tucked into the corner, a teenage couple kiss and eye the door for parents. Standing by a table is a man waiting for his wife. She finishes her drink slower than she needs to. He sighs and waits. Finally she rises and leads him away. He smiles valiantly at Ana and follows his wife with a grim acceptance.

At the door they stop and move to the side to let someone into the bar but the gesture looks exaggerated. They swing a full yard out of the way and the man raises a hand in apology even though it is he and his wife who are allowing the person to pass. When Ana sees who enters the bar she thinks two things. She knows she has seen him before and she understands why the couple acted that way.

★

She doesn't recognise you from last night which is good but, of course, is also pretty bad. One way or another you manage to order a Coke. Her body, it's just sinful. She's tall, not far off six foot, and she's got the hat-trick. Face, tits and body. Her wide shoulders are needed for her tits that sit gloating under the uniform. Her legs are long and when she walks for the Coke her arse is hard to ignore. But her body is just what it is. With a few hours, and a full tank of petrol, you could match it in Peterborough.

It's her face though. When she comes back with the Coke you're like a kid. You look at her in wonder, scoping for anything, however small, that might not make it what it seems but there's nothing to be found. The mouth you could go into. The cheek-bones could be discussed. You could spend hours on the eyes that flick from colour to colour or the hair that swings as she moves. But there's no point. There's no point in trying to get to grips with her features on an individual basis when the whole lot together ends up like that, with the smile and the look. She knows, she's got to know, what she's doing to you here.

She asks for your room number and you need a couple of shots but you get there and she takes a note of it before leaving the bar, walking through the door to what's probably the kitchen. You look round nervously, expecting everyone in the room to have been watching you and her, but the small mob in here are just getting on with things. The room feels empty with her gone.

You sit on a stool at the bar. You could go to one of the tables, but fuck it, you've not come down here to sit at a table and you don't really want her to come back and see you go for one. You're worried you might not walk normally in front of her. You're worried you might have lost all sense of balance. Things don't feel normal.

You drink your Coke. It'll be good to have the option of ordering another when she comes back. The bar's spotless. Glasses dry in the tray and the ice buckets are full. She's a worker, this one.

When the kitchen door opens you frown at the spirit bottles. You scratch the back of your head. She passes by and your eyes don't follow. You look at your Coke and drink some more and only when you put the glass down do you look at her. She's at the end of the bar, wiping the draught pumps. When she finishes she hangs the cloth over the neck of a tap. You're glad you've got something to say but now you wonder if this is a bit odd in itself. A grown man drinking a glass of Coke every five minutes. How's that going to look?

You're not sure what to do but you are sure of other things. You're sure, for starters, that you're getting hot again. You're sure that you're going red. You're sure that suddenly the stool feels like one big pin and you're sure that she's coming towards you. You're sure of all those things but you've got no, no idea what –

'Where are you from?' she asks.

Her voice is worth more than all the other voices you've ever heard put together.

★

There are few people left and no tasks remaining so Ana talks to the man sitting at the bar. She finds it interesting that he drinks only Coke at this time of night and she finds it interesting that he is so vast. His size has been made, created over what must have been years. His shoulders are humps of intent and his arms strain with the muscles he has given them to carry. He should be threatening but he's not and Ana cannot decide why. She speaks far more than she'd have intended if she had prepared for this moment in advance.

★

You tell her you're English and that you're from Peterborough. She asks if it's near London. You tell her it's forty-three minutes by train. She asks if you work in London. You say that you work on a building site in Peterborough but you're a mechanic by trade. She says that she has a friend in London who she grew up with in Hungary.

'Hungary?' you say. 'So how did you end up here then?'

You want to ask her name but it almost feels too late.

'I am looking for someone,' she answers.

'Who?'

'A man who knew my family,' she says. 'I am trying to find him.'

'OK,' you say.

She goes to do a job that doesn't look too urgent. That went well, you think while you wait. You try not to watch when she heads out to collect glasses from the tables. You must have met a woman like her before, you must have done, but you can't think of one.

'How long have you been here, in Ibiza?' you ask when she's back.

'I came in March.'

Six months she's been here, which explains the tan. You're not sure, but you can't see Hungary being tropical.

'How long are you staying?'

'Until I find this man,' she says.

She looks exhausted. You ask her what time the bar closes. You're still hoping she might say something about you coming in last night, but she doesn't. She tells you the bar closes at two.

There's not much more to say and you decide to quit when it doesn't feel that you're too far behind. You stand up.

'Well, lovely to meet you,' you say. 'I'm Craig.' For a moment, just a moment, you nearly use your real name.

'I'm Ana,' she says.

She gives you one last smile and you hope that's not because you're leaving.

★

Ana watches the man go and feels an anger coming. No matter her boredom there was no need to have said these things. It is late and this is some excuse but it's with annoyance that Ana turns to the final glasses of the evening.

Monday

With the puking and whimpering she sounds like a dog. It wakes you up but you don't open your eyes. Why would you?

★

The sun has little power but over time these early mornings have marked themselves upon Ana. Her hair bears streaks of blonde and her tan is constant, neither fading nor darkening between days. When she leaves Ibiza it will take time for the sun's work to disappear.

Crickets waken each other and the first of the day's car horns sound from the street. Sometimes the caretaker's here, peeking at Ana and lifting flies from the pool with elaborate twists of his net. Today she's alone. Her watch sits on the table and counts down the hour she grants herself. The watch is to stop Ana from dreaming, from letting her mind wander too far.

Even now she fears a day when she'll choose not to leave after the hour. That instead she'll lie here and watch the hotel come alive around her. That she'll let life happen and perhaps slip into it herself. Back into a life she abandoned when she flew from Hungary to Jerusalem with the man's name that brought her here.

The watch shows ten minutes left, but Ana reaches for her shirt. Today she leaves early.

★

The two thoughts run into each other in your head. You can't take much more of this and you can't take any more at all. You get out of bed and pull on the first clothes you find. You grab your wallet. In the bathroom she's put down a towel to protect her knees. Settling in for a while, she is. She looks like she's praying. Her hair's pulled to one side, her body rocks in front of the toilet. What a fucking business.

'I'm going out,' you tell her.

Turn round and apologise, you think, you hope. Turn round and apologise. It wouldn't exactly be cause for a street party but it would help. It would stop things being what they are right now which is bottom-of-the-barrel territory. Turn round and apologise. She turns round. Her face is whiter than the tiles.

'Well, that's a great help, Craig. Thanks a lot.'

Her eyes dagger at you but then she's back to the toilet and the gagging. You walk out the room. Something just happened but you're not sure what. In the lift and the reception you blink and breathe with the anger. In the street you feel different. Light, sort of. New.

*

For Ana, religion meant exhausting nights in Komoró. Her mother had not been a sleeper. Every evening she would dress as if for bed and go through with Ana's father. During the night, Ana would hear the door and a chair being pulled out from under the table. On the nights when her mother was crying, Ana would go to join her.

She learnt not to ask where the hurt came from but instead to sit by her mother for long, torturous sessions with the Tanakh. There would be boring speeches from the Torah with her mum resting her finger on the page to translate hesitantly into the Magyar while the young Ana fidgeted.

When she grew older, Ana would sometimes ask her mother to talk at night of Komoró in the war. Ana would ask for the muddled stories of her grandparents and others going north on long trains. She'd ask too about Pál Teleki, who the teachers at school mentioned quickly, hurriedly and only when they had no other choice.

Her mother's voice would falter while she closed the Tanakh and said this was not a conversation for now. Only at the very end, when she lay in bed and the neighbours queued outside, did she relent and tell Ana about those trains and where they had led and that she too was on them. And then Ana would know why her mother cried and why, every night, the darkness arrived with such power.

Her mother had clung to religion for her own reasons but for Ana it was a distraction. She did not like to hear of destiny and grand plans and hidden hands. She wanted facts. And yet, in recent months, she's started to believe in fate. She didn't mean to, it certainly wasn't deliberate, and it's entirely the fault of this car.

Every time this car fails to start, a debate begins in Ana's mind. She decides that she should have expected the car to fail and this, in some way, would have forced it not to. Or, if she's worried about the car starting, she concludes her concern has somehow spread to the engine. Today she's too tired to take a position either way so she turns the key without any thought. Not only does the car not start, it doesn't even appear to try. Ana feels the same fury and helplessness she always does and, today, a panic because today there's one house she wants to go to more than anywhere.

Ana cries. This is unexpected and unusual and she struggles to react. It feels like the distant experience it is. She looks unsuccessfully for something to use against the tears and then cradles her head in her hands, leaning to the window in exhaustion. The man has to knock on the glass more than once before she looks. It would be hard not to recognise him. Ana rubs her eyes with the sleeve of her shirt. There's no option but to open the window.

'You OK, love?' he asks. Into her hesitation he slips, 'It's me, Craig, we met last night.'

'I remember.'

He bends towards her and this makes him even larger. His shoulders are wider than the window.

'My car is not working,' says Ana.

'Is that all?' He smiles and it's an unlikely, shy smile from such a man. 'That's hardly worth crying over, is it?' He straightens. 'Right then, we'll get this fixed. Open your bonnet.'

The man, Craig, walks round the front of the car. He frowns at the bonnet, as if trying to see through it to the problem. Ana pulls the lever. She's stopped crying. It already feels strange that she was doing so.

★

If we're going to be honest here then you can't believe your luck. If you'd walked out the door and bumped into her holding hands with some lucky bastard and eight of their children you'd have been happy enough just to see her. To stroll twenty yards down the street and find her bawling her eyes out over your sole area of expertise is a pools win on your birthday.

The car's Spanish but not too old and this island's not big enough to hurt the mileage unless she's been doing laps of the place for a laugh. If the engine's not starting then you're looking at the carburettor, exhaust or some local strife in the ignition.

You want her to see you work so you lift the bonnet, pin it in place and stand sideways on. You go through a couple of faces, kind of serious at first and then some nods and smiles to show her you're clocking the problem. In truth you don't have a clue. Unless the engine was on fire then it's strictly guesswork from up here but you're giving her a little blast of what you're all about. When you finally pull your eyes over to her you're hoping to catch a bit of appreciation but she's staring at something off to the side. A wall. She's looking at a wall. She can watch you and she can watch a wall and right now the wall's winning. You smile as you duck under the bonnet.

It's not a bad little get-together down here. 1.8 litres. 4 cylinders. It's been bolted in centrally which helps when it comes to checking the connections. Some of the foreign cars that used to come in the garage, well, you'd have to be a midget to get in behind the engines that they stuck to one side for some bollocks about fuel efficiency. The amount of fuel saved by doing that could be saved by parking further from the kerb.

You get the basics out the way. Oil, water, battery. All fine. You come out of there and now she's watching. She's approaching happy, which is a rapid improvement, and there's no doubt, no one could deny, that you're a part of that.

'Here, love,' you say, 'have you got a radio in there? Can you turn it on to check the battery?'

She frowns and her frowning is like other people laughing.

'It's not the battery,' she says. Her accent comes and goes. 'I'm not stupid, you know?'

As she says that she offers a little smile and it is, no joke, one of the best moments of your life.

Jesus Christ.

You get back behind the bonnet before you do something else. Like tell her you love her or burst into tears.

★

While Craig works, Ana checks her notes and lines up addresses into a list. With some effort she pushes the house with the yellow gate to the end. First she will finish with the road to San Vicente and those houses that have been empty and silent over recent weeks. There is a lot of driving, they are scattered relics from past days, and she ignores the fact that presently she can't drive anywhere. This man, Craig, has a confidence that she'd like to share.

★

You give the crankshaft the once-over and the bearings feel fine. If they break loose then the crankshaft won't turn and the engine goes on a sympathy strike. Carry on, carry on. You move to the pistons and, as you work your way through the process, you feel something which you suppose must be a bit of nostalgia because under a bonnet was always a good place to be.

Back at the garage you had two choices. Keep busy or talk to the boys. Some of them never shut up, it was like their wives wound them up at the back before they left in the mornings, and after a couple of hours of Bradford City and this and that you'd escape under the bonnets. The boys left you to it. They wouldn't have bothered you anyway with your size, but they certainly didn't bother you when you started up with Sam.

That first day, your first day at the garage and the first day you set eyes on Sam Albright, you thought he was some old duffer wanting to know why his indicator wouldn't go off. Then a few of the boys went across and shook his hand but he was already looking over at you.

'Who is this strapping young fellow, and is he aware of the struggle?'

Those first few months you just did a bit of driving for him. You still worked at the garage but more and more he'd be pulling you out in the afternoons to take him over to Stockport to meet a couple of enthusiasts or through to Birmingham to see the first of his converts down there.

He never talked to you about it. You sat in on the meetings and you bought into it just like everyone else but he never went at you when it was just you and him. He'd ask about your old man, who he said he'd known, and he'd talk about the Germans bombing Rawson Market by mistake during the war.

You enjoyed driving Sam. The meetings in those days were the hardest he would ever do. A handful of men in the back of a pub, not knowing why they were there and not trusting Sam and certainly not trusting you standing there twice the size of them. Sam was a magician back then. He'd leave that first lot pumped up and promising they'd have fifty men the next month. The next month you'd drive Sam back and he'd get a standing ovation just for entering the room. Time and time again, he turned shit into gold right there in front of you.

No one could resist him. The garage was owned by two brothers who came in on Fridays to do the money. They owned a few garages and one drove a Merc and one drove a Beemer and they were decent lads, truth be told. They'd given you a job and you didn't have a single qualification. 'If nothing else he can do the lifting,' one brother told the other and they stuck you on £70 a fortnight.

Then Sam came in and soon enough you were driving him a day a week. Then it was two and the brothers couldn't ignore it any more. One morning you were underneath a blue Maxi when you saw their shoes and they called you to the office.

They said things were getting a bit out of hand. They said they knew Sam was popular with the boys but they couldn't keep paying you full-time wages. You passed all this on to Sam and, come Friday, he turned up at the garage. He stood there in the middle of the forecourt until all the mechanics went over because there didn't seem any other choice. Finally the owners came out the office and they had no choice either. Sam stood there like a magnet.

He started talking. He talked about local people and local businesses and how the two had to support each other. How they depended on one another. He talked about a movement and how the earlier people joined a movement the more they benefited from doing so.

'Be at the beginning of history, gentlemen,' Sam announced, and even at that stage it didn't seem strange that some old boy with a comb-over could stand in a garage on Davidson Street and say these things on a Friday afternoon. 'If you become part of the movement then the movement will become part of you.'

The garage owners looked at each other and asked Sam to join them in the office. Ten minutes later he left, winked at you and shook everyone's hands on his way out. The brothers called you in and shut the door and said, 'You're working for Albright now, kid. We'll still pay you, but you're working for Albright.'

And that was you done as a mechanic, four months in.

You look at the engine with those four months' experience. There's only a few things go wrong with motors. Bad fuel mix, loss of compression and loss of spark. You start with the fuel mix, rubbing your finger up and down the rubber pipe. No clogging so the air's there but most of the time it's stupidity that ruins the air mix. No petrol. You bang the tank and it washes up the side through the dirt. There could be impurities in there but for now you move on to the compression.

Loss of compression comes from the bird's nest of pipes under the engine. The pistons are fine. The valves look OK and you run a hand along the cylinder to check for a hole. In Bradford, where the sky as good as weeps for nine months a year, you'd be looking for rust but there's not a touch of it out here in the sunshine.

Your options are dropping away and that's not exactly ideal. You pull open the cylinder head to see the spark plug and laugh with relief. The poor little bastard must have started complaining a while back, but no one's been listening. Now it's taken the coward's way out, committing suicide by crunching itself into a metal ball.

'For you the war is over,' you say, pulling the spark plug out the cylinder.

You walk round to the window and hold it up.

'This is your spark plug, or at least it was.'

She laughs.

'It does not look very good.'

'Not too clever, no,' you smile.

'Is this easy to fix?'

'Piece of piss,' you say and think that you really shouldn't be swearing. 'Let's go and find a garage, I'll bang a new one in and you'll be good to go.' You've never said *good to go* before in your life and you don't understand why you've started now.

'*You* will fix this?' she asks.

She says it like you've got no arms.

'I told you last night,' you say, 'I'm a mechanic. I work in a garage.'

You do something with your hands. Presumably, you imagined it would look like a mechanic at work. You look like you're doing the breaststroke.

'I don't remember.'

Some people would be offended by her saying that. You wouldn't be offended if she said that then kicked you square in the balls.

'That's OK. Yeah, I'll do it for you. No problem.'

'OK,' she says, 'so we'll go to the garage.'

★

Since Francesco, it's very rare for Ana to be in company. To walk down the street with anyone would feel foreign. With Craig, it's different still. People react to him in surprising ways. They turn a corner and a man's nearly upon them. Without hesitation he steps into the road to let Craig pass. Two local women stand at a bus stop. They ignore Ana and look at Craig with intrigue.

When he asks a man for directions to a garage Craig speaks so politely that it surprises her. The Spaniard makes some sense of what Craig's asking and points vaguely to the beach, which seems unlikely to Ana.

'You don't speak Spanish?' she asks Craig while they walk.

'Spanish?' he answers. 'I'm still working on my English, love.'

She laughs. The sun slides through the streets, the morning's progressing but she doesn't mind. They arrive at the beachfront and Craig approaches a taxi driver locking his car. Craig points at the car's engine and gets his message across in that same, patient voice. The driver points confidently to a row of shops at the other end of the beach. This, also, seems unlikely to Ana who has seen those shops before.

They pick their way through the tourists and dog walkers.

'You've been down here before?' asks Ana. She's surprised that it's her who's starting the conversations.

'Yeah, last night, for dinner,' he answers, then catches himself, lowering his head for a moment.

Perhaps, Ana concludes, this is the reason for his silence. He must have a family back at the hotel and now he's found himself using his morning in this way.

'Do you want to go back?' she suggests. 'I can have the people at the garage fix the car?'

'No,' he answers tensely. 'No, I'm fine.'

The shops the taxi driver pointed to sell alcohol and clothes to the tourists. There's no garage here. An old woman stands in the shade of an awning, gathering herself for the journey home. Ana asks her in Spanish for a garage. The old woman points back the way they came and names a street. Ana laughs and turns to Craig. She thinks Craig's smile is a little strained. She's glad for his sake when they find the street and the garage and their adventure is over.

*

These people, they have to be at it. They have to be trying it on. First you stopped some boy back up beside her car, put on your most acceptable voice and told him you needed a garage. He points down to the beach and you think, 'Is that right, pal, a garage on the beach?'

It seems unlikely but, you know, this boy lives here. So you get down to the beach and of course there's not a garage on the beach because if there was a garage on the beach then it would fucking struggle. You want to run back and find the boy and say, 'Sorry, mate, were you under the impression that I owned a *submarine*?'

So you ask a taxi driver. If you want to find somewhere, after all, then ask a taxi driver. That's the rule, especially in a little place like this. In a little place like this a taxi driver should know what's in people's *cupboards*. The taxi driver points you, as sure as you like, to a row of shops at the other end of the beach.

Off you go again. You're getting wound up and that leaves you quiet. She asks if you've been down to the front before and you tie yourself in knots by saying you were down for your dinner last night. Obviously that sets off a few questions in her head about who you're here with, or who you're supposed to be here with anyway, and sure enough she offers to go to the garage solo.

You nip that in the bud and then you're at the shops and no, there's no garage here either. She, Ana, she goes and rattles off some Spanish to an old bird who dispatches you back the way you've just come. Ana seems to be holding up OK, and you manage to produce some sort of smile, but all you want to do is run back to that taxi driver and ask if he knows how pointing works.

Ana leads you to a street and here's the garage. What credit you gathered under the bonnet has been well and truly blown on the journey here. Time for a comeback, you decide. The boy behind the counter chats away in Spanish, and chucks his eyes at her at every opportunity, but you're already at the racks. You find their spark plugs and match up a set to the frazzled piece of coil.

'Just these, mate,' you say. You'd probably have paid too but she's already put money on the counter.

When you leave the garage she steps into the road and smiles before she speaks.

'It should be easier,' she says, 'on the way back.'

You laugh at that. There's a sharp blast of acceleration and a kid on a motorbike comes down the road. You reach a hand to her shoulder and, with the touch of a finger, guide her back up to the pavement.

*

The car's too hot. Ana rolls down the windows and lets her door hang open. She sits sideways in the driver's seat, her feet dangling towards the pavement while Craig bangs metal against metal. He swears in English, softly so he thinks she can't hear. She pulls her skirt higher, enjoying the sun on her skin.

Craig mutters and swears some more and then he's up and closing the bonnet. She watches him walk round the car and sees his furtive look at the hotel. He must be getting worried now, she thinks, about this time away from his family.

'There we go,' he says. 'Shall we give it a try?'

Ana turns the key and the engine starts. Craig looks even happier than her.

'Thank you very much,' she tells him and she's wondering what else to say when he speaks.

Then it's just his question and the noise of the engine he fixed.

*

The second you got under the bonnet you checked the hotel. You found your balcony and the curtains were closed. You took

130

longer than you needed to with the spark plugs, tapping a spanner against the pipes while you tried to form a plan, but now you're finished and no plan's been formed. You close the bonnet. Her brown legs stretch from her seat to the pavement. You have a last check on the balcony. The curtains are open. Open.

You say it before you have time to stop yourself.

'Can I come with you?' you ask.

Her response isn't too promising, in that she looks absolutely terrified. You keep talking because what else are you going to do now – run away?

'If you're trying to find this man then you should let me drive and you can, you know, concentrate.'

You can see the red folders and notes on her passenger seat and can't think what else they could be. You gesture at them helpfully and she slides over a protective hand in response. She doesn't look too close to getting round to speaking.

'The spark plugs should be fine but I'd rather see them after a run, you know?'

Now she's looking straight ahead. If anything, this is getting worse.

'I don't have much else to do,' you say and produce an odd laugh. What are you doing? 'It would be nice to see some of the island,' you add hopefully.

If she never speaks then will you never stop talking?

'OK,' she says. It's not much of an OK. It's not much of an OK at all.

'I can come?' you ask and sound so much like a kid that you want to excuse yourself, walk round the corner and pull your own tongue out.

'Yes,' she says and this time, believe it or not, there is the trace, the smallest trace of a smile. 'You can drive me.'

She gets out the car and switches sides. You cram into the driver's seat and push it back until it clicks. She scoops the folders into her lap.

'So,' you ask, 'where to?'

'I'll show you,' answers Ana. 'This way for now.'

She points behind you.

'Right then,' you answer.

You tug the steering wheel, tap your foot on the accelerator and the car arcs round. You're driving. You're on the wrong side. Everything is on the wrong side.

★

Ana's glad to give directions because it offers escape from this new madness. She never even considered taking Francesco out on her search and he knew, or thought he knew, what she was doing. There would have been no real danger in taking him and yet she hadn't seen it as a possibility. Now she is on her way with her folders, her notes and a stranger. They leave Es Cana and she guides them onto the San Carlos road. It stretches before them with flat fields either side.

'You are here with your family?' she asks. She doesn't know what she wants the answer to be.

'No,' he says, 'on my own.'

'Oh,' answers Ana and Craig realises that he has to say at least a little more.

'I lost my job back in England,' he adds. 'I thought I could do with a holiday.'

He's not looking at her, his attention is on the road and Ana admires the care of his driving.

'Have you been on this road before?' she asks.

'No,' he replies, 'we came another way from the airport.'

'Then you should enjoy the fields,' says Ana. Craig glances at the sweep of olive trees that run to the first of the hills.

'Lovely,' he says and looks back at the road.

Cars pass by heading to Es Cana. Craig makes a strange noise, a low groan.

★

This has to be a nightmare. If it isn't a nightmare then the impression that it's doing of one is absolutely uncanny. Painting two lanes on this road was a criminal act. You've got about three inches to play with at either side. Every time a car passes you sit here, at the wrong side of the car on the wrong side of the road and think they're coming right for you. You could shake hands with the drivers when they pass if they weren't all going so very fucking fast. This isn't a system, you decide bitterly, this isn't any kind of system at all.

She starts firing questions at you and you want to ask her to just, please, give you a bit of time to adjust to the fact that you're driving a car on the right-hand side of a glorified pavement while Spanish boys take your paintwork off at sixty miles an hour. At one point she suggests you look at the fields. It's all you can do not to tell her, not to turn round and tell her that if you look at the fields the two of you will end up in those fields sitting upside fucking down.

★

'This is San Carlos,' Ana tells him.

Craig wasn't driving quickly to begin with but he starts to slow a long way from the crossroads. Ana can't stop herself from looking at that opening, rising stretch of road to the yellow gate.

'Into the village?' asks Craig, seeing the crossroads' options.

'No,' she answers. 'You should see more of the island first.'

He pauses in thought. Ana can't remember the engine ever sounding this strong.

'Would you like to drive?' he asks her.

She smiles at Craig's politeness.

'No, it's OK,' she tells him. 'On you go.'

Craig takes the turn so slowly that they nearly stop. The road climbs away from the village and out the valley. Ana shifts her back to the car's door and consults her list. First of the remnants is a house just north of San Vicente. They reach the top of the hill and the sun is there to greet them. Ana presses her head to the leather and closes her eyes, enjoying the warmth and the rare rest.

*

The driving gets better which is to say you're no longer about to take delivery of a nervous breakdown. It helps that she's having a kip because more questions from her would have meant more lies from you and that's not a pressure you particularly need right now. You risk a look at the notes she's been trying to hide. Names and addresses. Some scored out, some with scrawled details beside them. The folders are thick with paper. She's been busy.

It's not an easy job she's given herself. These hills are covered in trees and you can't remember the word but they're definitely the stubborn type that keeps their leaves all year. It's not a big island but with the hills and these roads it must be a hard place to find someone. And a good place to hide.

You hit a town without trying and when you go through the gears she wakes up and yawns. It's a nice enough place with the same drill as Es Cana. There's the beach, some old buildings and then the new hotels looking a bit guilty in among them.

'San Vicente,' she tells you.

She points you round the town then up a road that threatens to go narrow on you again before she asks you to stop. She leaves the car and walks towards a house. If she'd thought to ask, you could have told her not to bother because this place has slipped someone's mind. The curtains are drawn, the windows are filthy and the garden's not winning any prizes. She gives the door a few bangs then she's back.

'No luck?' is what you say. It's just the latest piece of genius from you.

'No.' She smiles patiently. 'Now we go back.'

You retreat round the town to the road you came in on but it's not long until she sends you off to a mud track. It's a tricky little set-up and the wheels go from under you on a bend. You steer into the skid and bring the car back under control, if that's not too ambitious a word. She doesn't react at all, just stays looking at her notes and you realise that morale is taking a dive. You shouldn't be here and she's starting to realise it.

At the end of the track is a farmhouse owned by an old boy in a hat who tells Ana something she writes down. You have a bit of time to think about what to say when she gets back in the car and what you come up with is: 'Success.'

You don't make it sound like a question so if she doesn't reply it's just about OK.

'Success,' she answers but there's not much behind it and you're back ploughing through the mud in silence. By the time you reach the road you're thankful for the tarmac but nothing else because this really isn't going too well. Whatever was here is being lost in instalments and the day's future is spelling torture.

'I did not tell you,' she says, her face turned to you, 'that it would be exciting.'

When you see the smile your pleasure can't really be gauged because there isn't a scale known to man. You manage a grin then fix on the road to stop the terrible words that could come from you right now. You drive past the hills, past the trees. Coniferous. There you go, that's what they are.

*

135

Of all the concerns, of all the obstacles, it is his age. That's what holds most of Ana's worry. If he's alive, if he's here on Ibiza, then he will be seventy-one years old. It is just another statistic working against her and the result is an awful thought. She needs him to have had a healthy, happy life. Not for the first time, she directs this idea away.

These lingering addresses are far apart and conversation seems to have left them for now. The silence, thinks Ana, is welcome for them both.

★

One of the problems in driving for Sam Albright was that he changed his car every couple of months, so every couple of months you'd have a new motor to get used to. Sam said he changed them because of *the security services*. He talked about *the security services* a lot and for a long time you thought it was part of his performance but it turned out Sam was on the money.

You had taken him down to Nottingham. You sat in a Wimpy while Sam walked round the car park with some bearded lad who you'd later see at Bradford Square wearing a 'Local Organiser' badge. Sam wrapped up his chat and you finished your Wimpy Half Pounder and met him at the car. A few minutes into the journey back to Bradford you clocked a white Volvo a couple of cars behind. Out to the dual carriageway then onto the M1 and the Volvo was still there, tucked in two cars back.

You didn't say anything to Sam. He was reading the *Daily Express* for a start. Instead you waited for Barlborough Services then took the exit late and went up the ramp fast. The Volvo turned in but it was way back now and you darted into the car park, stuck the car in the corner and jumped out. Sam shouted for fags and you jogged into the services building, slipped into WH Smith and stood at the window.

The Volvo crept into the car park. They hardly looked at Sam that first time round, but they'd have seen him reading the paper. On the second circuit the Volvo's driver went slower still and the passenger pulled out a camera for photos that couldn't have offered much more than the front page of the *Daily Express*. On their way out they passed right by the services building. You stepped back from the window but you saw the suits and the haircuts and thought that they weren't your average plod.

You didn't tell Sam because then you'd have had to get used to a new car every week. You ignored it and to be fair it went away until four months before Bradford Square, when John Dickinson walked across the forecourt of the Shell garage on Albany Road. You didn't tell Sam about that either.

And now, suddenly, you're a driver again. You're getting used to a car, taking directions, pulling in, waiting and driving without talking because questions don't get much of an answer. It's not so bad though. Sam Albright never looked like her and Bradford never looked like this.

But now you're starving and once you think about that you can't think about anything else. You've eaten nothing all day and your body is, quite rightly, asking you some proper questions. A good few houses have come and gone, you must have nearly worked your way back to that village in the valley. San Carlos she'd called it and you're sure you saw a restaurant behind the church.

'Many more to go?' you ask, nice and friendly.

'One,' she says.

*

There have been times today when she wanted to free herself of his company but now she remembers why he's here. What is strange is that there is no doubt. She could direct them back to the hotel, drop him there and come back alone. These options don't linger for more than a moment. This is why he's here and her directions take them to San Carlos.

'Into the village?' he asks at the crossroads for the second time today.

'No,' she answers. 'Above.'

She points to the left and the break in the trees.

'There?' asks Craig, uncertain.

'Yes.'

He steers the car in.

'Fuck me,' he says. Ana's smile is quick and private. This road would make anyone swear.

★

There's a point about halfway up when the potholes hit a foot deep and you think that she has to be taking the piss. She must be conducting an experiment into how far a 24-year-old man from Bradford can be pushed before he loses it entirely. You're existing outside yourself, looking at this big lad bouncing up and down and banging his head off the sun visor and you're thinking, 'What's that boy all about?' And now you're here at the end of the road, with the engine whining to a stop, and you're looking at Fort Knox and thinking that something, something is very wrong indeed.

'What's in there then?'

'I think it's his house, the man I'm looking for,' she tells you.

'You've been here before?'

'Yes,' she answers.

'And there was no one here?'

'No.'

You get out the car and walk to the yellow gate. It's solid, locked, seven feet high, and that's just the beginning. There are cameras and the walls are topped with wire. This place is sending a message and the message isn't very polite.

'I want to go in,' she says beside you.

You want to ask if she's a professional pole-vaulter.

'Have you tried that?' You point at the intercom.

'There's nobody there,' she replies. She's looking right at you. 'I want to go in.'

'Break in?' You say it more for you than her. 'Nah, come on, love, why don't we try again tomorrow?'

What is this now? Do you think, do you *really* think, she's going to have you back tomorrow?

'They won't mind,' she says. 'I have been there before.'

'Inside?'

You point to the gate, to beyond the gate really, and she nods. It's such obvious bollocks that you can't ignore it.

Jesus Christ.

OK.

You run to the gate, jump and get your hands around the top. You hang for a moment then pull yourself up, get your elbows over and take a look. The gate could be opened easily enough from behind, there's just a piece of wood holding it in place. From the gate the hill continues and takes the road with it. Between trees you see white walls and a wooden deck on stilts. You drop down.

She's not looked at you like this before, or if she has then you've missed it.

'You've been in there?' you ask.

'Yes,' she answers.

'So you know what it looks like?'

She stops, bites her lip.

'Listen, love,' you say, 'I'll help you, but you need to tell me what's going on.'

This new look of hers could, believe it or not, be something close to respect.

'Let's go down to San Carlos,' she says.

★

Lies, real lies, didn't come in to Ana's life until Budapest. She arrived at university with a bag of clothes that made her feel awkward and from a very different place. In Komoró there had been problems and arguments but they were set always against honesty. She arrived in Budapest having watched her mother die and now she was in the city and among the city's boys.

They dressed in European clothes, dark denim and leather jackets, and smoked endless Gauloises. They talked loudly of summer trips to Berlin and the Dschungel nightclub, and their motorbikes clustered in University Square.

But they were children. When Ana walked into lecture halls their heads flicked to her instinctively, like disturbed animals at a waterhole. They'd crane their necks to watch her find a seat, then retreat into giggles and whispers.

They came to her, one after another. Muddled conversations in corridors while they scanned for witnesses, weak jokes in the canteen queue. There were notes slid under her dormitory door and drunken shouting outside her window at night.

Imre was different. He was quieter than the rest and his approach was built on doleful respect. Ana was lying in Vidám Park's lower meadow, reading of Pál Teleki, when Imre asked for permission to sit beside her. They talked all afternoon and every day for three weeks. At some point Ana told Imre she was a virgin and it was just another step, another stage. The conversation moved on.

Three weeks after they met in Vidám Park, Ana sat on the jump seat of Imre's motorbike while he drove her over the Csobánc hills to Diszel. For dinner Ana chose rabbit and Imre made fun of her country choice. He ordered champagne and drank nearly all the bottle himself. He swayed a little on the walk back to the inn.

He closed the bedroom door and went for Ana straight away. Sex was not as bad as she'd feared. The sharp pain slowed to a throb and he didn't take long. In the morning he was hung-over and made them leave before breakfast. When he dropped her at the dormitories he didn't turn off the engine, kissing her lightly on the cheek before driving away.

The following morning Ana thought Imre would be waiting for her in the lecture hall. She expected him to be sitting away from the other boys with a seat kept free beside him. Instead, heads turned, whispering and giggling came louder than ever and there he was in their celebrated middle. Ana walked a long way to the back of the room and she didn't speak to Imre again.

It wasn't anger that Imre gave Ana – her mother's final days had given her enough of that. What Imre gave her was concentration. It thinned her motivations for university right down to acting on what her mother had told her as she lay dying. That meant English and History and long, extra hours in the library which had eventually brought her to this restaurant, in this village. And in front of her is a man she doesn't know, and in her mind are truth and lies and a battle for how to mix the two.

'I am from the very north of Hungary,' Ana begins, 'a village called Komoró. In 1941 the Germans came to our country's border. They wanted to travel through Hungary to take Yugoslavia.'

Craig's thick hands are on the table. Worms of skin make up his frown. He is probably bored already, thinks Ana, and there is a long way to go. She shortens the story where she can. She tells him that Pál Teleki, Hungary's prime minister, told the Germans that they couldn't enter. He promised to shield Hungary from the war and the people called him the Great Protector. The people believed their prime minister because they had nothing else to believe. The front page of the *Budapester* read 'Teleki Will Protect'.

Ana tells Craig that Pál Teleki received a phone call telling him that the German tanks had crossed the border. He put down the phone and wrote a note. *We have allied ourselves with scoundrels*, wrote Pál Teleki, *I am guilty*. And then, Ana tells Craig, Pál Teleki shot himself dead.

'From then on there was only fear,' she says.

She tells Craig about 1944, when the German tanks came back and this time they were not just passing through. The radio said the Hungarian people were safe. When the tanks came into the mountains the mayor of Komoró announced that the Hungarian people were safe. Ana tells Craig that the mayor did not mean all Hungarians.

'Not us,' says Ana. 'Not the Jews.'

Craig's eyes twitch.

'My mother was seven years old,' Ana continues. 'She and my grandparents, and all the other Jewish families in Komoró, were picked up by the Germans. They were put onto trains.'

★

You're falling.

You're falling.

Down a mountain.

Out a plane.

You're falling a long way and not even God could catch you.

★

'The trains took them to Poland,' Ana tells him. 'To Auschwitz.'

Craig stirs in his seat.

'Concentration camps,' she adds, unsure if she needs to.

At least he's still looking at her, still listening, but she supposes he has no option.

'They were divided into two lines. The workers and those too weak to work. My mother and her parents were sent together into the workers line. They needed children's hands for some of the work. This was less than a year before the Russians liberated the camps. Everyone from Komoró who was sent to the workers line survived. They all came home.'

Ana sips her water. She hadn't ordered food and she was thankful Craig finished his so quickly, to let them speak without the Argentine lurking around the table.

'My mother was a child, she found this boring. She sat down, dug into the soil and threw some dirt that hit a guard. He dragged my mother into the other line. When her parents pleaded he said one of them could swap with her. Both my grandparents stepped forward because they didn't know if the other would. He sent them both to the other line. Both of them.'

Ana is becoming aware of her voice. She's surprised to hear it so flat.

'A few days later my mother saw her parents through the fences. They were sitting together with their heads shaved. That was the last time she saw them.'

She's relieved to reach this point. At least now she can offer Craig some understanding of why he is here and listening to this.

'After the Russians came they were all sent back to Komoró. My mother was adopted by her neighbours, the Töröks. They told her that her parents had gone to live abroad.'

The sun picks out the shine of Craig's sweat.

'When my mother was sixteen, the Töröks invited some of the other survivors to their house. They told my mother everything. They even gave her the name of the guard who sent her parents to the other line. Jakob Binder.'

143

Craig's left hand moves across the table to his glass. It's his first movement in what seems a long time.

'My mother did not tell me about Jakob Binder, and what happened at Auschwitz, until the days before she died. When I went to university in Budapest, I found a project in the History department called "The Auschwitz Testimonies". In 1976 they had taken oral testimonies from all the Hungarian survivors they could find. I read them all and the name I saw the most was Jakob Binder. He sent people to their deaths for any excuse you can imagine.'

Craig's eyes are on the glass held tightly in his hands.

'Last year,' continues Ana, 'I travelled to Jerusalem to see a man called Moshe Geigler who hunts those Nazis still alive. He told me Binder had come here, to Ibiza, and showed me old photos. Binder might still be here today, he might not. This is what I've been doing,' she says. 'It is Binder that I'm looking for.'

Craig almost looks pleased and Ana knows this is because he can sense an end.

'And that's his house,' he asks, 'with the gate?'

'I don't know,' answers Ana honestly. This has all been honest, so far. 'But I think so.'

Craig looks above her head to the hills.

'And if we break in,' says Craig, 'what then?'

'If it's him, then we say we have the wrong house, leave and I tell Moshe Geigler. Mr Geigler will arrange the arrest.'

Craig folds his arms into a wall of flesh.

'That is all I want to do,' says Ana.

There, in the final sentence. That is the only lie she tells him.

★

Sam Albright.

He noticed. You never listened to any speakers apart from him, you didn't go to anything that he didn't tell you to go to and you never put money in the buckets. And, more than that, you didn't join in. You waited in the car. Everyone else would be inside, drinking and singing songs about niggers, and you would be in the car park listening to the football phone-in on Bradford 103 and waiting for Sam.

Sam noticed that and he'd already decided what to do with you. You were driving him back from a meeting in Wakefield when he asked if you were *fully committed to the struggle*.

'Yeah,' you said, unsure if he was serious.

'Really?' he asked. 'You believe in the struggle? You believe that we are under attack as a people and that the future of the race is in our very hands?'

'Yeah,' you answered, your hands tightening on the wheel.

You watched the road but smoke and rum told you his face was close. You wanted to tell him that you believed in the struggle because he believed in it. You wanted to tell him that you believed in the respect and the power and the fact that you owned a piece of it, however small. You wanted to tell him that you only really believed in him and wasn't that enough?

'I have an idea,' said Sam.

He said you were to become *a true figurehead*. The tattoos took six months in all.

Now you're sitting here, with this girl who has stolen your mind, and because of Sam Albright your back holds the sunburnt memory of a particular tattoo from a rainy Bradford afternoon with Sam looking up from his paper and saying, 'Very nice, now that one is very nice indeed.'

The gates and the sign. *Arbeit Macht Frei*. Auschwitz.

Sam Albright didn't have any tattoos.

She's watching you, waiting, which is fair enough. If you handed someone a grenade, you'd expect a reaction. You look at the village square. You look at the restaurant's sign. The Argentine. You think about the Falklands, about Thatcher. You look back to Ana.

145

'That's terrible,' you say. 'Really bad.'

Really bad. You're on form here. She looks uncomfortable and you're worried she's going to regret what she's told you so you play the only card you've got.

'All right,' you tell her. 'Let's go up there and see if it's him.'

The relief travels through her.

'Thank you,' she says. Her face is flushed by the sun behind you. 'It'll be dark soon,' she adds. 'We should go now.'

★

Ana would have let Craig drive again but he hung back when they returned to the car. She feels unusually nervous steering from the space. It would never be good to crash but right now would be too cruel. Carefully she takes them free of the village and they're getting close to the turning when she sees it.

A police car would normally mean nothing to Ana but because it's today, and because of the location, things are very different. The police car's tucked into the opening. Even if Ana still wanted to drive up there she couldn't. She looks to Craig and he fails to remove his fear. Ana keeps her foot steady on the accelerator. They see the policeman at the same time. He stands with his hands on his hips, looking at the still body of a dog below him.

'He has hit a dog,' says Ana. Craig's relief is obvious and Ana feels his agreement before she speaks.

'We'll go tomorrow, in the morning?' she asks.

'No problem,' he answers.

They drive in silence back to Es Cana, where Ana parks a few streets from the hotel. It would be another worry if a colleague saw her with a hotel guest.

'So,' he says, unclipping his belt, 'shall we meet here at ten o'clock?'

It's a lot later than she would have chosen but, she realises, it is not just her involved any more.

'OK,' she says. 'See you tomorrow.'

He gets out of the car and walks away with the knowledge she's given him.

*

When you start up the hotel steps you feel like you're heading up the staircase at Wembley to lift the FA Cup. By the time you get to the top you feel like you're about to be hanged because at some point on those steps you remember what you're walking towards.

The hotel reception's packed with punters bound for home. One of the reps stands on her tiptoes and shouts, 'Half an hour to the bus, everybody, half an hour.'

This lot are ready to go. Pink-faced and knackered, they stand in their crumpled clothes and see out the last of their time in paradise under the reception's harsh lighting. You pick your way through and you're heading for the lift when you hear music from the pool. You duck out for a moment – anything to delay what you know is coming.

There's a fair amount of people around and straight away you're getting a few looks. People who you just about recognise from the last couple of days look at you then away to the other side of the pool. That's where the action is, no doubt about that.

The kids from yesterday have music on, a blaring piece of shit that has them up and dancing. Their young bodies shake in a wave of brown skin and few clothes. Among the movement you see a flash, just a moment, of a yellow top with a thick black stripe across it.

She bought that top from House of Fraser in Peterborough high street. It was her birthday and you gave her £20 and she took it without thanking you and went and bought that top. She'd worn it to her sister's house, to a catastrophe of a barbecue where Claire had shown her their new bathroom suite and she'd announced she had to go home *right fucking now please, Craig* because of a migraine. The highlights of the drive home were the deep scratches she left on your arm after you stupidly tried to turn the music down.

You walk round the pool and people whisper as you pass. Some of the kids see you coming. They knock over cans and bottles when they back away. Soon the only dancers left are her and the brave young recruit with her. She's got her hands round his shoulders and her eyes are closed while they kiss. One of his hands is steady on her arse but the other one is more ambitious. It's inside her top, over her right tit. You're close enough now to see the fingers working away under the yellow.

Finally one of his pals helps him out with a hissed 'Darren!'

Darren turns, sees you and gets in a terrible mess trying to bring his hand out her top. The suddenness of his yank means he manages to pull the thing down and there are her tits now, bobbing away and getting involved in the party. Darren tries to pull her top up and, in doing so, he's pushing her tits back inside with his bare hands. His friends watch in disbelief.

She's properly pissed. It takes her a bit of time but once her top is back in place she finally looks at you. What doesn't help (but what would?) is that she smiles.

Darren looks like he cannot believe that every day in his life has somehow added up to this one. He must have a truckload of thoughts going through his head but they only amount to a muttered, 'I didn't, I mean, I wouldn't have.' He clasps his hands on top of his head.

'Give me the key,' you say to her.

'Fuck off,' she says.

Darren looks at her with genuine hurt. He wants to ask her why she is doing this to him.

Sadness is what you feel, as well as the more obvious material. You look at her and think how far things have journeyed to get to this. She leans down and picks up her shoes. She pecks Darren on the cheek which nearly finishes him off and when you walk away she's beside you. Everyone within a hundred yards is watching now which isn't ideal but, under the circumstances, it's like getting dirty looks on the *Titanic*.

In the reception the rep shouts, 'Twenty minutes till the bus, folks.'

There's not a word in the lift then you're in the room and she goes for her suitcase, throws it on the bed and starts piling her clothes in. Just like that. You're not sure what to do. You don't want to stop what seems to be happening. You sit on the wicker chair which has a bit of a grumble about that decision.

'Put the TV on,' she says without looking at you.

Somehow it makes sense for you to do this. You get up and turn on the TV and the screen warms up by the time you're back in the chair. It's some discussion programme, politics by the looks of it. Four Spanish men in suits sit round a table arguing away, pointing at each other and getting wound up. They've all got moustaches though, all four. It's hard to get away from that, hard to ignore it. Surely before the show started, did they not take one look at each other and say, 'OK, hold tight, this is ridiculous'?

She fetches her stuff from the bathroom then, without pausing, takes the bottle of champagne that you bought on the plane, wraps it in a cardigan and places it in her case. £14.99 well spent, you think. She leans on the case and it's painful to watch her get the zip round. The problem, of course, is she'll struggle to carry the thing.

She looks at you just long enough for a nod. You're up like a shot and lifting the case down, then pulling it on its wheels to the door. You're in the corridor and she's behind you and now the two of you are standing next to each other in the lift and all that is said in the lift, the only conversation, is:

Her – 'What about all your gym stuff?'

You – 'I'll call you when I'm back, we'll sort it.'

The Lat Attack cost £199.99. The Shoulder Moulder cost £124.99.

The reception's emptying, the bus is here. She walks to the rep. Her shoulders are slightly hunched, she's not wearing much of a travelling outfit and you hope she won't be cold when she gets back to England. She speaks to the rep and it's not a long conversation and she turns to you and she smiles to tell you that it's OK, that you can go.

You turn back to the lift and you're in there pressing the button and already your breathing isn't right. The door closes and something's happening. This is unexpected. You concentrate on what there is to do. The corridor, the door, the room. Take off your clothes, turn off the TV, get into bed, turn off the light.

Now there's nothing. It wasn't just a smile. She looked scared. Standing there in that little top from House of Fraser with a suitcase that's half the size of her. She was scared. You're alone in the darkness and you're crying. You've had a few minutes to know this was coming but even so it's mugged you.

Tuesday

'Jakob Binder,' whispered her mother with her eyes half closed. The room was dark because light had started to hurt her. Just the day before Ana had changed the bedding but already the room smelt of decay and ending.

'That was the name of the guard.'

It had taken two days for her mother to remember the name. She had slipped in and out of sleep but every time she'd awoken wanting to return to Auschwitz. She'd talked of the trains and the fences, the gates and the sign. *Arbeit Macht Frei*. She talked of the fear and the freezing cold. More than anything she talked of the nights filled with screaming that had caused her a life without sleep. Now she spoke of the man whose white trousers she'd struck with a child's fist of soil.

'Jakob Binder.'

There's darkness, confusion. Ana can't see what's coming next.

★

The knife's on your throat. That first touch wakes you and then there's more. Metal taps your arm, runs across your belly and messes with your cock through the nylon of your boxers. Pricks and jabs. Nothing serious but serious enough. These are knife merchants, with voices.

'He's a big bastard.'

'All right there, kiddo?'

'Sam Albright says wake the fuck up.'

They roll you over with the knives, piercing your skin to force you off the bed. You hit the ground face down and look up to see splinters around the lock of the door. They clamber on you like monkeys. One holds your legs, another mounts you and pulls your hands behind your back. Someone sits cross-legged on the floor and holds your head in his hands, his fingers spread hungrily round your scalp. He's controlling you now and there's not much you can see other than his folded legs and, behind him, the trainers of someone standing away from the action. That makes four of them.

'An amateur, that's what you are,' says the hero holding your head. 'Dead asleep with a plastic lock in the door.'

The accents are Scouse and that's hard to believe because Liverpool was Sam Albright's worst nightmare. The people he needed through there weren't exactly up for lectures, they just wanted paid.

You'd drive Sam to meet Scousers who'd nod and pretend to listen then ask if Sam needed stolen cars. A few months before Bradford Square you drove Sam through again. He'd been lined up to meet a serious mob who had the right sort of influence. Sam told them that the movement was unstoppable. He told them about the estates he controlled in cities across the north, and how it was time Liverpool heard his message. This time the Scousers showed some respect. They offered to nick him *buses*. On the way back to Bradford Sam said you wouldn't see Liverpool again. 'They haven't got the right spirit,' he said bitterly. 'They can't see the wider picture.' He sat and shook his head, holding the blank membership forms he hadn't had the chance to give out.

But now you're seeing Liverpool again.

'How did you find me?' you ask, because conversation is better than any alternative.

'How d'ya think, kiddo?'

The voice comes from above the pair of trainers. He's the boss.

'Go on,' you say.

'Your man Dickinson.'

Something turns within you.

'Oh yeah? What's his first name?'

'Why would we know?'

'What does he look like then?'

The fingers squeeze your head. This boy with the folded legs wants to remind you he's here too.

'Dickinson, that's all we know. He sold you out, son.'

'What does he look like?'

At the trials John Dickinson stayed through the back and watched it all on a monitor. One day you pointed at the monitor and asked him if it was like watching *Rumpole of the Bailey*. He said it wasn't. He said *Rumpole of the Bailey* didn't have actors as good as Sam Albright. Dickinson wasn't a bad lad. It wasn't him, this wasn't him.

'I knew it,' you say, 'I knew he'd do me.'

'Hi, yeah, we've got him.'

The trainers have moved to the table. He's on the phone. The fingers tighten further on your head and ease your face to the tiles.

'Take it easy,' says the voice above you. 'Don't you worry about that.'

His nails are a crown of thorns. The phone conversation proceeds the way you'd expect.

'Yeah, piece of piss, he was sleeping.'

'No, on his own.'

'Yeah? Here?'

He's surprised but you're not. He's talking to someone who Sam's given word to and Sam's word is only going to go one way. It's two years since the trial, give or take, and he's got another eighteen years to go. Twenty years minimum the man was handed. Now he's got you he'll just want it done.

Without warning and without reason the fingers lift from your head and after this everything happens very fast. You look to the right. The trainers are owned by a skinny man who holds the phone and looks past you to the door. You look to the left. The door's open and a hotel maid stands in the corridor and opens her mouth, waits, then closes it again.

With everything you can find you push your right shoulder into the floor and use it to pivot your left shoulder upwards. The two on your back sway to the right and there's enough momentum for you to roll them off. You spring to your feet and they scurry to the door and slam it shut in the maid's face. When they remember they have them, they lift their knives. One of them is a decent size but he's only the second biggest in the room.

The boss is still holding the phone. He's certainly not taking charge of this development. The boy who was enjoying himself so much with your head scrabbles to his feet, finds his blade and runs over to the others. So now you've got three Scousers and three knives between you and the door and one Scouser who's too scared to even hang up the phone between you and the glass, the balcony, the pool.

You pick up the chair.

'Come on then,' one of the three shouts, not to you but to his pals.

The three of them come at you blades first. You thrust the chair at them, they flinch back and this gives you the space you need. You throw the chair at the window. It turns in the air, reaches the glass and keeps going. The window shatters in an oval and you're off and running. Three steps on the tiled floor, a limp hand from the boss that slaps your chest, one step on the patio, a palm on the balcony and you're up and over and in the air.

Four storeys high. Three nights ago she called you outside and you peered at a dark block of water that seemed right below you. Now you look and it's set back a few yards. With the speed you went over the balcony you've probably bought that distance but this, this is going to be very close indeed.

Someone screams.

This is the shallow end. This is the fucking

★

Her father was outside talking with the neighbours. It was just Ana and her mother.

'Binder,' said her mother again, 'Jakob Binder.'

Now that she'd arrived at this memory she didn't seem able to go past it. Her lips were cracked. Ana lifted water with a spoon and tipped it in.

'Coffee,' whispered her mother.

Ana held the cup at a shallow angle. Her mother drew her tongue along the china, enough for a taste at least.

'The name of the guard was Jakob Binder,' said Ana's mother. Her eyes were clouded, her skin grey as life sighed from her.

'Why did he have to take them both?'

Ana wakes. Somewhere a woman screams. The tourists are already up and playing at the pool. The sunlight seeps round her curtain at an angle Ana hasn't seen before. She remembers that she didn't set an alarm because today is starting late. At ten o'clock, with Craig.

★

You hit the water but, put it this way, your entrance isn't exactly Olympic standard. Arse first is how you arrive, with your legs out in front and your hands pissing about somewhere. The first loser is your right hand which catches the pool's edge on the way past. Then comes the water and then comes the pool's floor and you hit it bastard hard.

You stop, you have to stop, but you stop that fast that you feel like you're going back the other way. Your whole body snaps and a pain zips up and down your spine while you remember you're underwater. There's no knowing how you get to the surface but when you stand your left foot pulls away in fright. You perch on your right leg, throw your good hand to the pool's edge and you breathe.

You lift your right hand. Move the fingers and it's not so bad. You send this instruction down your arm and the response washes your body in pain. You'll come back to that. That's a work in progress. You move to the steps which are easier than they should be because the water helps with your weight. Out the pool and you're on your knees. You try to stand but it's just not happening and there are too many reasons why. Now you're flat on your back and that's a little better but you're making a strange old noise that you're not in charge of.

Oh but you're finished, lying here on the hot stone.

★

The water turns warm in her hand and Ana steps into the shower. The memories travel from her sleep – her mother's busy funeral, her father's hand shaking until she took it in hers, and then Rabbi Solowitch calling her back to pull the envelope from his pocket. She had read it that night while her father slept. Her mother's handwriting told her only where to go. She took a torch to the cellar and found the loose brick and the bound parcel.

The banknotes went back thirty years. It had taken her mother three decades to save this money and she had done so in secret. Over time her plan for the money must have changed but the envelope showed how it ended. There were the instructions to find the money, an application form for the university in Budapest filled out in Ana's name, and nothing else.

Ana told her father, who was a good man but bad with his money, that she had the chance of a scholarship. She gathered recommendations from her teachers and Rabbi Solowitch and took the overnight train to Budapest, staying awake and feeling every few minutes for the money within her coat.

The university gave her an interview and she paid her fees in advance. Maybe it was this that led to her acceptance, but when the letter arrived in Komoró a week later she read it for her father and added a sentence about the phantom scholarship.

Hints of what would become her father's depression had already arrived, but Ana felt no choice but to go to Budapest. She left him on the train platform at Komoró, his arm raised in a stiff wave. Then it was university, the shame of Imre, and three years in the library. It was towards the end of those three years, after she'd found the Auschwitz Testimonies and Binder had come to life in front of her, that she found Moshe Geigler.

There was a short article in the *Budapester*, two paragraphs on how Geigler had tracked down a Nazi concentration camp doctor in Brazil. Ana went to the university's collection of international newspapers. The *Wall Street Journal* called Geigler 'the Nazi Hunter'. The British *Times* said Geigler had a list of every Nazi still alive. *Le Monde* described his *siege*, headquarters, in Jerusalem. Ana called the international operator and together they found the number. While the phone rang, she could hardly breathe.

'Moshe Geigler,' he said.

Ana told him in English about her mother, about Komoró and the trains.

'This is Hungary?' said Geigler.

'Yes.'

'So,' he said, 'Auschwitz. What is it you want?'

The *New York Times* had described Geigler as 'curiously lacking in emotion'.

'Jakob Binder,' said Ana. She would have said more if he hadn't spoken first.

'You should come to Jerusalem,' said Geigler. 'That would be best.'

He hung up. He would tell her later that he had dozens of calls a day. It was easier to tell people to come to Jerusalem, to work out who was serious.

The water's turning cold. This is what Ana gets, a few minutes in the morning and the same in the evening. The staffrooms work off different pipes to the guests above. She closes the tap and the water coughs then slows to a dribble.

★

There are faces above you and behind them is the sun.

'Are you OK?' asks some genius. Yeah, I'm fine, mate. Just dropping in.

'Has anyone called an ambulance?' another boy shouts in a way he must have seen someone shout on the telly.

You push yourself up into a sitting position. Your back's in disbelief but when it realises what you've done it goes for you properly. This takes you out the game for a second and you obviously shout something a little daring in content because people pull away in fright.

You steady yourself then swing to the side and onto your feet. The pain comes in chunks. You track your eyes up the hotel. Four storeys high you see four heads. You look at the Scousers, they look at you and then one after another they flick out of view. That's them coming.

'You shouldn't move,' offers the same boy, the TV fan.

'I probably should,' you say.

There's a gate to the street. You try and take it easy on your left foot which doesn't seem to appreciate the gesture. It makes it clear that it really doesn't want to be involved at all.

★

It doesn't usually take Ana this long to prepare. She tells herself it's because today there's no rush and no point in reaching her car earlier than they've arranged. But the extra time is not spent on her notes or practical matters. She adds make-up that would never usually appear during the day. She pulls a brush through her hair twenty times each side like she used to do with the Gera sisters before the dances in Komoró, where Rabbi Solowitch ran between couples to pull teenage hands back onto shoulders.

Ana chooses the jeans she bought in Budapest on her twenty-first birthday. She found them in a boutique on Váci Street and the price left her guiltily eating soup for a week. She adds a loose T-shirt and stands in front of the mirror. It would be dishonest to say that Ana is unaware of her effect on men but it is an effect that slips to and from her mind. When it does register it's usually as an unwelcome hassle. This morning she is aware of it, and this morning she is glad for it.

★

This isn't going to be a marathon and it certainly isn't going to be a sprint. To say that you're walking is an exaggeration. You're moving your feet and the best bit is when they're in the air because every time they land it sets off another protest that leaves you reeling. You count your steps. To think they won't catch you is just daft, but you count your steps so you don't think of that.

161

Here's a corner and you're round it. If you turn enough corners, make enough choices, then that's more and more that they've got to get right. The tarmac's cold against your bare feet. It wasn't Dickinson, how could it be? You need to find where she parked her car. It's not the best plan you've ever heard but you're in the kingdom of the blind right now. You get round another corner and this is a street you've seen before. You count your steps to the end and there it is.

Her car sits all alone. Behind it are bushes and trees and the start of the countryside. You don't know why she parked so far from the hotel but you're glad she did because those trees will do for now.

You're crossing the road when a car comes fairly moving towards you. It stops in time but there's not much room to play with. The Spanish boy at the wheel looks stumped and it's hard to blame him. He's nearly run over a boy who's standing in a pair of pants, dripping wet, and with an arm dipped in blood. You give him a wave and he waves back and you both pretend this is perfectly normal before you go your separate ways.

You push the trees' dry branches to the side and work your way through to a patch of grass. You try to sit but your back's not having that so you lie down on your belly. You can see under the trees to her car. You'll wait here. It's been maybe fifteen minutes, no more, since you woke up. If you were asked to describe your morning you'd say that it's been very busy.

Your body's coming out the shock. Now there's just the pain and a great tiredness. It wasn't Dickinson, it couldn't be.

If you just lie here then she'll come.

Stay awake.

★

Something's happening. Two of the pool attendants speak to a manager who stands between the receptionists and asks, 'Where?'

Over and over and each time sounding more incredulous than the last. The Spanish staff enjoy a crisis and Ana doesn't want to know about this one. The last time she saw such a scene it was a confusing argument about towels that involved hours of shouting. She carries on through the reception to the street.

Ana checks her watch. Her route is awkward, cutting through the thinner streets, where the restaurants take deliveries at their back doors. She emerges onto the wider road at the village's edge to see her car by itself. She gets in, turns on the radio then turns it off. She looks at herself in the mirror. Ana checks her watch.

Half an hour later her mind is a narrow place. She knew quickly, after five minutes of waiting, that he wasn't going to come. That sparked a difficult period of panic followed by a daze and now her brain is a battleground. She's decided this is too big to be handled immediately so each time her mind produces a new angle on the disaster she coolly shuts it down.

She dilutes her focus to the most simple of tasks – turn the key, start the engine, look for passing cars, then go. In this manner, like a robot, she drives to San Carlos where she parks and walks without thought into the Argentine restaurant. She sits at a table she has never used before. She told Craig everything. She told him everything, and now, and now this.

The Argentine walks out the restaurant smiling and clapping his hands together.

'Coffee,' says Ana in a sharp voice that surprises her and certainly surprises the Argentine, who retreats back inside looking wounded.

The folder is the next escape. To stop her thinking of Craig she thinks of other men.

Jakob Binder.

Moshe Geigler.

★

You're lying on your back, with your bad hand held over your chest like a broken wing. You twist your head and look. Ana's car has gone. Your mouth is drier than you'd have guessed was possible. You have to fight to swallow.

Her car's gone. OK. You sit up and that gets the usual standing ovation from your back. Your left ankle's twice the size of the other one. Your right hand's not keen on an active role. But her car's gone. You're so fucked in a general sense that it's hard to concentrate on how fucked you are physically.

You try to stand suddenly, as if you're selling a dummy to the pain, and what a mess you make of it. You grab a branch and your body twists and you're standing on your good foot and shouting with pain. A pine cone, you're standing on a pine cone. You kick it away and put down your other foot, with the ankle like a wellington, because you might as well confirm matters. Sure enough, you lean an inch of weight on it and the ankle near enough explodes. The bruising was coming up purple last time you saw it and now it's black.

Here's what you've got to get yourself out of this – one ankle, one hand, a back that's definitely up to something, no money and no clothes. You hold onto the branch and think about her car. It was pointing to the left, so you should walk to the right. That's the direction you came from yesterday and that's where she'll have headed. There's only one place she'll have gone.

You look for the thickest branch going and rip it from the tree. It comes off nicely and the length is about right. Off you go with your walking stick, watching for cones and trying not to think how this whole scene must look. A car passes by behind the trees. What if it's a police car? What if it's an ambulance? Would you stop them? You should but you know why you won't. Because, when they ask you to give them the slightest clue what you were up to, you'd have to make a decision on John Dickinson.

The sweat pisses from you and there's so far to go.

★

Moshe Geigler's office was in Jerusalem's college district, overlooking the botanical gardens. He was drinking tea at a desk that peeked from beneath a swarm of documents, books and photographs. His eyes danced about behind the thick glass of his spectacles, his hair was nearly gone and he moved like an older man while picking his way between pillars of paperwork to greet her.

'You have come from Hungary?' he asked.

'Yes,' said Ana.

'This is good,' he replied quickly, efficiently.

Geigler shuffled to a cabinet, his hand reaching for support from a pile of German newspapers. He selected a file and muttered to himself on the tricky journey back to his desk. While he manoeuvred through the room Ana looked only at what he carried. Sideways on, and moving through air, she saw BINDER.

Her legs weakened under her and she sat without being asked on the only chair free of books. Geigler took off his glasses and pinched them within a cloth, rubbing them clean between thumb and forefinger. He slipped them back on, opened the file and plucked out a photo. He placed it on the desk and turned it for her.

That first photograph was sepia and faded. A group of soldiers, standing in a row and looking at the photographer with curiosity, were in front of a wooden hut and a fence of stretched barbed wire. It was hard to make out faces but Ana's attention was elsewhere. Between the brown of the other soldiers one man wore white, spotless trousers. He was a step in front of the others and while they

165

slouched and frowned, his back was straightened, his heavy chest lifted and his eyes looked through the years to Ana.

Geigler's finger slid to the man.

'Jakob Binder,' he said. 'This photo was taken at Auschwitz in 1943.'

He read from the file.

'Binder is believed to have left Auschwitz without permission on 10 January 1945. He was seen with other suspected fugitives in Koper on 21 January.'

Geigler looked up.

'Koper is a port city on the Mediterranean coast of Slovenia.'

Ana nodded, unsure if she should say that she knew this.

'The Nazis had many sympathisers in Slovenia's White Guard,' continued Geigler. 'On 23 January 1945 eight trawlers full of fugitives set sail from Koper. One had engine failure a mile from port. Three were stopped by an American frigate off the southern coast of Sardinia a week later. The other four made it to Spain.'

Geigler turned a page.

'Ah,' he said. He placed his hands flat on the table. 'OK, yes, I remember.'

He leant back in his chair and clasped his hands over his chest.

'I started this in 1962.' He gestured around the room as if he were showing Ana great riches. To her it looked like the home of a madman. 'In 1964 I received a letter from Ibiza. Now, do you know where Ibiza is?'

'No,' answered Ana. It was hard not to smile at this strange man, who spoke to her as if she were a child and had eyes that changed shape behind his glasses.

'Ibiza is a Spanish island, in the Balearics,' said Geigler. 'This is the letter I received.'

He briefly touched his glasses and Ana thought with dismay that there was to be more polishing. Instead he lifted a letter for inspection.

'This man was a socialist, a dangerous ambition in the Spain of Franco. He worked at the harbour in Ibiza and wrote to tell me of the Nazis he knew to be living on the island. One of those was Jakob Binder. He said, now . . .'

Geigler frowned at the letter.

'Jakob Binder arrived on Ibiza in 1945. He bought a house and was often seen in the old town. That is all.'

Geigler replaced the letter, swapping it for another. When he raised this new document, a photo fell to the desk and Geigler held it beneath the page.

'I wrote back asking for more information on the Nazis he had seen, including Binder,' he continued. 'He told me what he knew of the others and for Binder he sent me this.'

Now he produced the photo which was black and white and taken at an odd, snatched angle. It showed a middle-aged man sitting at a felt-covered table, his face half hidden by his hand lifting a cigarette to his mouth. He wore a dark suit with a lighter shirt open at the collar. In front of him on the felt were a drink and a pile of plastic chips.

'Turn it over,' said Geigler.

On the back of the photo was written: *Casino de Rey, Ibiza, 16 April 1964.*

'Binder was on Ibiza in 1945 and he was on Ibiza on 16 April 1964,' said Geigler. 'That is all I know.'

'You never had another letter?' asked Ana.

'No,' answered Geigler. 'I wrote but I did not hear back. I fear our socialist was uncovered.'

'Have you looked for Binder there, on Ibiza?'

'No,' he replied. 'One day, I hope, but for now' – he waved at endless piles of paper and photographs – 'I have stronger leads and only this one pair of hands.'

'He will be living there under his name?'

'Of course not,' chided Geigler. 'He will have arrived on a

foreign passport, probably Swiss or Austrian, and who knows what name he will have used.'

Ana had no other questions.

'We always need help,' said Geigler.

Ana knew every time he said *we* he meant only himself.

'Please,' she said, 'can I have this?' She held the photo from the casino.

'I cannot,' Geigler told her. 'It belongs with the file.'

'I will go to Ibiza,' answered Ana. 'I will look for him until I know.'

'How can I be sure of this?'

'Because I came here,' she replied. 'And because I have read every single one of the Auschwitz Testimonies at the University of Budapest. Have you?'

In her taxi to the airport Ana wrote everything Geigler had told her in her notebook and slid the photo from the casino between the pages. She flew back to Budapest only to collect her things and then it was Barcelona and the Spanish lessons. Then it was Ibiza.

★

After a lifetime, the road splits. You don't know where it's going to the left but you know exactly where it's off to on the right. It's the long road to the village, San Carlos. From memory you'd say ten miles. You look back to the trees where this little outing began. You can still see them, even though there's a sea of pain between you. Ten miles could be called ambitious. Ten miles could be called ludicrous.

Among a decent spread of problems is the road itself which is flat and open all the way. At some point the Scousers are going to fire up there and you won't exactly be hard to spot. The fields either side of the road are all the same – red soil, the odd olive tree and a handful of desperate-looking sheep. Not a huge amount of cover for an eighteen-stone man in his pants.

You make the nearest gate, lift it out of the lock and swing yourself through. The soil's soft beneath you. The first few steps are a novelty and after that there's no novelty at all. Your stick sinks into the mud like a flagpole while you lurch onwards. You look drunk.

This field's a good hundred metres long. People get medals for running this distance and those cunts only take ten seconds. One morning last summer you sat and ate your breakfast and watched Ben Johnson take the gold in South Korea. You watched him before the start, with the veins lifted in his arms and that twitch he had, the cracking of the jaw. This one's at it, you said to yourself. And that was before he took the gold, and that was before the press conference and the tears and the steroids.

You could do with some of them now. The dusty pills you bought in Gold's Gym in Bradford then the vials of clear liquid you injected into your arms and calves until Dickinson made you stop. You wonder if John Dickinson took Sam Albright's money. The field's grooved and your left foot keeps catching the humped soil and sending decent reminders up your leg about the state of play. If this was a story then people wouldn't believe it, no matter how well you told it.

During the trial they moved you every night and the only rule was you had to be less than an hour from Bradford and the courtroom. So that brought in Oldham, Rochdale, Huddersfield, Blackburn, Leeds, Wakefield, Barnsley and so on. It was a new hotel every night but truth be told you didn't notice much difference. You were taken to court early to talk to Dickinson and the prosecutor, you stayed there afterwards to talk to Dickinson and the prosecutor, and then you were taken back for room service and *Wogan*.

You'd lie on the hotel's bed and eat room service and Wogan would sit on his leather chair and smile and get his guests to tell stories. Sometimes he'd cock up by chipping in something from the story that hadn't come up yet, so you'd know they'd practised the story out the back. But that was fine, as long as they told it well.

Your feet are sinking deeper into the mud and you don't know if the soil's getting softer or you're finding it harder to pull them out. Your eyes are attacked by sweat. You take your mind to Wogan, to Wogan and you. You're sitting opposite him wearing the suit John Dickinson bought you for the trial. Both you and Wogan have a leg swung over the other. You're pals really, more than anything. It's not just business is what the scene is saying.

'And you were in this field?' asks Wogan, his eyes shining in the studio lights. He's already smiling.

'That's right, Terry,' you say, 'a field full of mud.'

'Well, they often are,' says Wogan and he gets a big laugh from the audience which is fair enough.

'I suppose you're right, Terry,' you say.

'So, come on now,' he says, 'you were in this field?'

'Yes, Terry, I was in a field trying desperately to escape from four Scousers who hadn't exactly taken a shine to me.'

'Liverpudlians can be' – Wogan slips the audience a look – 'difficult.'

The audience lap that up. Their laughter fills the studio.

'Scousers, Terry.'

'Oh, I think we'd better stick to Liverpudlians.' He reaches forward and taps your knee in warning.

'No, Terry,' you say, quieter, 'Scousers.'

'Now –' he says, he sounds like a teacher.

'Terry?' you cut him off. You lean in and hold his tie. You tug it gently, bringing his face to you. 'They're Scousers, Terry, and they want to kill me.'

Wogan's mouth opens in an 'O'. The studio audience don't say fuck all because your behaviour is completely unexpected.

★

170

From the terrace of the Argentine, the hills seem emptier than before. Ana doesn't see the houses, only the trees in their ancient spread from hill to hill. So many of the people on this island are visitors, she thinks, whether they come for a week or fifty years. She has been here only for one summer, but in that time surely no one has seen as much of the island as her.

Ana considers how her friends must have spent the summer. The Gera sisters in Bupapest will have boyfriends, jobs and lives. Kianna is in New York. A friend told Ana that Kianna was paid $500 for every photo shoot and rented an apartment with three bedrooms. Even the other girls from school in Komoró would have been busy. Alida Szabó, the most stupid girl Ana had ever met, had apparently married a lawyer from Mándok who drove a Mercedes.

And Ana, at twenty-two years old, had spent her summer using up what little money she had and chasing a ghost. All she will be left with, she thinks bitterly, is that car. All she owns is a car that cannot be trusted and a future that is black with worry. With some effort she halts these concerns. There is still some chance, she tells herself with little conviction. She flicks open the folder and finds the photo.

In her first weeks on Ibiza she carried the photo in her purse wherever she went, as if she would see a man in the street that would need immediate comparison. She thought she'd be showing it every day to people in the houses she visited. In fact, there had only been a handful of occasions when she'd got that far in the conversation and each time it had been met by nothing. The photo has not left the folder for weeks.

When the Argentine brings her the bill Ana tips him more than she should. Leaving the restaurant feels strangely final.

*

Yards from the field's edge you hear the car. You stop and stand like a scarecrow and, to be fair, right now you'd make a good one.

171

Over the wall you see the car's roof slow to a stop. You cover the last, awful stretch of mud and you look. The car's empty and the driver's door hangs open. An old boy carrying a sack walks into the next field. The sheep clock him and show a decent turn of pace to swarm round a wooden trough. That's where he's headed. The car's engine ticks over which means he's left the keys.

With a hand on top of the wall, you hop to the gate and knock it open. After the field, you're grateful for the firmness of the track. The car's a banger but at least you've seen it move. You angle into the driver's seat. The keys are there and you realise with surprise that this could work.

The old boy's facing you but he's bent over his sack while the sheep mob him. The gearstick quivers to the engine. You pull the door closed. You check over your shoulder. You look down at the pedals which are old and raised high and will need a level of force that your left foot can't provide just now. You tuck your left foot away, put your right foot on the clutch and slide your stick down onto the accelerator.

You find reverse and push the stick. The pedal gives slowly and then suddenly. The engine near enough shouts the old boy's name and sure enough he's up and waving as if there's been some terrible mistake. The car rears and you remember the handbrake. When you release it, the car swings backwards into the opposite wall.

You flick into first gear and what's strange is that the old boy, the farmer, he's not moving. He's dropped his sack, the sheep fight over it at his feet, and he's looking at you with his hands on his hips. He can't have expected this when he left the house, you think, and the insurance form will be a cracker.

You jab the stick and the car glides down the track. The San Carlos road's approaching but you don't want to break up this arrangement by stopping. You slow and turn hard and the car skips onto the tarmac, the tyres hold and bring you straight. The open window sends a breeze down your aching back. The road's surface feels like a carpet. You hold the stick firm on the pedal, keep the wheel straight and coast up and over the hills to San Carlos barely believing your luck.

It's when you start the drop into the valley that you recognise the arrival of a proper test. You pull out into the other lane. If a car came round the corner then things wouldn't look too clever but you need the space and a stall wouldn't be welcome. You wait for the gap in the trees then lean down with the stick, switch into first gear and whip the wheel. The car goes a little spastic but once it hits the drive, with the slope and the gravel, it understands where you're coming from and agrees with your choices. The wheels spit stones and give you just enough pace to send you upwards.

It's fair to say that the farmer's car isn't a natural match for this road. What suspension there is seems to go on strike and every pothole is another assault on you. Your ankle's being banged about, your back's getting handed surprises and you're more than happy to see the clearing and the gate ahead. That's when the tyre goes. The car's arse drops and you turn to see strips of rubber ping into the air. You've lost most of your speed already so this just makes matters a little embarrassing. The car stumbles into the clearing, has a little cough and then goes to sleep.

You open the door, clasp the roof and pull yourself out with your one good hand. You sit in the dirt, your back resting against the front of the car. You wonder how the farmer got home. You look back down the road. It's a surprise you made it up but that just means you can't make it down.

She's not here.

*

At first Ana believes he's dead and other people would think the same. His head hangs motionless over his body which is naked apart from underpants. One arm's coated in blood and an ankle is swollen and discoloured. When she slams the car door in her rush to go to him, however, Craig looks up and says, 'Hello, love.'

'What happened?' she asks.

'I was in a fight,' he tells her and his voice seems softer than she remembers. 'Some English boys this morning, they were still drunk from last night.'

'Are you OK?'

'I think so,' he answers. 'More or less.'

Ana looks at his injuries and, in doing so, at his body. There must have been a lot of these other men, she thinks.

'It was early,' he says. 'I wasn't dressed.'

In Ibiza Ana has learnt not to be surprised by the British. About the drinking and the situations that can create.

'Let's go in,' says Craig.

'The house?' answers Ana, knowing and hoping that is what he means.

'Yeah, if there's anyone there you can say you need help for me.'

'How will we get in?'

What she means is, how will he?

'Drive your car up there,' says Craig, nodding at the gate. 'Use it to climb over, open the gate then come back for me. I can't walk.'

'I can open it?'

'It's easy,' answers Craig. 'I saw it yesterday.'

Ana is not going to question this opportunity. She drives towards the gate until she nudges the wood. She climbs onto her bonnet and pulls herself up. Through the trees are a house and a wooden platform raised on stilts. She checks the ground beneath her and jumps. The gate's held in place by a plank of wood gripped by a hook on each side. She lifts it, throws it to the side and tugs on the hooks. The gate opens. She pulls it wide then reverses her car back beside Craig.

'I can't carry you,' she says.

'No,' he says, 'you can't.'

Craig takes loud breaths, as if about to go underwater, then rises onto one foot. He feels his way round the car and sits sideways, his bad leg crossed over the other and swollen ankle raised. He lies back and his legs drag in far enough for Ana to close the door.

'I will go slowly,' she tells him.

'Thanks,' he says, his hands gripping his knee.

Ana drives through the gate, closes it behind them then takes the car up the steep drive. The house is only one floor but spreads over flattened land fronted by the platform.

'Wait here,' Ana tells Craig.

By now, Ana believes that she knows when she knocks on the door of an empty house. There is an established air to the silence, and that is the case now. She knocks again and reaches for the handle which gives way and the door swings open. She's in a large room with old furniture and heavy curtains lining one wall.

'Hello,' she shouts into the murky light, in English then Spanish.

The house is cold. She walks to the curtains and tugs them apart. Sunshine floods in through glass doors leading to the wooden deck. She's looking for the lock when the voice sounds behind her.

'Hi,' he says.

From the sweat and the panting, his journey from the car must have seemed long.

'Thought I'd better join you,' he says, 'in case.'

'Wait,' Ana tells him.

Craig grips the door frame while she hurries round the room, pulling cushions from chairs and collecting them on the floor. She arranges an attempt at a bed.

'Come here,' she says.

Craig hops heavily to her and Ana guides him onto his back. He groans and his eyes squeeze shut in pain while he settles. Ana lifts a rug from a chair and lays it across him.

'OK?' she asks and there is a delay until he opens his eyes.

'Yeah,' he answers in this new, soft voice. It is strange for a man of his size to seem vulnerable.

'I have to do a few things,' says Ana. 'They will hurt a little.'

★

This is reality, there's no doubt about that, but it's a funny kind of reality. You feel like you're dreaming but you can't be because it's so very sore. You can see her move around your body, you can feel her busy hands, and you can certainly feel what they're doing.

★

All the men in her family's street had laboured on the farms outside Komoró. They went to work together, walking silently towards the fields with their lunch in string bags by their side. The work on the farms was often unsafe and many times there would be injuries. Men would be carried back by the others and laid across a kitchen table for the women to tend to.

Ana has seen Craig's injuries before and she knows what she's looking for when she searches the house. From the tidy kitchen she fetches a bowl of water and some cloths. From the cupboard in the spotless bathroom she takes a roll of bandaging and bottle of disinfectant. She returns to the kitchen and opens the fridge.

For a moment she is overcome. The meat is rancid and the smell overpowering. She slams the door closed and leans over her knees, persuading herself not to vomit. She finds a glass and fills it with water. In a cupboard are some biscuits. She carries this final load through to Craig, considering the odd contrast between a house kept so clean and rotten meat in the fridge.

Ana begins by wiping the blood from Craig's arm and ankle to find the true injuries. The hand has three broken fingers, maybe four. She rubs in disinfectant, which makes Craig's body straighten in pain, then looks around the room until she sees the bookcase. Taking a heavy paperback, she cracks the cover free and tears thin strips before sliding them between Craig's fingers. Over this arrangement she wraps the bandaging.

His ankle is swollen black and nearly twice the size of the other. She asks him to move his toes and he does so with only a grimace so she knows it's the ligaments within the joint that he's disturbed. She removes the blood and then works in the disinfectant, a move that has Craig squeezing a cushion with the white knuckles of his good hand.

'Wait,' says Ana and returns to the kitchen. The freezer gives up enough ice to fill a small bag and she returns to place this on his ankle. She ties it in place and moves up his body. Washing the blood and sweat from his face proves awkward with Craig blinking and trying to look past her, so after this she finishes.

Ana knows he may need proper help, his movements suggest there may some pain in his back that she would not be able to see, but for now he will be OK. She knows that it is for her own needs that she is thinking this way. She knows that she might require him; she hopes that she will.

'Have these,' she says and places the biscuits and water beside him.

'Thanks,' he answers.

Ana stands. It's time to look at the house properly and to answer the only question left.

★

She's kneeling beside you and holding a passport in front of your face. The passport's old. It's the size of a phone book for a start. The photo is of some boy in military uniform.

'Binder,' she says.

She shows you the front cover, with Switzerland picked out in

177

gold, and then the personal details inside which don't say anything about Binder.

'Look,' she says, and points to an entry reading *Kössler*. 'And now here.'

She holds a letter open for you. She's properly excited and her eyes are alive with something. The letter looks formal and it's in Spanish. You're not quite sure what she's expecting you to do with this.

'It's from the hospital in Ibiza Town,' she tells you. 'He has had tests. Cancer. Then they asked him to go in for more, here.' She points to a date. 'Four months ago.'

'OK,' you say.

'Look,' she says, and points to the name on the letter. Kössler.

'OK,' you say again.

'It is Binder.' There's something delirious about her. You consider if she's been at the drinks cabinet. You heard banging, and her voice.

'Is it?' you ask.

She brandishes the passport next to a new photo. The new photo shows some boy sitting at a table at a casino. He's lighting a fag so you can't see his whole face but you can see more than enough to know it's the same man.

'That's Binder?' you ask.

'Yes,' she says. She points to a collection of mail on a table. 'That is his mail. It goes back to this date four months ago.' She gestures to the letter. 'He has not come back from the hospital.'

'He could be dead,' you tell her.

'No,' she answers. 'I have called the hospital. I said I was a relative.'

'He's there?'

'He's there.'

To her side is something else, an envelope that you can see is stuffed with banknotes.

'It was hidden with his passport,' Ana tells you. 'I am going to give it to Moshe Geigler.'

You look down at your body and wonder where the pain's gone.

★

Ana places the mail back on the table where she found it neatly stacked. Someone has been checking on the house, a neighbour perhaps, though they obviously forgot about the fridge. It is late now, and they will leave in the morning. If they are discovered she will form a story around Craig's injuries.

She returns to his side. His eyes are closed but he's awake. His chest is raised above the rug. There is still blood spread around it where he has touched himself with his damaged hand. She takes the wet cloth and begins to wipe over the vastness. Over his shoulders she sees the beginning of some sunburn on his back. His chest is two bubbles of hard flesh. His stomach is ridged with muscle. She removes the rug. His underpants are dirtied with blood and, strangely, with what looks like the red dust of the fields.

She moves to his legs, stroking downwards with the cloth. As she does so she feels him tense and when she looks back up his body his penis has raised within his pants. He looks with embarrassment at the ceiling. Ana's mind moves in ways that surprise her; she feels control slip away.

She pulls his underpants down his legs and places them to the side. She settles beside his crotch and takes hold of his penis. It's alive in her hand. It feels and looks like just another of his muscles. She stands and pulls her top off, then unbuttons her jeans. Craig watches her with what looks like alarm. She slips off her pants then bends down, lifting one leg over him.

For a moment she hovers there above him, her hand back on him and guiding him until he touches her wetness.

'You want to?' she says.

He takes two, maybe three, attempts to speak.

'Yeah,' he says.

★

You wish this was hurting more. That would give you somewhere to point your mind other than the matter at hand, but your injuries seem to have taken a little break right when you need them the most. From the first sign, the first whisper, that this was on the cards there's been a possibility that the game could be all over at your end.

She's on top with her legs wrapped tight over yours and it's hard to be clear about your role. Your cock's inside her, though you're very much trying to forget that fact, and she's rocking back and forth and seems to be enjoying it but you're not entirely sure if you've been given partnership status.

You reach a hand for her bra, and feel no older than twelve while doing so, and she pushes it away. You take that with a fair amount of relief. You want to tell her that you understand and agree with her decision.

She pulls back a hand and unclasps her bra. That's why you were sent packing, so she could do it herself, and there they are. Right in front of you and swinging in time to her movements. You lift your hands and hold her tits as if they're diamonds. If you'd ever held diamonds, that is. Or tits like these.

Her fingers trail across your body. You drop your hands to her hips and there's a rhythm that grows stronger. She's grinding into you. You think about your cock, about what it must be dealing with right now and how little time it had to come to terms with the situation. It received as much warning as the boys at Hiroshima. You think about them, the little Japs going about their business with the A-bomb falling through the clouds, and you think that she's like a mushroom cloud up there right now.

You're waiting patiently for a sign that you can wrap things up with a bit of dignity and it finally arrives. She speeds up further, and you're fairly sure your thighs are now alight, and then she jerks to a stop and looks at the ceiling. You take a chance that she's done and send word down to the front line. She slumps towards you and by the time she lands on your chest you've come inside her far harder than is decent. She's hot against your skin. Her hands scarper to your cheeks. She drags her face up and her mouth is by your right ear and she says, 'You need to do this for me.'

And you think, do what? You look down and you can see her bare arse and you think, well, thank Christ I couldn't see that or we wouldn't have made it this far.

'Will you?' she asks.

You're both waiting for your answer.

'We should get some sleep,' you reply.

Behind her, through the glass doors, comes the dawn.

Wednesday

This is the first day the sun's not been around in the morning and that's fine with you. Over in the next valley the clouds are lower than the hills. Here it hangs like a ceiling above you and San Carlos down below.

You sit on the German's seat on the German's wooden deck and you can't knock the set-up he's got here. 1945 she reckons he bought this place. Forty-four years he's looked down at the village and you can't imagine much has changed. The roads will have been here before the cars. The houses flow off the church walls so they're clearly vintage material. The village, San Carlos, has just sat and got old while the German has watched and done the same.

This is a view that you'd want if you were hiding. If they came for you then you'd know about it, and the village is laid out beneath you like a board game. You look at the restaurant on the edge of the village square.

Getting out to the deck wasn't so bad. There's a bit of stiffness but your ankle and hand are bound that tightly that they've lost the capacity to shock. Your back's still lively but, as long as you're slow and give it some warning, it seems to be giving you a fair chance. She's patched you up well but, let's be fair, she's done it for a reason.

You look at the restaurant again. The Argentine.

You stand with care and walk inside with more. She's singing somewhere through the back of the house. She said she was going

185

to get ready and you were sure not to ask what for. That's a conversation pending, no doubt about it. You find the phone which is old and has a thick cord coated in wool.

The telephone code for the United Kingdom is 00 44. Thank you.

It takes a bit of time and the ring sounds far away.

'The Dickinsons.'

'Hello, John.'

The pause is a clue and then his voice gives the answer.

'Hi,' he says. 'Everything OK?'

His voice tells you very firmly that everything is not OK. Not OK at all.

'Not really, John, no.'

'What's up?'

'I'm in Ibiza, in a village called San Carlos. I'm here at a restaurant . . . the Argentine. I'm fucked, John, there's some Scousers around, on Sam's money. You've got to get me out of here.'

'San Carlos? The Argentine?'

'Yeah.'

'Stay there. Don't move, don't speak to anyone. I'll have the Spanish police pick you up, just give me five minutes.'

'Cheers, John,' you say and that's that. No big goodbye. You replace the handset and return outside to sit and wait.

You think about John Dickinson. You think about his kids. You remember the conversations during long car journeys about school fees and tennis lessons. You remember him talking once, late at night in a hotel bar and him with a whisky and you with a coffee, about his wife having it rough with some illness and having to chuck in her work. By the time you see the car coming down the Es Cana road you're fine with what's about to happen. You're just an observer.

The car loops round the square, past the restaurant, and parks out of sight behind the church. The Scousers jump out and circle the church in pairs. They approach the restaurant from two directions, moving quickly with their hands in their pockets, and slip inside.

You think about John Dickinson. Just a copper really. Special Branch but a copper all the same. With a copper salary and expensive kids and a wife who can't work. Then there's a hundred grand, right there, waiting if he wants it. He's the only person in the world who knows how to find you. All he'd have to tell his boss is that you can't be found.

You only told John Dickinson that you were going on holiday, you didn't tell him where, but you know he followed you through the bank card. £180.75 at the airport and then the reception at the hotel. You didn't exactly make it hard for him. Now the card's gone and he's gone and you don't have fuck all. The Scousers trickle out the restaurant. They have a chat then walk back to their car. They drive out of San Carlos a lot slower than they arrived and this time they take the road to Ibiza Town.

You hear her coming through little slaps on the wood. She's dressed only in a towel and she sits, carefully, on your lap.

'This is not painful for you?'

'No,' you smile.

You'd accept a decent quota of pain if it meant her sitting there and she's not using much of it. She slips a hand round you and her fingers tap the back of your neck. Her hair's wet. She's not got anything on her face and she looks even better for it.

'It is a nice view,' she says.

'Yeah, lovely,' you answer.

The Scousers' car slips between the hills. You think about John Dickinson telling you to call him directly from now on. You think about John Dickinson saying he'd wanted to come to Peterborough and tell you in person about the £100,000 and you wonder how that meeting would have ended. You think about John Dickinson. Nothing personal. A great big bastard shame, but nothing personal.

★

Ana's surprised about how long it takes Craig to ask for her intentions. When she found him outside on the deck, she presumed he'd at least enquire about their plans. When she returned from Binder's bedroom with the largest clothes she could find and handed them to Craig, she thought he'd ask what he was dressing for. And when she tidied the house to remove any sign that they'd been there, making it clear that they would not be back, she anticipated several questions.

Instead Craig silently pulled on Binder's clothes. A green silk shirt that got over his chest with nothing to spare, shorts a little higher than they should be and sandals just large enough to fit round his ankle, which the ice had brought back down in size.

Ana saw an infant in Craig's movements when he followed her to the car. His whole body slumped from side to side, his hands reaching out for balance, but he moved with more freedom than yesterday. It's only now, when she gets in the car beside him and places the hospital letter and the envelope of money in the glovebox, that Craig finally asks.

'We're going there, to the hospital?'

'Yes,' answers Ana, fastening his belt.

Down the madness of the house's drive and through San Carlos there's no further conversation. Ana has been past the hospital, which is beside the island's only motorway at the edge of Ibiza Town, many times. It is no more than twenty minutes. That is how long she has to prepare him.

'In Auschwitz there was a pair of sisters,' she says, her hands steady on the wheel for the long, straight road south. 'From Mándok, the next town to Komoró. They were ten and twelve years old when they were put on the trains. One of the sisters gave her testimony to the university in 1976.'

From here, on the flat plain that leads to the sea and Santa Eulalia, Ana can see the island's whole sky. Today it is a dome of greys, the clouds stretching from the sea on one side to the hills on the other.

'The woman said that on their second day in Auschwitz her sister had coughed during the morning inspection. Binder marked her as a TB suspect and sent her to Special Treatment, the gas chamber. It was where he sent all the pregnant women too. He said it was a bonus, two Jews instead of one. I read many accounts of this.'

Craig lifts his left arm to the rest. He looks straight ahead.

'These were not orders he was following,' she continues. 'This was just Binder, these were his decisions only.'

Ana looks at Craig long enough for him to have to look back. His eyes slip over briefly. He shows uncertainty and Ana knows she is running out of road to remove it.

'My mother did not have a full night's sleep in her life,' she continues. 'Until the day she died the darkness meant Auschwitz. The darkness meant Jakob Binder.'

★

More and more and more she tells you. All these poor bastards yanked out of one line and stuck in another and then that was their lot. She tells you about the gassing, about lungs swelling until they burst. She talks about the bodies being burnt and the chimneys and the smoke and the screams, and in the middle of this endless river of misery, she tells you, was her mother and the German. Jakob Binder.

You're sitting here in Binder's clothes and there's no doubt in this world about what she is asking you to do. Finally she stops talking and, slowing at a junction, she places a hand on your knee and looks you up and down.

'You like the clothes?' She smiles.

You laugh with relief and you look at her smile and what the fuck are you playing at? Why is there a decision? You look at her and think of last night. You look at her and think of tonight. You don't have anything else and you're not sure how you forgot about that because it's fairly important. You don't have anything or anyone else.

This won't be hard. You're talking about an old man and a hospital where it probably makes the local paper if someone comes in with a stubbed toe. And it'll be deserved. The boy's got it coming. That's part of your thinking, though you'd be lying if you said it's your main concern.

This is her war but you'll fight it for her.

★

Would she be here without him? It's not a question that Ana can easily answer. She could have climbed the yellow gate before, when she was alone in front of it, but she never did until he told her to do so. She could be driving to the hospital without him, but not only has she chosen not to, she is preparing him for something she always believed she would do alone.

It's hard for her to think past the hospital and what awaits them there. But when she does, when she allows herself the slightest notion of afterwards, Craig is still there. That is what surprises her the most.

Above them the clouds have broken and rain hits the windscreen in dotted streaks.

'Rain,' says Craig.

'It is the first for weeks,' she answers.

They're on the motorway that wraps thickly round Ibiza Town. The hospital appears in the distance, hedged between the island's few factories. Together it's a jarring sight, a reminder that Ibiza isn't just an island of beaches and hills. It's a place where people work and a place where people die.

Ana flicks the indicator and slows for the entrance to the hospital car park. Craig's left hand flashes across. His arm is dead straight, his hand tight enough on the wheel to stop her moving it with both of hers.

'Keep going,' he says. 'Fuck.'

In the car park, one vehicle faces back towards the entrance. Two men sit in the front and a further two in the back. All four look at Ana's car. One of the men, the front passenger, is pointing to her or maybe to Craig.

★

There's only going to be one hospital on the island. The last these boys saw of you, you were after doing a double pike into a shallow end and now John Dickinson's told them you're looking for help. It was going to be the police or the hospital they tried next and you can't believe you didn't see this one coming.

'Keep going,' you tell Ana. You smile when you say it, in a fairly desperate suggestion that this is all standard, knockabout stuff.

She's not exactly troubling the speed limit but at least you're moving. The Scousers skid out onto the road behind you. Their car must be a hire job. It looks new and probably has five years on this crate.

'They are the men you fought with?'

'Yeah,' you answer. 'OK, love, we need to go a bit faster.'

You hear from the engine that she's flattened the pedal. The motorway bends and there's a slip road ahead that points away from the town. That's really your only shot.

'Go off there,' you tell her.

It's impressive really, the way she gets it. She only brakes at the last moment and arrows in a racing line for the turning. The slip road runs off between fields. You and her look in different mirrors for the Scousers so together you see their car make a late, clumsy exit to join you.

'Right,' you say, which should be followed by a plan but you don't have one.

She's doing what she can, her foot's still down, but they're closing on you without trying. The road worsens under you, as if the motorway money's running out by the yard. You're heading for the nearest hill. That's not a bonus.

'Can we talk to them?' she asks you.

'Not really, no,' you reply.

Four of them with blades and you in this state. There's no way. Would they go for her too? It's hard to say. You think about opening the door, rolling out, and at least doing her a favour. It wouldn't be difficult, just a case of unclipping your seat belt. It's probably too late now, they're right behind you. The front passenger is the skinny boy with the trainers. He's smiling and you can't really blame him.

The rain's falling hard and she's struggling to find the right setting for the wipers, so it takes a moment to see the road roll upwards. She's slow with the gear change and your speed takes a hammering. You groan up the hill and you're saved by the road getting tighter so they can't pass by.

They ram the back of you, which might be deliberate and might not be. She doesn't seem scared and, stranger still, she doesn't say anything. She just clicks the wipers and the rain beats the windscreen while you watch the road go from tarmac to mud.

You're over the top of the hill and heading down the other side. Her foot must have been against the floor all this time because the wheels struggle through a puddle before finding purchase and sending you shooting down the slope.

You look behind to see that you've bought a bit of space over the Scousers but you know that won't last long. You look ahead and, well, you realise that the Scousers don't matter any more.

You're nearly at the bottom of the slope and the road is just water and even if you were going slower you'd never make the turn.

You lean to the side, as if by doing so you can keep the car on the road.

Beyond the road are the trees.

'No,' is all she says.

*

Ana still holds the wheel but her grip loosens. She has no control over this. The road is raised for the turn and so between the road and the trees there is a moment when the car is in the air.

She isn't wearing her seat belt. She fastened Craig's but forgot to fasten her own.

Everything goes very quiet.

The trees.

*

The trees cradle the car in their branches, soaking up the speed while the seat belt feels like a wire across your chest. Your knees crack the dashboard and your head punches the window then flicks back and gives the same treatment to the headrest. The noise arrives afterwards which seems strange until you see the action to your side. You have the best seat in the house for the arrival of the Scousers' car.

It reminds you of something you saw once on the *News at Ten*. You were in Bradford and you must have been ten years old, give or take. The news item was about car safety and they showed a car full of plastic people crashing into a wall. The boy talking over the action said, 'These are crash-test dummies, not real passengers,' and even at that age you thought that he must have been having a laugh, seeing as they were made of plastic and didn't have faces.

But watching the Scousers, it's hard to think that they're people because they look like those dummies. The car stops but they keep moving in unison. The front passenger, the boss, he snaps to a stop but the other three are just a collection of limbs as they smash forward then back then forward again until they're left spread about the place.

It's surprising how quickly the silence returns. You're facing the Scousers. Your shoulder's popped out. When you try to turn and see Ana your shoulder tells you that you can't. The side mirror's been bent and shows all you need to see of her. You can see hair and blood and the blood's winning.

*

There are a hundred noises but they are pulled together into a bang, an explosion. It is the same with the pain. There is too much of it, from too many places. When her body stops moving it is twisted and wrong. Her breathing goes away. She cannot see and coldness forms at her feet and begins to travel upwards.

Ana thinks of the day at Coches Felices and Francesco kicking the tyres. She thinks of the hotel and how they will react when this phone call arrives. She thinks of her father. She thinks of her mother. She thinks of this man beside her. Craig. She knows so little about him and yet it is with him, and only him, that this is going to happen.

One by one, parts of Ana surrender and her mind hides in what is left.

She found Binder. She found Binder. It was not a waste, it was not a dream. She found him.

It's coming now. Her head seizes because there is no air left.

It does not come with any more pain.

*

The man's fingers pinch your face.

'Can you hear me?' he's asking. 'Can you hear me?'

Your eyes are heavy. A siren, people shouting. Unless this boy was out walking his dog in white overalls, he's to do with the sirens. He bothers your neck to check your pulse.

'You are OK,' he says, and it's hard to break through his accent and find out if that's a question.

'My shoulder,' you reply.

His hands stray over you and take control. His fingers are on your shoulder but it's not where it should be.

'Breathe,' he tells you and you're halfway through doing so when his hands stiffen and there's a click and a little fire beneath your skin.

'There,' he says. 'It was dislocated.'

You're facing the Scousers' car which is empty and not pretty, what with the bits of Scouser lying around. There are ambulances and other boys in overalls and then a police car arrives at some pace and skids in beside them. You're glad the police are late and the medical mob is in charge. Your new pal reaches over you and unclasps your seat belt. You could turn round now, turn round and look to your side, but you don't.

He tightens a bandage round your head that you can't remember him putting on then taps his fingers down your leg.

'OK?' he asks, every few seconds, and you nod.

He runs them up your back.

'OK?'

You nod. You're no cripple, that's something. He lifts your bandaged hand and gestures to your ankle.

'What happened to you?'

'I fell down, mate,' you tell him, 'the other day.'

'Who did this?' he says, meaning the bandaging.

You don't say anything but you must have shown something because suddenly he loses his confidence. He's not a professional any more. He's just a man shitting himself about telling something to a much bigger man. You look, you have to really, at her seat. It's black with blood. Blood is on the window. On the dashboard. On the door. You turn back to him and he's too slow looking away.

'Dead?' you ask.

'Come,' he says, tugging gently at your hand.

'Dead?' you ask.

He looks over his shoulder to the others but no one is going to help him here. He's scared. You put a palm on his shoulder, smudging the white with blood.

'It's OK,' you tell him. 'She's dead, right?'

'Yes,' he says.

'OK,' you answer. You squeeze his shoulder. 'It's all right, mate, don't worry.'

You're not sure why you say that. He looks relieved, stands and shouts to the others. Your mind looks with desperation for something to stick in ahead of what he's told you and you're glad when something does. You reach to the glovebox, lift out the envelope and push it into your pocket. Now there's nothing but what he's told you.

He asks for your hands and pulls you to your feet. You lean to your good side and he gets the hint, ducking under your arm and guiding it round his neck. He directs you to the ambulance and you keep your head down when you pass the police.

The steps into the ambulance are a challenge so it's only when you're in there and sat on a plastic bench that you see the Scouser sitting opposite. There's some blood on his clothes, probably not his, and his arm's in a sling but other than that he's got away with scratches. That's why he was in charge back in the hotel room then, he's the only one bright enough to wear a seat belt. He knows you're here, he could hardly miss you, but he's very interested indeed in those trainers of his.

The boy in the overalls, a paramedic you suppose he must be, pulls the doors closed and shouts to the driver. The ambulance jolts back onto the track and creeps up the hill. The paramedic walks up the swaying cabin and leans into the driver's section, talking to him in Spanish. You can think about Ana or you can speak to the Scouser. You lean towards him and he braces himself.

'Where are your mates then?' is your opener.

He shakes his head.

'All of them?' you ask.

He doesn't say anything. You suppose it's not in his interest to confirm that it's just him. Of the four who as good as killed her, it's just him left.

You sit back and put your head against the metal but it bumps with the road so you lift it clear.

'Listen to me. OK?'

He nods, still concentrating on his trainers.

'Oi,' you say.

He looks up. He's whiter than he was when you got in here.

'The coppers will be at the hospital,' you tell him. 'We don't know each other, OK? We're on holiday.'

He has to swallow before speaking.

'Right,' he confirms.

The ambulance shakes in the mud.

'They were my brothers,' he says. 'We were all brothers.'

You see her for the last time in the hospital car park. The other two ambulances cough up a couple of stretchers each and the last stretcher to be lifted out, while you hobble through the car park, is her. You just have one look, a couple of seconds all told. Her hair is coming out the side, hanging below the blanket that's blotched with blood. You wish you hadn't looked at all. An old boy in the car park crosses himself. You go in one door, she goes in another.

In the hotel reception a doctor sits you in a wheelchair.

'This is our biggest one,' he smiles. He knows about her, that's why he's so friendly.

The Scouser's put in another wheelchair beside you. The receptionists stand and watch because they can't have many days like this. Four bodies before lunch. You're wheeled to the lift and the Scouser is beside you while you rise through the floors. The doctor pressed the top button and that's the fourth storey.

It's a big space with rows of beds and then bang in the middle is a raised area with desks. A welcoming committee of nurses descend on you. You're taken to a bed halfway up a row while the Scouser is wheeled right up to the end. That means you're in between him and the lift and that's something that the Scouser is very much aware of. He rabbits away to the nurses, who shake their heads and get him onto the bed.

They're busy with his arm which must be broken the way he winces. Your shoulder's stiff enough to stop much movement but it's on your right side so that hand wasn't up to much anyway. It's your head that's the mystery. You feel it through the bandage and the doctor clocks you and comes over.

'Please do not touch your head,' he says. 'We will do stitches now.'

He calls to a couple of nurses who wheel him his kit. He selects a syringe and pulls your bandage off. You think about the Jock doctor digging out the tattoos Sam gave you. When John Dickinson came to pick you up he'd brought blankets and pillows from his own home to put over the car seat. John Dickinson did a lot of things like that, which he didn't really have to do.

The syringe goes in and out. The doctor waits a couple of minutes then gets sewing. It takes longer than you think but you're glad of that because just after he starts two Spanish coppers walk into the ward. The nurses have a word with them and they take one look at you and make for the Scouser. While they talk to him you don't look over, not for a moment, which isn't easy but you don't want there to be any connection between the two of you.

'All done,' says the doctor and the nurses wipe you down and you notice they don't let you see your head before they wrap it up again. They turn your head, your back twinges and the doctor sees your response.

'You have a little whiplash,' he says, 'from the crash.'

You want to tell him that your whiplash is from the shallow end of a swimming pool.

'It will pass,' he tells you. 'A few days perhaps.'

'OK,' you say and he leads away the nurses.

The police see their chance and over they come. One's younger, one's older, and the youngster kicks things off.

'What is your name please?' he asks with his pencil ready above his notebook.

'Lee Wilkie,' you say, and he writes it down.

Lee Wilkie was the bigger of the Wilkie twins and when you were a kid he was the best football player on the estate. Even on the gravel patch behind Presto's supermarket on the Clepington Road, Lee Wilkie could run as fast with the ball as without.

The police ask why you're in Ibiza and you tell them you're on holiday with your girlfriend. They ask where you're staying and you tell them you're staying in Es Cana. They ask the name of the hotel and you tell them you can't remember. That's a day or two's work for them right there, and that's all you'll need.

'Where is your girlfriend?' It's only the younger one who's talking.

'She left yesterday,' you tell them. 'We had an argument.'

'An argument?'

'Yes.'

'Why?'

'The woman,' you say, 'that I was with in the car.'

'We're sorry about her,' says the young cop which is decent of him but is immediately trumped by the older one chipping in with a cracking one-two which starts with: 'Who is she?'

Then, seconds later, with a hand raised in apology: 'Who *was* she?'

'I met her in Es Cana,' you tell them, 'in a bar.'

You wait for them to ask what bar and you tell them you can't remember. You tell them, with a bit of a sad smile, that you were drunk. They want a bit more on her and you tell them the wrong name, wrong job, wrong nationality. If she has ID on her you'll say she lied to you. You'll say she must be married.

The older copper points to the Scouser.

'Do you know this man?'

You give them a touch of confusion.

'That man? Only that he was in the other car.'

'How did you crash?'

It's all the older cop now.

'It was raining, we went off the road.'

'Where were you going?'

'Just for a drive, she was showing me the island.'

'You were going fast?'

'Yes,' you say, 'she was going too fast. I told her to slow down, but, well . . .' You feel no guilt saying these words. They're not exactly going to give her a ticket.

'We will be back tomorrow,' says the older cop but you don't believe him.

'OK,' you reply.

They go and talk to the doctor. The younger cop gives him some fairly forceful instructions while the older one holds your gaze until you give up and push back into the pillow.

★

You ease the rest of the sandwich to the side. You're hungry enough but this is just grim. The bread isn't bread and the meat isn't meat. You think, not for the first time, about a kip. The Scouser's been sleeping for a couple of hours. You'd be gambling if you did the same. You try the coffee. You can confirm that it is hot liquid but nothing more than that.

The excitement over your arrival is a memory. Nurses flit between patients and a TV in the corner shows a programme that seems to consist of Spanish women crying. The day continues without four people it started with. The Scouser sleeps while, a few floors below, his brothers must be on ice. You lie here in hospital pyjamas while somewhere there's a woman who was more than you ever thought of having and now she's dead. There's no limit to how long you could think about Ana and no limit to what it might do to you and for that reason you lie and watch the Scouser.

As things stand, you're both here for the night and your body can't understand why you won't let it sleep. You need to remember the Scouser though, remember that it would be a gamble. You close your eyes not to sleep but to check. You tell yourself you'll wait ten minutes. In fact it's two at the most until you hear him call softly for a nurse. He's a cheeky bastard but he's also a decent actor. There's a discussion where he talks a lot quieter than the nurse and then two pairs of feet pass the end of your bed.

You open your eyes to see them walk away. The other nurses are busy with patients so you swing your legs out of bed and set off after them. At the end of the row you see him thank the nurse before slipping into the toilet. The nurse stands outside for a moment, not sure what to do with herself, then heads off to the other end of the ward.

You wait. He comes out the toilet quickly with his head bowed and makes for the lift. He's holding some tissue to his face which is a nice touch and means the first he knows of you is when you clamp a hand on his shoulder. He swears.

'Back you go,' you say.

What's surprising is that he thinks about his options. You smile in case the nurses spot you. They'd be over quick enough and it should look like a friendly chat. They wouldn't know that you're holding his shoulder tight enough to feel the bones.

'OK,' he gasps and you let him go.

You follow him back to the beds. He wraps himself in his sheet. You're not going to fall for that again, which probably means he really will sleep now.

It's a pork chop you suppose but there's something not right with it. It's almost a dead circle for a start. You think that it doesn't matter where you are in the world, you really don't want to be having your dinner at a hospital. You drink the water and eat the Spanish attempt at a chocolate bar.

It's dark outside but only just. The daytime nurses clocked off and the two that replaced them are very much the B team. One has already turned her chair to get a better view of the telly which, believe it or not, seems to show the same programme. It's been seven hours of crying. The other new nurse walks so slowly you'd think she should be in one of these beds.

The Scouser's not having a good time. About an hour ago a doctor brought him three plastic bags. They had a quick chat and the doctor left the bags at the foot of his bed. There can't be much doubt that's his brothers' gear down there and the Scouser's looked emptied ever since. You hope they don't bring you a bag.

A few of the older patients have already chucked it for the day and as soon as they fall asleep the nurse sets off at her breakneck pace to pull their curtains closed. You've been willing the Scouser to sleep and finally he turns over. It takes the nurse a bit of time to see him and then a bit longer to cover what for her is a half-marathon to go and draw his curtains then get back to her desk.

You tilt your head to the pillow and do a passable impression of sleeping. She takes on the expedition to your bed and you hear the curtains run round the rail. You're up and out your bed and pulling the curtains an inch apart. The nurses are chatting, both turned to the telly.

You file out through the curtains, creep over the tiles and slip into the Scouser's cubicle. He's sleeping, properly sleeping, with his mouth open and one hand hanging off the bed. You put your hand over his mouth and he jerks awake. His eyes look like they could burst.

'Listen to me,' you whisper.

His mouth's busy under your hand.

'I need you to listen to me, OK? Keep quiet and listen.'

He nods and you remove your hand.

'You're going to leave here and get a ferry to the mainland. You can get back to England from there. When you get home you're going to tell Sam Albright that you boys killed me. You're going to tell Sam Albright that the four of you killed me and got rat-arsed to celebrate. Are you fucking listening?'

'I'm listening,' he says, his voice dry from sleeping.

'Tell Sam Albright that your brother was too drunk to drive and took you off the road. I know Dickinson's involved. Sam will get him to check on the car-crash story and it'll play out fine. Even if Dickinson hears about the other car it's not my name they've got.'

'OK,' he says.

'Tell Albright you buried me in the hills. You don't know where because the hills all look the same but tell him you put me down deep.'

You can see his wheels turn.

'You'll get the money,' you confirm. 'You might as well come out of this with something.'

'And you'll be safe,' he says, his voice stronger now.

It's a brave thing he's done here, speaking up like that, but he wants to point out that this is a deal and you can understand his position.

'If you do what I say, then yeah,' you answer.

'I'll do it,' he tells you. 'My brothers had kids, you know, they'll need the cash.'

'Right,' you say. 'Do you have a passport?'

He pauses before answering.

'I've got four,' he says, and points at the bags.

'I thought so,' you say and it's odd that you feel awkward. 'Your brother, the big lad. I need to take his.'

He reaches down for the bags and the passport is in the second one he checks. There's a small patch of blood on the cover that you both pretend not to see when he hands it over. He sits up in the bed. The bags, with their scraps of his brothers, are on his lap and he looks like he's about to fold.

'Here,' you say, 'we don't have time for that. Get yourself ready, OK? Two minutes.'

'All right, mate,' he says.

Mate. The boy's lost it. You dart back over to your cubicle. You put the passport in the envelope with the German's money, then go back to the curtain and it's not long before the Scouser appears. Clever lad, he's rustled up an outfit from his brothers' stuff and between them they've offered a pair of trousers and a shirt unmarked from the crash. Right now, you're still in pyjamas. The Scouser has one of the plastic bags in his hand, presumably with four wallets inside, which is fine by you. It's in your interest that he makes it home.

The nurses lurk at the desk and you're settling in for a wait when a patient has a coughing fit and they both go to the cubicle to investigate. The minute they're behind the curtain, you and the Scouser step out and move swiftly between the beds. You get to the lift and you're worried about it making a noise but the doors shut silently and you push for the third floor. You're hoping for a similar layout and you get it, with the lift opening to rows of beds and no nurses in sight.

'There must be a fire exit,' you say.

'There,' says the Scouser, pointing to a glass door and a staircase.

'On you go,' you tell him. 'Get the first ferry in the morning.'

'All right,' he says. You've never liked the Scouser accent. It sounds like they're singing. He reaches out a hand and it's the strangest thing in the world that you shake it and say 'good luck' and, at some level, mean it.

The Scouser legs it and you concentrate on your surroundings. If someone's been in this place for four months then you're guessing they'd have their own room. You go back into the lift and try the floor below. Straight away, you're sure you've got the right place. This floor is a grid of tight corridors between rooms with patients' names scrawled on paper signs.

At the end of the corridor is a nurse, hunched over a desk and writing in a pool of lamplight, so you turn the other way and work your way up and down the passageways. It's mostly Spanish names, first initial then surname, and from behind the doors you hear snores and more coughing. There's a lot of coughing in hospitals, which stands to reason.

You've done a few passageways when you reach the end of one. It's the last room before the windows and written in black pen on the sign is *D. Kössler*.

The door isn't fully shut and you open it with the tip of your finger. The room's small and well lit with moonlight. There's a wardrobe, a table, a seat and then the bed.

Sometimes you forget that old boys can still carry a bit of heft. When he was young, the German must have been capable. His arms lie outside the sheets and have some shape to them while his chest, which rises and falls as he sleeps, shows heavy work in the past. He's put decades into his tan and his hair's greyed but thick enough. The pyjamas are the same as yours and a plastic tube runs from the back of his hand to a bag hooked on a pole.

You close the door and sit on the seat beside the bed. There's a tiny whistle to his breathing. On the wall is a clock and you look in time to see the second hand glide past midnight.

Thursday

When Dickinson drove you out of Bradford, for two months of hiding before the trials, he put himself between you and everything you left behind there. He got you to sign a form. *Power of Attorney.* Then he went away and spoke to your landlord, your doctor, your dentist and your bank. Dickinson didn't let you speak to them yourself. He seemed to think there was a risk you'd have a panic, that you'd tell some boy at Bradford Building Society that you'd shopped Sam Albright and you'd greatly appreciate it if he'd keep it to himself.

Dickinson went to the nursing home as well, so when they called, they called him and then he called you. He said your mum had been moved to Bradford Royal and things didn't look good. You weren't exactly surprised. Alzheimer's wasn't a story that offered many twists.

'They're thinking it's days, I'm afraid,' Dickinson told you. 'I'm sorry.'

'Not your fault, John,' you answered.

This was a few weeks after the trials so you'd not been long in Peterborough. You didn't know the roads, the directions you gave Dickinson were hopeless and he was late arriving. You sat on a folding chair in the cold flat while the sky turned dark outside. On the drive north you spoke about football to stop him speaking about her.

The pair of you got to the hospital at two in the morning. Dickinson hadn't phoned ahead because he said that would be *an unnecessary risk*. In your mum's ward he showed his badge and said that no one could leave the room until he did. The doctor and his nurses weren't happy but a Special Branch badge is a bit of a conversation stopper.

The doctor said your mum *wasn't responsive*. You wanted to ask how many exams he'd passed to notice that. A nurse led you to the bed then ducked away. You sat with your back to them because you knew they were watching. You sat with your back to them and you looked at your mum.

She'd been in the nursing home for a few years, burning through what you got for her house, and you'd only seen her maybe a dozen times. You'd been busy with Sam Albright while your mum went nicely mad. She'd stopped recognising you but at least in the nursing home you could recognise her.

Sitting in the Bradford Royal you wondered what was going on inside her body. Her cheeks looked like they'd been burst and she had bones showing through her face that you'd never seen before. She'd got herself a belly, a little ball under her nightie that made you smile it seemed so daft on her. Your mum checked out the ceiling with her eyes big and blinking. Her head nodded every so often for no reason at all.

Across the polished floor you heard a doctor tell John Dickinson, 'This is completely unacceptable,' and John Dickinson reply, 'That is his *mother*,' because he was a good lad, John Dickinson, and it's sad what happened there.

'Hello, Mum,' you said.

You didn't expect a reply and you didn't get one. You sat on the plastic chair and considered your mum and the decades that she had with your dad, a set-up that must have been a lot less fun than she'd hoped it would be.

You thought about your mum outside the Reform Street butcher's. She didn't want them to see her waiting so she'd stand at the bus stop over the road. When she spotted the red stickers going on the meat your mum would nearly get run over so you got your cheap steak. Every day she did that and every day she pretended she'd been hanging on for a bus.

Before the Alzheimer's came you used to nip round and see her every Thursday night. She'd go and make tea and you'd leave £40 on the mantelpiece next to the photo of your old man. You'd sit in your old man's armchair and stay for one cup of tea and ten minutes. When she asked about the garage you made out you still worked there and when she asked about your girlfriend you said you had one and she was called Maxine. Then you stood up and kissed her on the head and you said before leaving, 'Don't you worry, Mum, don't you worry about nothing.'

The Alzheimer's came like lightning. Her sentences wandered up dead ends. She got confused and soon she just abandoned ship. Long before John Dickinson took your name away your mum had swapped it for all sorts. Sometimes it was your dad's name, sometimes it was a name she'd read in the paper and sometimes it was a lucky dip. Archibald, she called you once.

'Who the fuck's Archibald then, Mum?' you asked, because it was funny sometimes, when she said these things.

'*Archibald!*' she hissed, pointing at you with a shaky finger. 'Language.'

The good thing about the Alzheimer's was that it arrived before the trials. By the time they came along she was in the nursing home but she might as well have been living on the moon. Every day it made the front page of the *Bradford Mail* and it still passed her by.

Watching her in the hospital that night, with Dickinson and the doctor fighting in whispers behind you, you wanted to lift your mum up. You wanted to straighten her back, stretch her lungs and fill them with air. You wanted to breathe for her.

You waved over the doctor who was pleased to get away from Dickinson.

'There's nothing else you can do?' you asked him.

'I'm afraid not,' said the doctor. 'It will be in the next twenty-four hours. I'm sorry.'

'It's not your fault, mate,' you said again and the silence grew until he left.

You thought about the dinners you'd had when you were a kid. Your old man made it a hundred yards out of work before he was kidnapped by a pub so it was only ever you and your mum at the table. It was covered with a plastic coating that something got under, causing a speck of green mould to appear at your side and grow a little more each week. One day you came through from the sitting room and your mum had turned the table round so the mould was at her side. It got bigger still and then you came through one evening and she'd got a spare sheet and torn it in half to make a tablecloth.

Your mum didn't speak much at dinner. You ate your food and she sat looking worried. She'd pull her hands under her chin and stare at the macaroni which would be too stiff or too soft, or the mince that went down like mud or the sea of beans with a puddle of HP Sauce in the middle. When you looked up at your mum she'd smile, trying to stop the worry spreading over the table with the mould.

'Mum,' you said in the Bradford Royal.

There wasn't much light but there was enough to see her.

'Mum,' you whispered.

And she turned her head. Your mum turned her head and smiled at you, just you, and you smiled back. You stood up and bent over her strange body. You held her hand and kissed her on top of her head and you said before leaving, 'Don't you worry, Mum, don't you worry about nothing.'

You walked to the door that you'd entered by and Dickinson jogged to catch up with you. On the drive back he told you that the funeral was *a necessary risk*. He said that he would make sure her death wasn't in the paper and bring in the Manchester coppers you'd used for the trials.

'No Bradford police, obviously,' he said.

You told him you weren't going to go to the funeral. He said he wouldn't put you in a position of danger. You told him you didn't care if Sam Albright was the bastard organist, you weren't going to the funeral.

Your mum lasted two more days. John Dickinson phoned and told you. It was a Saturday afternoon. You went for a walk and ended up in a pub. The Moon Under Water next to the Dixons in Peterborough high street. Her friend came and asked if you were a weightlifter. You looked over and she was beautiful, that night in the Moon Under Water. Then there were the dinners, the house and the Friday night with her sister and Roger that had somehow brought you to Ibiza where you sat and watched this German sleep.

Ana told you he'd been here for four months and looking closer you can see he's not well. The tan hides a lot but his skin's tight and thin and there are little bursts of blood all over him. He's lain here while poor Ana ran around like a lunatic – up and down those hills, banging on doors, day after day. She must have driven past this place a hundred times. A hundred times she could have stopped and found him. Not now she can't.

She's not going to leave you. It doesn't matter how little time you were with her, because it's not like the clock's stopped on that. When the car hit the trees you didn't forget her, did you? She's going to be with you for a while yet and you know, really, that it's going to get worse. Time tends to make things look better so God only knows what it'll do with her and what the two of you could have been.

It wouldn't be hard to do this for her. You could stick a pillow over his face or yank that tube out his arm and see what happens.

He's an old man hiding behind lies. His past is filthy but, to be fair, so is yours. What could seal it, what could let you do this for Ana, is that the more you look at the German the more you're seeing *S. Albright – Party Leader, Treasurer. Membership Number: 1*.

And you're back to that morning five days after Bradford Square when it seemed like you were about to take over the: world.

The National Committee met at ten in the morning. The Coventry organiser had left his house at dawn and he told you this like he wanted a prize. The meeting was in the back room of the Cuckoo's Nest pub in Thornbury. You minded the door while the National Committee sat at a long table and a couple of them screamed for London.

'Trafalgar Square,' they said. 'Come on, Sam, Trafalgar Square.'

Sam told them that he admired their ambition but London would have to wait.

'The movement's funds have been greatly depleted, gentlemen,' he said. 'Now is a time to take stock and replenish our reserves.'

He told them to return to their home areas and *redouble their efforts* in collecting subscriptions. Then he went off onto something about Admiral Nelson and then he stopped speaking and they gave him a round of applause. The Coventry organiser smiled as he walked past you for his epic journey home. Sam said you and him had to wait at the Cuckoo's Nest for more leaflets to be delivered. After half an hour of waiting he got quiet and edgy.

'Enough,' he muttered and walked to the car.

You drove Sam back to Dawson Street. He told you he was going to have a bath and then make some calls so not to come for him until six o'clock that evening. He closed the car door, opened his gate, walked up his path and let himself into his house. You drove halfway home then realised that you'd left your jacket at the Cuckoo's Nest. It was a nice, lined bomber jacket and you got hot even thinking that someone might have swiped it. When you walked into the Cuckoo's Nest, the landlord held up your jacket in one hand and a brown package in the other.

'Your jacket and Sam's leaflets,' he said.

The leaflets were heavy and wrapped tight. The package said 'Bolton – Leaflets for Sam'.

The Bolton organiser had sent his apologies for the National Committee meeting. He and a few others were forever sending Sam leaflets or membership forms. Every few days you'd pick up a package from a friendly pub or you'd be sent somewhere to collect it by hand. Sam said they were *too sensitive for Her Majesty's Mail*.

It was only twenty minutes since you'd taken Sam home so you drove back round to his house. He wasn't a fan of you coming to his door. You knocked hard but he obviously couldn't hear you from his bath. You thought you'd leave the package on his step but then you saw the lock was only a Yale. That surprised you, what with all Sam's talk of *the security services*. Your mum's house had a Yale and you'd been slipping it open since you were twelve years old.

You made a decision. Slip the lock, leave the leaflets on the bottom of the stairs and explain later if you needed to. You pulled your Bradford Building Society card out your pocket and pushed it corner first into the gap. Down and up and then push. The door swung open and you walked into an empty house. You thought you'd broken into the neighbour's. You stepped back outside, checked and came back into Sam's place, the house in Dawson Street where he'd always said he'd lived.

The house was empty. That's not to say that it was sparse, or there wasn't much going on. It was empty. There was nothing there but rooms. No kitchen, no furniture, no bulbs. You felt your way up the staircase to find two more blank rooms and then an attempt at a bathroom. There was a toilet bowl on its side and a sink that was bolted to the wall but didn't exactly look hopeful. There wasn't a bath.

You left the house and found a phone box. You rang the number that you'd always rung for Sam's house on Dawson Street. He answered on the second ring.

'All right, Sam?' you said.

'Hello, lad,' he answered.

'Where are you?'

'In the house,' he replied, sounding angry that you'd asked. A TV played in the background.

'The leaflets arrived,' you said. 'I'm just round the corner from you, I'll drop them off.'

'Not right now, lad,' he told you. 'Come at six like I said.'

You went back to your flat and ate some food with your mind on holiday. At five you drove back to Dawson Street and parked at the top end. At half past you saw Sam walk down the street and slip inside the house. At six you drove outside and beeped. This is what he'd drummed into you, to always stay in the car and wait for him to come out.

'It's just safer,' he'd said at the time. It hadn't made much sense then but it made a lot more now.

Sam came out of the empty house and waved as he walked down the path. You wondered if he'd bothered taking his jacket off. You gave him the leaflets from Bolton then took him to a meeting in Huddersfield with the local organiser there, a boy called Jamie who'd met Sam a few years before and quickly pulled together a hundred members. Jamie was a strange case. In the National Committee meetings he never said a word but Sam went to see him more than any of the others. You waited in the car outside a breaker's yard while Sam and Jamie sat talking on the bonnets of wrecks. Then you drove Sam back.

'Anything else?' you asked when you approached Bradford.

'Nope,' said Sam, 'Just home.'

It was only nine o'clock when you dropped him off at Dawson Street.

'You'll get the end of the football,' you told him.

It was the League Cup quarter finals, live on ITV, with David Coleman in the chair.

'So I will,' said Sam, smiling.

You let Sam get inside then drove a hundred yards and pulled in behind a Transit van. Through the wing mirror you watched him leave the house and walk towards you. There was a moment of concern as he got closer but he strode right past with his collar pulled high over his face and round into Brook Street. You waited a minute then followed in the car. You were turning into Brook Street when you saw a brown Jag steer out of a parking space. Through the rear window you saw that same collar, pulled high around Sam Albright's face.

You couldn't say exactly how many times Sam had told you that he'd never driven a car, but you knew it was a lot.

You followed Sam out of West Bowling, through the terraced streets of Wibsey and then into the Buttershaw estate. He made for the dual carriageway where you nearly lost him before spotting the Jag sweep off onto the Queensbury road. You were out of the city between rough fields, sad mixtures of concrete and grass that couldn't be much use to anyone. In Queensbury you kept a car between you while Sam worked his way through the town's tight streets and took the road to the moors.

They're just an hour out of Bradford but you'd only ever been to the moors once before, on a school trip when you were a kid. The teachers told you that the moors were a *pristine wilderness* and that if anyone dropped a single piece of litter there would be hell to pay. Then they trooped you off the bus and gave you bits of paper to draw rock formations. One by one, the paper blew out of the kids' hands. You remember sitting on the bus as it drove away and watching half-finished drawings of rock formations blowing all over the *pristine wilderness*.

Following Sam that evening the moors looked bigger than you remembered, with the long humps of grass running off to the horizon. The other cars had drifted away and the darkness was coming down properly up there. The only lights you could see were Sam's brakes and he'd not worry about a set of lamps this far behind.

There was the odd house shadowed to the side of the road and when you saw Sam's brakes light up and stay lit you slowed right down. He turned off through a gate and you drove past, nicking a quick look at the Jag drifting up to a decent size of house.

You drove round the next bend then killed your lights and slid off the road. The grass was solid under your tyres and you tucked in behind trees thick enough to hide the car. You jogged back to the house which sat in a large garden walled against the moor. The Jag was parked at the front door and you followed Sam's journey inside through lights turning on then off. A room downstairs, the hallway, a room upstairs for a while and then the house was back to black because, you realised with a feeling that wasn't welcome, that was Sam in bed. That was Sam home and you were standing alone out on the moors and wondering if anything in the world was real.

You returned without enthusiasm to your car. You couldn't risk turning on the heating for the sake of the battery and you were glad that you'd got hold of your jacket. You took off your watch. It was a Casio, a digital thing you'd bought one Saturday afternoon before heading up to Chicago nightclub. You must have thought it would be the last piece of the jigsaw to land Maxine for good, that the sight of a £14.99 Casio from H. Samuel would have her forget all about the estate agent in Whetley Hill and come home with you instead.

After setting the alarm on the Casio for six in the morning, you had a crack at sleep. Somehow or other, well into the freezing night, you managed some sort of kip. When the alarm went off it took you a bit of time to work out the ugly reality of what it was and where you were.

You climbed out the car and stretched, your hands on the cold metal of the roof and your breath forming little clouds. You moved stiffly towards Sam's house which in daylight looked even bigger and more jarring against the naked moor. From the gate, open curtains showed the house was already in business. You supposed Sam had a bit of a morning commute.

There were bushes in the garden that offered a bit of cover so you picked the nearest one, ran over and chucked yourself down behind it. The grass was wet with the dew and you wished you weren't wearing your new jacket.

It was Sam's voice you heard first. The bush's branches dripped water on your arms when you pushed them apart. You didn't have much of a view but there was Sam, carrying something to the Jag and slinging it in the boot. You could hear a woman but not see her and there was a third voice, a kid's voice, coming from somewhere.

Watching Sam through the branches, the wetness of the grass starting to seep through to your skin, you saw that he was changed, different. He walked in a strange way, laughed oddly and you could hear that his accent had taken a journey. He moved out of sight and the car doors slammed shut. The Jag started up, you heard tyres over gravel and then they passed by in front of you. You didn't see much. There was Sam nearest you, someone next to him and a kid bouncing up and down in the back with a hood over its head.

Sam Albright had told you that he had no family. Sam Albright had told you that the movement was his family. It was a line you had heard him use on many people many times.

You turned onto your back. The sky was a faint blue. The sun would take a while to get over the hills. You heard the car move across the empty moors then the silence return. You stood.

Breaking in was a piece of piss. Round the back you found a

loose window next to the door. You leant in and flicked the dead lock open, then walked into a better house than the one in Dawson Street. You started in the kitchen which reminded you of a page from the Argos catalogue that your mum would mark up for Christmas. There would be a photo of a kitchen with a table you could play snooker on and in the corner you'd see your mum had circled a wooden spoon. Sam had bought the whole page.

All the rooms in Sam's house felt expensive. The carpet gave way softly under your feet and the wallpaper was thick strips of detail. The place was immaculate, cleaned and scrubbed. You supposed Sam's missus probably didn't work.

There were bits of Sam downstairs, a bottle of his rum and the smell of his fags, but upstairs you found his stamp. In the bathroom were big bottles of shampoo marked Hair Reinvigorator and by the sink a set of combs were laid out like a butcher's knives. You laughed out loud, thinking about Sam standing there building his comb-over every morning.

Next door to the bathroom was an office of sorts. There was a desk and chair but you were looking at the chest of drawers which didn't belong in here. You opened the top drawer and it was full of small parcels of money. You opened the other drawers. They were all full of small parcels of money.

In every case, the packaging had been ripped open but you could see the writing and, even if you hadn't, you knew what these were. They were the parcels that you had thought were leaflets, or subscription forms, or some other bollocks you'd been told. You had brought all of them to Sam.

You looked through the drawers and found what you were wanting. He'd only got it last night but it was there with the others. *Bolton – Leaflets for Sam*

Inside was the same as all the others. Pound notes, fivers, the occasional tenner. Dirty from the hands that had owned them before they came to Sam.

You'd asked Sam once about the leaflets, about why there were always so many. He said he needed to check them before they went to the public.

'The movement's message must be consistent,' he told you.

The message looked pretty consistent now. You closed the drawers which were heavy with the money. On the desk were blocks of membership forms, notes for Sam's speeches and a diary. You were going to move on when you saw the tickets on a small shelf to the side of the desk. They were plane tickets, you saw that easily enough, but the destination was harder. Zurich. Germany, you decided. It was the dates that confused you. Sam, *S. Albright*, had flown there half a dozen times.

You sat on Sam's chair and worked it out. There had been no Italy, no trip to France to hear the radio adverts about the Algerians, no America and no burger as big as a dinner plate. Only Germany, only Zurich. You'd always dropped off Sam outside the airport, he'd never let you come in. Leeds Bradford Airport, Sam had told you, was *teeming with the security services*.

You decided that this was going to be a day that you would remember.

You passed the chest of drawers on your way out the room. It never occurred to you to take some of the money, you don't know why. You didn't feel too clever going down the stairs and then you got to the bottom and saw the photo and after that you didn't feel too clever at all.

The photo was framed and propped up on a table. It was probably lucky that you'd missed it earlier because if you'd seen it then you might not have made it upstairs. It was a family shot of Sam, his missus and his kid. His arms were around them both, gathering them in. It looked like it had been taken in a park. If you'd had to guess what Sam's missus was you'd go for Pakistani. That's the rough area, you decided as you stood on the thick carpet of Sam's hallway, that's certainly the region.

And the kid. When Sam spoke about kids like his, the son that he held in one arm, he used different terms depending on who he was talking to. At Bradford Square, with the police and the *Bradford Mail* listening, he called them 'the great unfortunates' who 'through no fault of their own' had 'nowhere to call home'. When he spoke in meetings to possible new members he called them 'cocoa kids'. When he spoke in meetings to established members, to the grinning loyalists, he called them a lot worse.

Somehow you made your body travel out the house, through the garden, along the moor, into your car and then the road down to Bradford. Even Bradford seemed altered. You saw buildings you hadn't seen before, people looked at you at traffic lights and your car seemed difficult to drive.

Find Sam. You tried a few places before rolling into the car park of the Ship in Braithwaite. The Ship was a shithole, and a long way from the sea, but the owner had been an early convert to Sam. Inside, the barman played the fruit machine and Sam sat drinking coffee and reading the *Daily Express*. You asked him for a word outside.

'What's this then?' he said in the car park. There was only one other car there, a red Sierra that you presumed must belong to the barman. You wondered where Sam had parked his Jag.

You told Sam that your mum was still in the nursing home and not coming out. You told him that the money you got for her house was nearly gone. You said you'd never asked for a boost before but you needed one now. You were only asking to borrow it.

'Just a few grand,' you said.

The sun was behind your shoulders and Sam's eyes flinched when he looked at you. Now that you'd seen the tools of his trade, you found yourself admiring the twists and gimmicks of his hair.

'Were you not there, young man?' asked Sam, his voice tired. 'Were you not with me in the Cuckoo's Nest public house yesterday morning?'

'Yeah,' you say, 'I was.'

'So you will have heard me say the struggle was running low on funds. You will have heard me say that, with great reluctance, we must go back to our loyal members and ask them to once again dig deep for the sake of the movement. You heard this?'

That wasn't the voice you had heard on the moors.

'I did, yeah,' you replied.

'So perhaps you can tell me, young man, perhaps you can tell me why you should have funds that we cannot afford? That while the movement is scraping together every penny it has, we should divert several thousand pounds for your personal use?'

You didn't look at Sam because you didn't want to kill him in the car park of the Ship.

'Fair enough,' you managed.

Sam pulled out his wallet. Taking his time, making it dramatic, he slid out a twenty-pound note.

'This is from me,' he said, 'not the movement. Buy your good mother some flowers.'

'Thanks, Sam,' you replied. You took the note and realised that you would have held it once before, bound up with others behind brown packaging.

'My great pleasure,' said Sam. 'Now, I have some speechwriting to do, lad, ahead of the next push. I'll telephone you in a few days and let us speak then about your mother. Perhaps there is something that can be done.'

He spread his arms, his wings, like a Messiah. Then he clapped and said, 'Good,' and walked back into the Ship.

You drove to your flat. In the joke kitchen with the single hob and the fridge that needed a day off once a week, you reached into a cupboard and pulled John Dickinson's card from behind the tins.

It was four months since he'd walked over to you at the Shell Garage in Albany Road. It was one week since you stood on the

223

back of Whyte's Fish lorry and watched Sam Albright speak to eight thousand people while the wood shook under your feet and you held your hands behind your back and all of Bradford knew who you were.

You drove to a phone box and dialled the number and John Dickinson answered. You said your name, your old name.

'You're just in time,' he said and then John Dickinson told you to drive to the Little Chef at Junction 40 of the M1 at eight o'clock the next morning.

You stand up and move beside the German's bed. You're not far apart in size. If you had to wear his years then you'd be in his range, there's no doubt about that. And one day he must have been the same as you.

'So,' said John Dickinson in the Little Chef, 'what do you know about, the money or the family?'

'Both,' you answered.

'I thought so,' he nodded. 'I thought you'd need to know both to call me.'

You didn't know how you wanted the conversation to start and you certainly didn't know how you wanted it to end.

'What do you want to hear first?' he asked.

'The family.'

'He's been married ten years, the kid's six, born just before Albright's last spell inside.'

'Sam's been inside?'

At a meeting in south Manchester, you had listened to Sam say that the movement must respect *every single one of Her Majesty's laws*. The only exception, said Sam, was if the movement was *provoked*.

'Right,' said Dickinson. 'Let me try again.'

Your breakfasts arrived. You'd ordered the full house but now

224

it arrived without the mushroom. You considered calling after the waitress but Dickinson was already off and telling you about Sam.

'Albright's a con man,' said Dickinson. 'He started off in Brighton – that's where he's from – thirty years ago. All sorts of stuff, and then he hit upon selling advertising space for newspapers he didn't work for. He did a few years, at HMP Ford in Sussex and then moved up to Leicester. He met his wife there then set himself up selling insurance for companies he didn't work for. Got away with it for years, made a few quid, then got picked up and sent to HMP Folmwood.'

Your thoughts waited in a queue.

The southern accent you heard on the moors.

The time you drove past Leicester and asked Sam why you'd never taken him there and he said it wasn't big enough, which made no sense at all.

The many occasions that Sam had told you he was Bradford born and bred. All the stories that Sam had from Bradford in the old days and yet the only person he'd committed to knowing from back then was your dead dad.

Sam Albright had you drive him all over Bradford because he said he didn't drive. He just didn't know the fucking way.

HMP Folmwood.

'Folmwood,' you say. 'Isn't that where the riots were?'

'The riots,' said Dickinson, 'were Albright.'

It must have been ten, twelve years before. You were cross-legged on the sitting-room floor. Your old man sat with his cans laid out like a castle on the table before him. On the telly some men were on a roof holding up a banner saying 'Rights 4 Whites' while smoke escaped from the barred windows below them. Your old man banged his hands on the living-room table and shouted, 'The workers have spoken!'

'It was only on the news for a few days before Harold Wilson forced it off,' continued Dickinson. 'He said the rioters didn't deserve "cheap infamy".'

Your old man loved anything like that, anything that turned over the police or the government. He told you once that you and him should lead a revolution. You were eleven and he was pissed every night by six o'clock. You remember thinking that you'd probably need a bit of help.

'HMP Folmwood had always had problems between the wings,' said Dickinson, 'but Albright turned it into a straight fight, white versus black. All he did was give some sort of speech in the canteen.'

'Sounds like him,' you replied.

You wondered when Dickinson was going to tell you what you had to do.

'The whole thing got out of control and, right before the Home Office sent in the riot police, Albright told the negotiators that if they quietly gave early release to him and four others it would be over in an hour. It was a devil's deal for the governor.'

'And they got it?'

'They did. Albright was released a few days later in the middle of the night and agreed to live well away from Leicester. Have you been up to his place?'

'Yesterday,' you said.

That morning you'd had to wear your old jacket to come and see Dickinson. Your new one was ruined from Sam's garden.

'Part of the deal between the governor and the Home Office was that Special Branch would be on Albright for a year. I picked up the phone and got the case. I found out he'd bought that house cash – it had to be the last of the money he'd hidden from his insurance scam. I waited to see what he moved on to.'

'When was this?'

''79,' replied Dickinson and he could see you were confused. 'You met him in '81, yes?'

'Yeah,' you said. 1981. Sam walked into the garage.

'He spent a couple of years doing mail-order fraud. I decided to wait. Mail-order fraud wasn't my job and I had a feeling Albright would go bigger. In early 1981 he started meeting up with the other four he'd got out of Folmwood.'

Dickinson reached into his suit and produced an envelope. He moved his tray to the side and put four photographs on the Little Chef table. You put your cutlery down.

They were all members of the National Committee. In each case you had been there when Sam had met them for the first time. These four had clapped the loudest at the end, been the first on their feet introducing themselves to Sam, first to sign the forms and encourage others to do so.

'He knew them?' You already felt stupid and you knew that asking was going to make it worse. 'He knew these boys before?'

'Yeah,' said Dickinson. 'This one's his favourite.'

He pointed to the photo of Jamie. The first time you took Sam to Huddersfield it was for an after-hours meeting in a pub beer garden. Sam talked about England being *swamped by waves of hungry mouths and thieving hands.* Jamie had led a standing ovation. At new meetings you stood right behind Sam so you were beside them for the introduction. You remember Sam and Jamie shaking hands, with Sam leaning forward to make sure he caught Jamie's name.

'It was all planned,' Dickinson told you. 'None of it happened by accident. They knew from Folmwood that they had something they could sell. These four went to Leeds, Blackburn, Bolton and . . .'

His finger hung over Jamie while he remembered.

'Huddersfield,' you told him.

'That's it. They took menial jobs, talked about this guy from Bradford with a few ideas, pulled along a dozen people to Albright's arrival in the area, and then that was that, Albright did the rest. You've heard him talk,' said Dickinson, 'we've heard him talk.'

227

Your breakfast wasn't going to be bothered any more.

'As things got bigger,' Dickinson carried on, 'these four managed it, pulled in the money and sent it to Albright.'

'That's all it was?' you ask, feeling like a kid. 'It was just money?'

'Do you have any idea how much he's making?' was Dickinson's answer to that.

The subscriptions, the endless collections.

Whatever you can afford, gentlemen, for the struggle.

'It's not just from members,' said Dickinson. 'We reckon Sam controls a hundred estates and some of your local organisers have gone a bit overboard. Protection rackets on shops, taxes on the dealers and the hookers. They think they're doing it for the greater good, of course, that Albright's leading them to the Promised Land and the money will get them there.'

You think about the other National Committee members. Not the four from the photos, the ones who really believed. The boy from Coventry and his four-hour drive for a meeting that lasted ten minutes, the boy from Harrogate who'd quit his job to work full-time on recruitment, the boy from Chester who named his kid Sam.

'He's made a million,' said Dickinson. 'Maybe two. Maybe three for all we know.'

'And he's nicking it?' you say. 'Keeping it?'

'Of course,' said Dickinson and he meant *of course*.

The packages, the packages you had fetched for Sam, always came from Leeds, Blackburn, Bolton and Huddersfield. It was you that took them to Sam. It wasn't hard for Dickinson to see what you were thinking.

'You've been driving Albright for six years,' said Dickinson. 'You've met all these people, you've offered protection to them all and you've handled the money. We followed you a hundred times. That's conspiracy, that's involvement.'

You think about the Volvo at the Barlborough Services.

'I didn't know fuck all about it.'

'I believe you,' said Dickinson quickly. 'These other four have been on holidays, buying cars, sticking their kids in private schools. You haven't shown any obvious sign of wealth.' He looked embarrassed and you wished your new jacket had been available for selection. 'But you're sitting on ten years. It's the criminal conspiracy laws, you see, the IRA laws. Albright could get twenty.' He reached for his coffee. 'But if he got twenty, then you'd get ten.'

'Or?'

'Or you drive to Bradford and pack a bag, I pick you up in two hours and you'll only go back there to stand in a courtroom and send this lot down.' He gestures at the photos.

Those four plus Sam, that's who did this. Five men brought eight thousand to Bradford Square. Five men got twenty thousand members. All those people, and all that money.

'They're talking about London,' you say pathetically, 'Trafalgar Square.'

'Who are?' asked Dickinson. 'Not these four, not Sam, I bet?'

'No, the others.'

'That's because they think he's real, that the whole thing is real,' said Dickinson. He was good enough to say it quietly, seeing as you'd believed that more than anyone. 'Albright could only hold a rally like that in Bradford, he's paid off the police there for years. Bradford Square was the only place he could have done that.'

You thought of the night of Bradford Square, of Sam's face in the street light outside the house in Dawson Street. *Did it go well?* His face showed pride and something else. Sadness. He knew that was the end. Everyone thought it was the beginning. Sam knew it was the end.

'So what's his plan?'

'Zurich,' said Dickinson. 'Switzerland.'

Switzerland. You were close enough.

'Albright's been travelling there regularly,' says Dickinson, 'stashing most of the money. Last time he was there he rented a house. His wife and kid flew there last night, one-way tickets.'

If you'd had a better view in Sam's garden you'd have seen the suitcases. But, even if you had, you'd not exactly have guessed all this.

'Albright's finished,' Dickinson told you. 'He's about to disappear and I doubt very much these others know it.'

That would be something, you thought, if Sam was about to do these four the way he'd done you. That would be something, though not very much. You thought about him the day before, in the car park of the Ship, telling you to wait for his call and that you'd talk then about your mum. *Perhaps there is something that can be done.*

'We're picking him up today,' said Dickinson. 'It's up to you if you're in the next cell. This is your only way out.'

'That's not why I'd do it,' you answered without thinking.

'I know,' replied Dickinson.

'Where would I go?'

'Anywhere you want,' said Dickinson. 'You'd be in the witness protection scheme from today. Relocation and £180.75 a week for five years from the date of Albright's conviction.'

'That's not why I'd do it either,' you said and Dickinson nodded.

The waitress came and took away your trays. She asked if you'd enjoyed your breakfast and you said that you had. You didn't mention the mushroom situation.

'He'd have to get the twenty years,' you told Dickinson. 'He'd need to die in there.'

Dickinson smiled because he knew you were in.

'If you do this then he'll get twenty, I guarantee it.'

You thought about your mum, you thought about Maxine.

'OK,' you said.

Dickinson called for the bill.

'What if I'd said no?' you asked him.

'I'm glad you didn't,' he replied and pointed out the window to a parked Sierra estate that was full of men that looked like him.

'I've got tattoos on my back and I want them off,' you said, sitting in the Little Chef at Junction 40 of the M1 on a wooden seat that was built into the table and didn't give you much room to play with.

The German's breath catches. He coughs and in the quietness the sound is like a klaxon. His eyes stay closed, his breathing returns to normal. He's still asleep for now.

In the wardrobe is what you hoped for and for a second time you dress in the German's clothes. You select a shirt, a pair of linen trousers, some grey leather shoes that could only be owned by an old boy and a sun hat that neatly covers the bandage on your head. You change out of the hospital pyjamas and your back throws up a few twinges from the whiplash and the last nip of the sunburn where the tattoos had once been.

You stand beside the German in his clothes. It's ten past four. You've spent quick hours together, you sitting with your past while he slept with his. Sam will be sleeping too, lying in a cold cell and happy because he's got you, found you.

'Did it go well?' Sam asked.

And you'd loved him for asking.

Your hand wanders to the plastic tube. It enters the German's skin under a plaster. There are little bubbles in the liquid and their movement shows that the tube's in use and giving him something he needs. You hold it in your hand.

'Who is this young man?' Sam asked. Your first day at the garage. Sixteen years old and you'd got yourself a job. Your dad was gone, your mum wasn't far behind, but you had a chance until Sam arrived to steal you away and paint his lies over your back.

The tube is flimsy in your hand.

'Who is this young man?'

He stole your life, Sam, he stole your life.

'Who is this young man?'

Someone switches on the German's eyes which go from closed to wide open without anything in between. It would be hard for him to miss you. He sees a monster in the night, wearing his clothes and holding his tube. His mouth opens like a fish looking for air. He says something in German. You reach over your other hand; it's patched and wrapped and the fingertips are stained with blood. You hold his chin lightly and turn his face towards you.

'Auschwitz,' you say softly, and the feelings that rise to his face are ancient.

He says something in German. You wish you spoke it because if you knew for sure then there wouldn't be a decision to make. There's no reason why Ana would be wrong and the boy's certainly scared but it would be hard for him not to be. He's rattling away and you recognise fear and guilt but, to be fair, you can't rule out that he's asking why the fuck you're wearing his clothes.

The table beside his bed is empty. No cards, no flowers. You realise you could be the first visitor he's had. He doesn't have long and he's waiting alone. He's telling you a story and it feels like a long one. You let go of his chin and place the tube gently on his bed. He sees the bubbles keep travelling into his arm but there's no relief in his reaction. What time he has left will be spent thinking of this and, if he's the man who Ana thought he was, then he'll have no choice but to go out thinking of Auschwitz. That's enough.

You walk out the room, stepping over the pyjamas abandoned on the cold floor. The corridors are empty and the fire exit takes you right down to the car park. You leave the hospital and, somewhere in there, Ana's body.

There are a few cars on the motorway, zipping by with their lights on full. Among them will be the odd taxi, finishing up with the nightclub crowds, but there could also be coppers and a man like you walking beside a motorway at night would be cause for questions. Besides, you know where the airport is from here. In the distance you can see the hills stop and beyond is the levelled land of the airport and the salt flats. A few miles, that's all it is.

You set off past the small factories to the wasteland at the edge of the old town. It's cold but it won't be for long, night's already losing its grip. You check your pockets for the German's money and the Scouser's passport. When you arrive at the first of the town's streets you pause under a light and see who you've become. His hair's longer of course, but that's fine. The Scouser was a big lad and his face will fit. He was called Sean O'Connor. Sounds Irish, you think. Makes sense. Four brothers.

It was only when you packed up your stuff that you realised how little you owned. You just about filled a bag then locked the door, slipped down the staircase and round the corner to Dickinson's car. He drove you down to Hendon, the police training centre north of London. Hendon's a copper factory with classrooms, lecture halls, dormitories, playing fields and a gym. Kids go in and coppers come out.

Dickinson scored you a private room in the dormitories. It was on the corner with a view over the playing fields and its own bathroom. Usually the private rooms were for supervisors and on your second day at Hendon some kid knocked on your door and announced that the hallway toilet was blocked. You told him you'd see what you could do. Dickinson and his team loved that story.

They were a decent lot, to be fair. There were four of them, younger than Dickinson and commuting up from London in good suits. You shared your days with them in a lecture hall where you drank tea and they took turns to throw you questions. They'd each been allocated one of the *suspects*. Dickinson had taken Sam. They told you what they knew and you told them what they didn't.

233

It would have got boring if you weren't learning as well and some of the stuff Sam's kids had been up to you couldn't believe. You knew about the window breaking and the graffiti but you were shown other stuff from all over the north. Black delivery drivers had been called out then beaten and robbed. Poofs had been chased down alleys and done over with blades. They'd burnt down Asian shops and then they'd burnt down any shop that wouldn't pay them.

Next up, Dickinson's team told you about Sam and Bradford police. That Sam's money had gone behind the bar at the police social club and that he'd sent two busloads of them to the hospitality at York racecourse. Bottles of whisky and champagne would be dropped off at police headquarters and he'd sent his favourite coppers on *holiday*. In return, they gave him a licence to rally in Bradford Square and a lot more.

'One night we saw two Bradford uniformed pull Albright over,' said Dickinson while his team laughed because they knew what was coming. 'He'd obviously been enjoying himself.'

You thought of some of the states Sam had been in when you dropped him off in Dawson Street. And then, of course, he'd had to drive home.

'They as good as carried Albright into the back of their car,' continued Dickinson. 'One of them followed in Sam's car and they went by convoy out to his house. Now that's service, is it not?'

You and Dickinson got on well. There was the day you were having lunch together in the canteen. The two of you sat in the middle of a room filled with eighteen-year-olds with shaving cuts and bodies like wasps.

'So,' said Dickinson, 'why would this lot think *you've* been brought here?'

'Practice,' you said and you laughed together.

He took you to have the tattoos off. That stopped you using the

234

gym so the evenings were long and the weekends worse. Dickinson brought you some books but you weren't into that, so he had a TV and video stuck in your room and handed you a Woolworths bag full of tapes. They were mostly Clint Eastwood or James Bond. You couldn't take Bond seriously so you went through the Eastwoods and then moved reluctantly on to the Bonds.

Weeks passed. On the lecture-room board they'd written the names of Sam and the others along the top. At the end of each day they stuck up possible new crimes under the names. The lists grew, particularly Sam's. Towards the end Dickinson was writing smaller and smaller as he tried to fit it all in.

On your last night at Hendon you were watching James Bond and thinking that if they weren't so spectacular in the ways they tried to kill him, if they just played it a bit more traditional, then they'd have a shitload more luck. The phone rang.

'Trials are set for next week,' Dickinson told you with one of his kids wailing in the background. 'We're moving you in the morning.'

Dickinson took you back north, to the first hotel in what would become a blur. Dickinson told you the charges. Between the four they'd got a mix of criminal conspiracy, extortion, incitement to riot, inciting racial hatred and theft. Sam had got the lot plus a bonus bit of tax evasion.

'Is there twenty years there for him?'

'I think so,' said Dickinson.

On the first day of the trials you had breakfast at a hotel beside Oldham then Dickinson led you outside where there were two vans full of armed police from Manchester. You and Dickinson rode in the second van up the M62. You leant to look through the driver's window when Huddersfield passed by on your right. When the traffic slowed for Bradford you asked the coppers about Manchester United. They had a Jock manager called Ferguson who everyone said was about to be sacked.

While the vans travelled through Bradford the coppers told you that Ferguson had to go. They all wanted Terry Venables to take over. You suggested they see if Kevin Keegan fancied management but they laughed and made it clear that the Liverpool connection would rule Keegan out. You were telling them about the time you saw Keegan score a hat-trick for Newcastle against Bradford City when a hundred hands hit the sides of the van and everyone started shouting.

You're pleased to see the tourist buses. The airport's car park is as good as empty and from a distance the building looks shut so when the buses pass you and make for the airport you're delighted. By the time you get to the entrance the tourists are out and collecting their bags. They're English, that's clear enough. The older ones look shattered, the younger ones are still living last night and it's not a happy combination.

Inside the airport the cleaners are working but the morning's flights are on the board. First up is Birmingham in an hour's time. The middle of the country, why not? You would only stay there to change the German's money then you could go anywhere. You're not sure where you'll end up but you're certainly not going to Peterborough. What's there? A Lat Attack, a Shoulder Moulder and an argument?

That's finished and gone and you wonder what she'll tell her sister. Probably that you got run over saving an orphan from being hit by a bus, then she'll ask her sister how Roger's doing on the orphan-saving front. It's less than a week since you sat in that restaurant with those three. Six days it's taken to get from there to this.

The Birmingham flight says Monarch Airlines beside it. You wonder if Majestik Holidaze is still in business. There's a row of airline desks and Monarch's the only one manned. He's a young English lad and doesn't look happy being here at this time. You

236

tell him that you've fallen out with your wife and need a one-way flight home. He's not interested in anything that you're saying. You pay cash for the ticket, which is in pesetas but doesn't sound cheap, and you tell him your wife has gone off with your credit cards.

'Fine,' he says and by that he means 'It's six in the morning, mate, I really don't give a fuck'.

The Spanish bird at the check-in is a bit sharper. She at least has the decency to give the passport a bit of a frown and look twice at your clothing. You decide not to bother her with the wife stuff. Up the stairs you find the local coppers manning the security check. You'd be more worried if it wasn't for those uniforms of theirs. It looks like the boy who made them had a bag of gold thread left over and was given ten seconds to use it up. One of them pats you down and another steps in front of you.

'No bags?' he asks with a thick accent.

You start your wife story and he gives up trying to follow it and waves you on.

The departure lounge is a good size but all the English sit tightly packed round the gate marked for Birmingham, as if they might somehow miss the flight if they were any further away. You sit beside them and listen to them moan. You open the passport. He was twenty-seven, three years older than you, and there was no doubt that he'd put the gym work into himself. A big lad he was. Shame.

There's a stir and a gap in the conversations around you. You look up to see that four very different coppers have arrived and are talking to the airline boy at the gate. Their outfits are a bit more realistic and the big difference is the guns. Even the younger, drunker tourists go quiet when they see them. Guns have a way of shutting the English up.

It was a riot and in a riot everyone is suddenly the same – the police, Dickinson, the people outside and you. For a moment there was no control. The van rocked, the police spoke into radios and Dickinson shouted at them, 'What's happening?'

The van's door handle jabbed up and down. It was made of plastic and you wondered how long it would last.

'What's happening?' Dickinson shouted again. He wasn't handling it well. The police talked into their microphones, pushing their earpieces in and squinting as they listened to responses. You seemed to be the only one who knew what was going on. Through the van's thin metal you heard them scream your name.

'We need backup,' said one of the coppers to Dickinson, 'local police.'

You laughed. Dickinson shook his head.

'Keep going,' he told them. 'Run the bastards over.'

You found out later what happened next. The six armed coppers in the other van got out and saw two hundred faces looking back. The coppers surrounded your van and their guns bought enough space for your driver to make the alley behind the courthouse. The coppers in your van jumped out and slammed the doors behind them. You and Dickinson sat in the darkness while he muttered various bollocks then the doors swung open and a copper shouted, 'Now, now!'

Dickinson set off for the courthouse like he was trialling for the Olympics but you didn't move. There were ten yards between the van and the thin line of coppers at the end of the alley. Beyond them were all the fingers and the fists and the threats and the promises. Some faces you recognised, some you didn't, but they seemed fairly united in not wishing you well.

'Let's go,' said the copper who was back helping his pals.

He and the others had pulled down their visors. They pointed their guns skywards in one hand and pushed your admirers back with the other. You stepped out the van onto the cobbles.

'Go, go!' shouted the copper.

The line wasn't going to hold. The police were as good as

wrestling now and their guns were just getting in the way. After the initial surprise, the rioters remembered that they were rioting in England and there wouldn't be any shooting today. The coppers might as well have been holding bananas. You looked at as many of the faces as you could. You smiled.

'Fucking go!' screamed the copper.

You walked to the courthouse, up the steps and inside. Dickinson called you from a room and locked the door behind you. He was sweating.

'I thought you were behind me,' he said, looking sheepish. It wasn't Dickinson's best day.

The police came running in, doors were shut hard and then they sat around you. They took off their vests and helmets and steam rose from their bodies. They panted for air, held their heads. One looked to you.

'Friends of yours?'

'Used to be.'

The head copper spoke to Dickinson. It was the first time you heard about *necessary risk* and *unnecessary risk*. They talked about varying routes, or the possibility of moving courts and private hearings.

'Listen,' you said. 'When will the money come up? Sam's money, when will that make the paper?'

'It'll be in the opening arguments,' said Dickinson, 'this afternoon.'

'Well then, lads,' you said, 'tomorrow we'll be able to drive here in a convertible.'

And that's what happened. Late that afternoon the prosecutor gave his opening argument and you persuaded Dickinson to let you watch. At the side of the court, tucked in behind the jury, he cracked open a door a few inches. Sam sat with two of his pals either side. He smiled, leant into ears and said things that had them smiling back.

The prosecutor brought up the money. Sam and the others knew it was coming. Then the prosecutor named the amount found in Sam's house and that sent a little jolt through the other four. Then the prosecutor talked about Switzerland and all five of them frowned. Sam shook his head and whispered assurance to the others. The prosecutor talked about *regular cash deposits* at a bank in Zurich.

'Lies,' called out Sam confidently and it was funny to hear his voice again. He went with his Bradford accent which you guessed was for the jury. The other four looked round the back of Sam's head to each other.

The next morning you read the *Bradford Mail* during the drive from a hotel in Rochdale. The front page said ALBRIGHT'S SECRET STASH. When the vans reached the courthouse there wasn't anyone there to meet you. A few days later you'd be taking your breaks in the alley, sitting on the steps with a cup of tea and one bored copper standing beside you. By then all the action was inside.

MR X TAKES THE STAND said the *Bradford Mail*.

The head copper has put his gun down and is at the desk with the airline boy. They're checking some paperwork together. The airline boy looks nervous and the copper puts a hand on his back to calm him. They go through what's there slowly, page by page. The other three stand and face the departure lounge, their eyes moving across the tourists before them.

You check the screen. It's 6.32 a.m. Boarding is at 6.50 a.m. You look back to the security check. It's the only way in and out of the departure lounge and it's fair to say that it's a one-way street.

You've got nowhere to go. What is going to happen is just going to have to happen.

It was hardly a secret that it was you. The *Bradford Mail* stuck with their Mr X stuff but Albright, the other four defendants and half of Bradford knew exactly who Mr X was. You'd gone missing the day of the arrests and hadn't been heard of since.

That didn't make your comeback any less of a moment. You stood in a corridor behind the courtroom. The strip bulbs made Dickinson look pale.

'OK?' he asked.

'Fine,' you told him.

'You're a hero for doing this,' he said. 'I hope you realise that.'

You didn't answer. A lad in a tie popped his head round the door.

'That's you now,' he said in a local accent and his look wasn't friendly.

'Good luck,' said Dickinson.

You walked into the courtroom and concentrated on finding the right seat. You sat down, spoke to the judge and got the business with the Bible out the way. Then you looked. The room was more than full. People were standing at the back. Sam Albright and his four pals sat in a row and looked at you as if you were God and the Devil tied together.

You spent a week in that seat. First came the prosecutor teasing out everything you'd given up at Hendon. On your last day with him he asked you five times, 'And can you see that man in the courtroom today?'

And five times you reached out a hand and pointed and said, 'Him.'

Sam was last. It was late in the afternoon. The courtroom windows were up high and sunlight ran diagonally across the ceiling. The prosecutor asked if you could see the man you'd spent a long day talking about.

You pointed at Sam.

'Him,' you said and Sam's eyes were slits.

The defence were next. Sam had spent a few quid bringing a QC up from London and to be fair the boy had certainly done his homework. The fact you were now a paid-up pal of the witness protection programme meant proving criminal behaviour on your part was irrelevant. The lawyer had to go after your character but that was fine. It just got a bit boring, that's all.

'This is just a collection of lies designed to save your own skin,' said Sam's London lawyer.

'No,' you answered.

'You are a fantasist, aren't you? An attention-seeker?' said Sam's London lawyer.

'No.'

'Is it not the case that you have been suffering from severe depression connected to your mother's ill health?' said Sam's London lawyer.

'Depression?' you replied. 'No.'

And so on. By the end he was toiling a bit but he had a few more angles left. He asked the last time you'd taken steroids.

'Not for two months,' you answered and the prosecutor stood up and submitted a medical report just like he and Dickinson had planned.

'Tell me,' he said, 'you were an active member of this organisation for six years?'

'Yeah.'

'And you benefited financially as a result –'

'No,' you cut him off.

'You – sorry?'

It was the one time he cocked up. You enjoyed it and you could see a couple of the jury did too. Sam should never have got a lawyer up from London. That was never going to play well in Bradford.

'I was paid by the garage on Davidson Street, not by Sam or anyone else.'

'And why would a garage pay your wages for six years if you weren't working there?'

'Sam's a persuasive man,' you said. 'That's why we're all here.'

Even a couple of Sam's men enjoyed that.

'You were a member,' said Sam's lawyer, and he was definitely losing it, 'of a racist organisation.'

'I wasn't though, was I?' you asked him. 'I thought I was, but I wasn't.'

'Why,' said Sam's lawyer and his smile didn't fool anyone, 'should these good men and women of the jury believe a word you say?'

'Because otherwise they'd have to believe him,' you said and pointed at Sam. Someone laughed from the press bench and the judge had to bang his little hammer.

When you left the courtroom the jury foreman, a fat lad in a golf-club jersey, nodded at you. In the corridor Dickinson was waiting.

'Well,' he said, 'it's a shame you don't drink.'

The night before the verdicts Dickinson stayed at the hotel. The two of you were up late, you drinking coffee and him drinking whisky. He told you that Sam was getting twenty years.

'With parole though,' you said.

'Maybe,' he replied.

Then Dickinson drank more whisky and told you that his wife was due an operation and she wasn't going to be able to work. He talked about school fees and mortgages and you stopped listening because you didn't think it meant much to you.

The next morning you sat at the very back of the courtroom and listened to the judge talk about an *evil empire* that had threatened to *unpick the moral fibre of the north of England*. You thought that, to be fair, the moral fibre of the north of England hadn't needed much unpicking.

Sam's boys got single figures. Five, two sixes and then a nine for Jamie.

When Albright stood up you thought how old he looked from behind. He'd always worn that pea coat which gave him a bit of a boost but in his suit he looked smaller and there was a slight stoop to his back.

'Samuel Albright, I sentence you to a minimum of twenty years' imprisonment.'

Sam turned, reached for his chair and sat down like the old man he was. People jumped up all over the court and you had to peek between bodies to see Sam taken away. He was looking around the room, searching the faces, but he didn't spot you before the coppers led him out the door.

That was two years ago, give or take, that last day in Bradford High Court. There have been a few bits and pieces since. Some genius painted you a gravestone on the side of your mum's old house and then Dickinson had calls from the prison governor to say Sam was getting close to various gangsters on his wing.

'He's planning something,' said Dickinson.

'He's planning something?' you laughed. 'Is that what my taxes get me, John?'

A rumour went round Bradford that you were in the Lake District and a carful of Sam's loyalists went up there and beat up some hotel owner who wouldn't hand over his guest list. Dickinson said that the fact Sam was down to a single carful of halfwits was a good sign but it wasn't, of course, because it forced him to go freelance with the hundred grand.

Sam was in his sixties, not exactly fighting fit and with nearly two decades of prison ahead of him. Dickinson had found out that Sam's letters from prison to Zurich had come back *Return to sender*. His missus had gone with the money and the kid. The hundred grand was his last stash, a final throw of the dice, and there was only one thing he wanted from it.

Standing in the house in Peterborough a week ago, with her in the shower upstairs and Teletext on the screen.

'He'll get some interest at that, John,' you'd told Dickinson.

You'd never have known where that interest would spread.

Dickinson gave you up, Sam sent four Scousers and you sent back one.

'Ladies and gentlemen.' The airline boy talks into a phone and it comes out the speakers above you. 'We can now begin boarding.'

People jump out their seats and jog towards the desk. You want to ask them why. You want to ask if they've been told that the first person on the plane gets to fly it.

The police are between the desk and the door, two either side so passengers have to walk between them. You join the queue and it doubles in size behind you to become a thick, muttering line of complaints. The time of the flight, the queue, how early the hotel sent them here, the waiting and then back to the queue. Round and round they go these happy English.

The first of the tourists pass between the police and you watch jealously the way they see the coppers as a curiosity, a little side-show on their way to the plane. How did they get served up those lives, those normal lives where police don't matter? You want to turn round, grab a few necks and ask who has the most to complain about right now. If any of this lot could trump your current situation then you'd be impressed.

You're getting closer. The airline boy checks the tourists off on his passenger list. It's the only paperwork on his desk so it's the only thing the police could have been looking at. Someone's turned on the heating inside you and your breath is coming out choppy. Your mind's off on a journey to somewhere very bad when you see the glass doors.

Past the police the glass doors to the runway have been well served by the cleaners and, when you look, they send a strong reflection back. The German's clothes, the German's hat. You look so strange, so ridiculous, that this yanks your attention away from your fear.

'Passport and boarding pass, sir.'

You hand him both. He checks the names, he doesn't even look at the photo, and gives them back. He's already speaking to the next passenger. You have no choice but to walk on.

Just the size of you would have them check you out. This is what you tell yourself. And then add in your get-up, the bandage on your hand, what's left of your limp. They'll want a chat at least, maybe a search. The German's money. How will you explain flying home with all that Spanish dough? You still haven't got an answer when you reach the doors, push them open, and walk out onto the tarmac where a boy in a fluorescent jacket points to the Monarch plane and says, 'That way, sir.'

It's a seat next to the window and you're happy with that. You stow yourself in there while the airline bird starts with the life-jacket routine. You're beside the wing so when the engines join in they do so under your feet. From the back of the plane some kids start singing. Behind you a couple argue about whether or not the boy remembered to pack some towels.

'They were on the balcony,' says the woman. 'Did you even bother checking the balcony?'

Someone presses their service button and calls out a drink order to the airline bird which you feel is a bit ambitious seeing as she has a life jacket round her neck and is demonstrating how to blow a whistle. The plane moves.

The other morning, sitting on the German's terrace and looking down at San Carlos, you thought about living with Ana in Hungary. About how that would turn out and what you'd do there. Now it's only England, but that's OK. There will always be work in England for a man like you.

Empty tarmac drifts by the window. You're the first people of the day to leave. In the distance the hill of salt remains in shadows that the sun hasn't reached. The plane stops and when the engines start again you think, without meaning to, that they *redouble their efforts*. That's the last of Sam, you decide, the last scrap of a man who you can leave here.

The plane takes off out to sea then begins a long turn back over the island. It's tilted to your side and there's a wall of water before the island reappears stretched before you. From up here the hills and the trees take over and the island seems older when you see it that way. Ana is down there and the only people with her will be the ones who have to fill in forms. Soon they'll be pulling out the same forms for the German, when he dies under a name that isn't his.

The plane straightens and climbs. The engines fight to take you higher and you appreciate them doing so. You watch Ibiza shrink and then cloud comes from nowhere and takes it away.

ACKNOWLEDGEMENTS

I'd like to thank David Riding and all at MBA, Beth Coates and all at Random House/Cape, my beautiful first reader Rhiannon and Mum, Dad, Alan and Carol for many happy Ibizan memories. I'd also like to thank José María Irujo, author of *La Lista Negra – Los Espías Nazis en España* (from which the book's epigraph is drawn), and the Raco Verd bar in San José, Ibiza.

NF